The
Bishop's
Daughter

ALSO BY TIFFANY L. WARREN

What A Sista Should Do
Farther Than I Meant to Go, Longer Than I Meant to Stay

The
Bishop's
Daughter

TIFFANY L. WARREN

GRAND CENTRAL
PUBLISHING

NEW YORK   BOSTON

Grand Central Publishing
Hachette Book Group
237 Park Avenue
New York, NY 10017

Printed in the United States of America

Grand Central Publishing is a division of Hachette Book Group, Inc.
The Grand Central Publishing name and logo is a trademark of Hachette Book Group, Inc.

ISBN: 978-1-60751-338-4

Book design and text composition by L&G McRee

Acknowledgments

I first must give glory to God for giving me the tenacity to pursue my dreams. He's blessed me with the most supportive husband ever, wonderful children, and friends who put up with me.

Brent, thank you for being there when I need you, for hauling books, and for bringing folk to my table at book signings! We're doing this together. Briana and Brittany—you two are such a help to me. I appreciate all that you do to help me at home and with your younger siblings. Brynn, Little Brent, and Brooke—Mommy loves you, too!

To my mother, Libby, and my mother-in-law, Linda, thanks for always telling folk about my books. Y'all publicize way after ninety days.

To my girlfriends Afrika, Tiffany T, Shawana, and Robin—y'all already know what it is! The rant sessions are in full effect. LOL! Thank y'all for listening to me. Thank you, Karen, Latoya, and Linda (the Hachette crew) for answering my questions and for treating me like I've sold a gazillion books.

Pattie Steele-Perkins, you are a great agent! I appreciate your concern for my career.

I have been blessed on this writing journey to find like-minded authors who have been mentors, friends, and prayer partners. Angela, Yolonda, Mata, Leslie, Latonya, Bonnie, Jacquie, ReShonda, Michelle, Vivi, Mimi, and Norma, thank you for your kind words and support! May God continue to bless you all.

Felicia Fontenot, you are an awesome woman! I feel blessed to have met you! And to the rest of the members of the Faith and Fiction Retreat staff—Kym, Karla, and Tonya—a giant thank-you! Zion PCC in Cleveland, I know you all are still praying for us; we're praying for you, too!

To all of the readers, book clubs, and book club presidents who have selected my books, I appreciate your undying support of African-American authors. I have to give a special shout-out to RAWSISTAZ, Spirit of Sisterhood, Prominent Women of Color, APOOO, Sisters with a Purpose, Sip N Read Café, Motown Reviewers Book Club, and the REGAL Sisterhood. Your love of books makes this dream possible.

I hope you all enjoy *The Bishop's Daughter*!

Chapter One

Darrin

I'm snatched from my sleep by voices.

They're coming from the living room. The first voice is Shayna, my lover, although she likes to be called my girlfriend. She is not my girlfriend. Haven't had one of those since high school.

The other voice is coming from the television. It's way too loud but not unfamiliar. I concentrate for a moment until familiarity becomes recognition. The voice belongs to that preacher Shayna likes to watch every Sunday morning.

Is it Sunday already?

I start a mental rewind in an attempt to recapture my weekend. Friday was standard. Edited a short story for a girl in my writers' group. She's entering a romance writers' contest and wanted my opinion. I didn't give it to her because I'm possibly interested in sleeping with her. I told her that the uninspired farce was poetic prose.

She won't win the contest, but she won't blame it on me. She'll accuse the judges of being amateurs and then come cry on my shoulder. I'll have tissues on hand— right along with the strawberries and champagne.

Also had lunch with Priscilla. My mother. The obligatory "good son" lunch that keeps me on the family payroll. I call her Priscilla behind her back but never to her face. She's petite, cultured, and polished but not above going upside a brotha's head.

We had the same conversation we have every week.

"Darrin, when are you coming to work for your father?"

"The day after never."

"You always say that."

"And I always mean it."

I love my mother, but I hate this conversation.

My father, Mathis Bainbridge, wants me to work in an office at Bainbridge Transports, shuffling papers, giving orders, and hiring overqualified people at ridiculously insulting rates of pay. He calls his company the "family business," but only one person in our three-person *familia* is interested in shuttling elderly people to doctors' appointments and on shopping trips.

It's not Priscilla, and it's not me.

"You coming to church with me on Sunday?" Mother also asked.

I let out a frustrated sigh. "I'll see."

My sporadic church attendance is Priscilla's other favorite topic.

"Don't you love Jesus?"

"Yes, Mother. I love Jesus."

That wasn't a lie. I do love Jesus. I just cannot say no

to a woman who wants me to take her to bed, and I have yet to hear a preacher tell me how.

Priscilla was extra irritated at our lunch date. She got borderline vulgar. "But you're willing to go to hell over some girl's dirty panties?"

I laughed then, and I'm still laughing. In Priscilla-speak, "dirty panties" was tantamount to cursing me out.

I replied, "Mother, please watch your language."

Saturday was worse. I spent the entire muggy and rainy afternoon at a 10K race to benefit cancer research. Put on a fake smile and interviewed the sweaty first-place winner, asking him questions that no one wanted answers to, all the while thinking, Why am I doing this?

There was a time when I was excited to have "comma, writer" after my name. You know, Darrin Bainbridge, writer. But the glamour that I'd envisioned has not yet materialized, and the less money I make with freelance journalism, the more my father threatens to chain me to a desk.

When I should have been winding down for the weekend, I blogged. Blogging is what narcissistic writers do when they don't have a book deal. Yeah, I'm just a bit narcissistic. Besides, people like to read what I think about social injustice, celebrities, and whatever else. Ten thousand hits a day on my blogsite can't be wrong.

The thing I love about blogging is that I'm anonymous. Like, last week I wrote a piece on Jesse Jackson and how he's more of a threat to African-American progress than the KKK. Then I chilled with him at a networking function the same night. No harm, no foul.

Since I can no longer drown out the television or

Shayna's hallelujahs, I open my eyes and concede to starting the day. I stretch, take a deep breath, and grin at the memory of last night. Shayna's perfume lingers in the air: a fruity Victoria's Secret fragrance purchased by me for my benefit but disguised as a spur-of-the-moment romantic and thoughtful gift. Yeah . . . I don't do those. But Shayna was pleased. So pleased that she stayed the night in my den of iniquity and is now watching church on television instead of getting her shout on in a pew.

I jump out of the bed in one motion, landing on the ice-cold ceramic tiles. My pedicured toes curl from the drastic temperature change. Yes, a brotha likes his feet smooth. Hands, too. What?

My apartment is slamming, and the furniture baller-style—especially for someone with such a low income. If it wasn't for the deep pockets of my parents, blogging and freelance writing would pretty much have me living in semi-poverty. But my mother makes sure I have the best of the best and a monthly allowance. I keep thinking that at twenty-eight, I might be too old for a six-thousand-dollar-a-month allowance. I'd be satisfied with less, but I'm not turning anything down. Priscilla's generosity (behind my father's back, of course) allows me to pursue my dreams, whatever they might be.

I pull on a pair of silk boxer shorts and walk up the hallway to the living room. Silently, I observe Shayna. She is rocking back and forth on the couch, her hands wrapped around her own torso. Embracing herself.

"You better preach, preacher!" she shouts at the face on the screen.

I mimic her movements and hug myself, too, but not because I feel the love. It's freezing in here. Shayna likes to turn the thermostat to sixty no matter what the temperature is outside. Freon-laced air rushes out of every vent.

"If you got breath in your lungs and strength in your body, you need to shout hallelujah!" shouts the preacher.

"Hallelujah! Hallelujah! Hallelujah! Hallelujah!" Shayna's four-alarm "hallelujah" sounds like one word. I am amazed. How can Shayna feel so worshipful when she just rolled out of my bed a few hours ago?

I'm curious. "Do you send this guy money? He's in Atlanta, right?"

Shayna looks up from the program and smiles seductively. Can she be any more blasphemous? "Yes, Freedom of Life is in Atlanta, and yes, I do send in my tithe and offering on the regular. I'm a partner." She motions for me to come join her on the couch. I don't.

"About how many members do you think he has?" I ask as the television camera pans to what looks like the crowd at a Destiny's Child concert.

"The sanctuary holds ten thousand," she declares proudly, as if it were her own accomplishment, "but there are about twenty thousand members and partners worldwide."

I'm in writer mode now. I can feel the wheels in my mind spinning. Probably something scandalous going on in a church that size. Pastor either skimming money off the top or sleeping with half the choir. Maybe blogging about a dirty pastor will attract some sponsors. Exposing rich black men pays well, and if he's truly grimy, I won't have a problem spending the money.

Shayna asks suspiciously, "Since when did you get interested in church?"

"Since just now. I could feel the spirit oozing into the bedroom, and I had to come investigate."

"I know you better than that. What's the real?"

Shayna doesn't know me at all, but she thinks she does. She assumes we have a deep bond because we've shared bodily fluids. There is more to me than my sex drive, but she'll never know that. She's not the wife type.

I humor her and reply, "Well, I think there has to be a story here."

"What do you mean?"

"I mean, this guy can't be more than fifty." I'm half explaining, half forming the story in my mind. "And he's got twenty thousand offering paying members? I bet he's living large."

Shayna frowns. "What's your point?"

"You don't think there's anything wrong with that?"

"Uh, no. Your daddy lives large."

I chuckle with disbelief. Didn't know she was one of *those* people. The ones who try to compare pastoring a church to running a business. For the fun of it, I quip, "Jesus preached for free."

"He didn't have a car note," she shoots right back.

"Okay, I see this might be hitting a little close to home, but I bet if I go down there to Atlanta, I can dig up a juicy story."

The thought becomes even more appealing as I put words to it. Atlanta is uncharted territory for me. Fresh stories, different scenery, and untapped women. The more I wrap my arms around the notion, the more it turns into a need. I *need* to get my butt down to Atlanta and break this story wide open. Blogging on location. Most definitely liking the sound of that.

Shayna leans over the back of the couch, pointing her polished fingernail at me for emphasis. "Whatever. Bishop Kumal Prentiss is a man of God, and he preaches the Word."

"Kumal Prentiss? That sounds like a hustler's name. And what do you know about the Word?"

"I grew up in church, sweetie. I'm not a heathen, like you."

"You're not the only one who was raised in church."

I'd had so much church growing up that if church was food, I could feed every one of those starving Ethiopian children who convince me every week to be their sponsor. If church was talent, I'd be singing like R. Kelly and dancing like Usher. If church was candy, let's just say I went to a lot of church. Every Sunday Priscilla dragged me, unwillingly, into the huge stone building. Me always screaming, "But Daddy doesn't have to go!" Her always replying, "Daddy's going to hell." She'd give me money for my Sunday-school offering and send me on my way.

I went through a phase where I enjoyed the services. I was thirteen, and my first crush, Alexandra, was fifteen and fully developed. I joined the junior ushers, youth choir, and youth department trying to get at that girl.

One Sunday morning old Pastor Davis preached on lust and hellfire. He'd said that if we didn't repent of our lusts and get baptized, we'd spend an eternity fighting fire. Since I had been drooling over Alexandra and her tight sweater for the entire service, I was terrified. Walked down that center aisle out of fear while Priscilla shouted, stomped, and danced. Went down a dry devil, came up a wet devil.

At age sixteen, I got tired of pretending that I could

walk the narrow road. I prayed about it. Told God that I would come to church when I knew I could live right.

Priscilla wasn't having it. I think she literally had a nervous breakdown when I told her I wasn't going back to church. She cried for days, walked around praying out loud, lifting God up and putting the devil under her feet.

I didn't budge. And for the first time ever, my father defended me. He stopped Priscilla dead in her tracks. He said, "Priscilla, you will not make my son go to church if he doesn't want to. Church is for women, anyway; it's about time he found a more productive way of spending his time."

The memory brings a smile to my face, makes me want to taunt Shayna about her hypocrisy. "And since you know so much about the Word, what does it say about fornication?"

She must be done talking to me, because she turns back to Bishop Prentiss, who has worked his congregation into a frenzy. Have to give it to him. The man has skills.

"You want something to eat?" I ask Shayna, ignoring her attitude.

Her face softens. "You know I do."

In minutes I've prepared a small breakfast feast. French toast on fresh French bread, garnished with powdered sugar, strawberries, and carmelized bananas, and a three-cheese omelet browned to perfection.

I can cook my butt off.

I arrange everything on the china my mother bought me for a housewarming gift. For me, it's not just the taste of the food, it's the look of it. Presentation is everything.

I can make a grilled-cheese sandwich look like a gourmet entrée.

Shayna's smile returns. She tosses her red curls out of her honey-colored face as she sashays barefoot over to the table. She looks as delicious as the breakfast, wearing her baby T-shirt and boy shorts. I feel a hunger starting inside me that has nothing to do with breakfast food.

Shayna's a cute girl, not stunning, but standing there at my kitchen table with her disheveled sexiness, she's irresistible. Then again, I have the same motto about women that I have about food: Presentation is everything.

"Why can't you be like the average guy and put everything on paper plates? This looks better than at the restaurant."

"For one, I'm not the average guy, and two, you wouldn't be so sprung if I was."

Shayna sits down and takes a bite before responding. Closes her eyes and chews slowly. I love the way she savors my culinary creations. She sounds like a baby relishing the first sips of a warm bottle.

"Is that good?" It's real hard to hide the cockiness in my tone.

"You already know it is!" she exclaims, smacking her lips thoughtfully. "What is it that I taste? There's a different flavor."

Her observation fills me with pleasure. "Oh, you've been around me much too long if you're noticing flavor nuances. I'm proud."

She licks her fingers one at a time. "Mmm-hmm. Maybe I have been around you too long, but baby, I am not sprung."

This woman is hilarious. Shayna is not only sprung; she's in love. I'm flattered, even if I don't feel the same way. She's been hinting that she wants to move in with me, but that is not going to happen. Rule number one of my cardinal rules is: Never turn a bedmate into a roommate.

"Okay, you're not sprung. I believe you. That's actually a good thing, because then you won't miss me when I go to Atlanta."

"So you're serious about this?"

I fold my arms across my chest and nod emphatically. "It is my duty as a journalist to expose the charlatans and inform the people."

"You better be careful. The Bible says, 'Touch not my anointed and do my prophets no harm.'"

"Look at you quoting Scriptures. I'm impressed. And don't worry about me. If your precious pastor is everything that he says he is, then he has nothing to worry about."

Chapter Two

DIARY OF A MAD BLACK BLOGGER

How many of y'all go to chutch? Naw, dog, I ain't mis-spelled nothing! Not church . . . but chutch? Let me break down the difference. Church is where you go to hear about the goodness of the Lord, hear some delightful singing, let the ministers pray for you, and go home feeling refreshed. Chutch is where you go to see what fly suit your pastor is gonna be sporting. Chutch is where your pastor rolls up in the parking lot driving a clean white Escalade with spinnin' rims. Chutch is where the ursher (again no mis-spelling) board is all wearing matching bedazzled jean jackets. Chutch is where Keyshia Cole is up singing with the praise team. And let's not forget the most telltale sign of a chutch. Chutch is where Profit or Profitess Such and Such is gone call for a thousand-dollar line at offerin' time.

My girl was watching some preacher on television this morning (still wearing her lingerie from the night before . . . but I ain't mad). I couldn't call it, though. He had a nice little crowd going, and some folks were definitely trying to get some deliverance. This dude might actually have a church. But since my fornicatin', tithin' and offerin'-paying FOTW (freak of the week for the newbies) is watching, more than likely, it's some good old-fashioned toe-stompin' CHUTCH!

Mad Black Blogger is OUT. Hit me up with ya' comments!

Chapter Three

Darrin

I'm sitting at my parents' table, doing the obligatory once-a-week family dinner. Priscilla likes the illusion that her family is in harmony and the two most important men in her life are the best of chums. I lock eyes with my father, Big Mathis. It seems like neither one of us wants to be here.

Physically, my father is an intimidating man. He stands six feet three inches and weighs nearly three hundred pounds. The hair on his head and face is a stark white. So white, in fact, that it's hard to believe once upon a time it used to be black.

I slowly breathe in and out, trying to calm my nerves under Mathis's intense stare. I will not start any arguments with Mathis. Will not engage in any arguments with Mathis. My mission is simple. I need the money for my Atlanta expedition, and I need to convince my father to give it to me.

Actually, it's not as simple as it sounds. Mathis Bain-bridge is a complex man. Priscilla is much better at reading him than I am, but over the years, I have picked up on clues to his temperamental mood swings. I like to think that I'm fairly accurate.

The key is the way he chews his food.

Sounds crazy, but it has rarely failed me. If he's chewing slowly, taking his time and savoring the meal, that means he's had a good day. A good day means the bank is open. If he's gnawing his food rapidly, like a caveman ripping into a raw brontosaurus steak, he's on the warpath. Consequently, the bank is closed.

Tonight he's chewing slowly.

"So, Dad, I'm working on a new story. This one is big."

He gives a favorable grunt as his reply. That means I should continue.

"It's about that huge mega-church pastor in Atlanta, Bishop Kumal Prentiss." I hope he can't hear the nervousness in my voice.

He scratches his hair and raises an eyebrow. I've got his attention. "The one who comes on Sunday morning?" he asks.

"Yes, that's the one."

Priscilla smiles. She loves a story about church. "What kind of story are you going to write about a bishop?"

"An exposé. My journalistic instincts tell me that there is a scandal brewing somewhere in that congregation."

"Why do you have to go all the way to Atlanta to write about a crooked preacher? We got plenty of them right here in Cleveland," states Mathis, as if he knows it to be a fact.

"Oh, you just hush your mouth, Mathis," fusses Priscilla. "I don't like the idea of my son digging up dirt on such an influential black man. He could become our next Martin Luther King."

Here *she* goes. I bite my lip, trying to maintain my composure while thinking of a comeback. "I guarantee you, Mother, this man is as slick as Bronner Bros. oil sheen."

Mathis gets right down to business. "And how do you plan to pay for this little adventure?"

Inside my chest cavity, my heart starts pounding and my breaths become faster and shallower. I can't let Mathis take this to our recurring argument. I've had this same conversation so many times that I call it the *Groundhog Day* discussion. I feel just like Bill Murray in that silly movie, where he keeps repeating the same day over and over and over again. Sometimes I gain a little ground, sometimes I lose a little.

"It's not an adventure, Dad. This is my career." My tone gives away my frustration.

"When you start making money instead of spending mine," says Mathis, laughing, "then we'll call it a career."

Déjà vu totally kicks in. I let out an exasperated sigh. "Mother, please talk to him."

"I don't know, Darrin. This story doesn't sound like a good idea. Why don't you write a piece about my Jack and Jill chapter? We've given a lot back to the community this year."

Great. I don't even have Priscilla on my side. We can usually double-team Mathis and wear him down. Looks like I'm all alone on this one.

"Dad, I promise this is the last time."

Okay, I don't really mean that. But I'm grasping for straws here.

"Right," says Mathis. "Until the next time."

Mathis grunts something further under his breath and goes right back to eating his food. And now . . . he's gnawing. But I can't stop now. I *need* to write this story like a hemophiliac needs a blood transfusion. (I know that's graphic, but I really need to write this story!) I feel something akin to desperation in the pit of my stomach.

"Come on, Dad. Aren't you just a little bit curious about what this man is doing with ten percent of the income of twenty thousand poor black folk?"

He wipes his mouth with his napkin. I think I've struck a nerve. Looks like he's seriously considering it.

I continue, "He probably drives a Bentley! Dad, you don't even drive a Bentley. And I bet he's never worked a day in his life."

Priscilla gasps. Her pretty little mouth goes into a frown. I'm upsetting her, I know. But it can't be helped. Sometimes in my battles with Mathis, she's an innocent casualty.

I boldly add another log to the fire. "You know what? I bet he's womanizing all the single women in his church."

Mathis glances at Priscilla. "Probably some of the married ones, too."

Priscilla glares at Mathis and slams her fork down on the table. Wait a minute. Did I just miss something?

"Your father," hisses Priscilla, "has accused my pastor of all types of ungodly mess."

Looks like the story might be right here. I haven't seen Priscilla this angry in a long time. Not since she caught me in bed with the debutante I escorted to the Jack and Jill cotillion.

"I stand by each and every one of those accusations, and I will until the day I die."

I can't help but ask, "What accusations?"

Mathis roars, "Let's just say that I caught your mother in a very compromising position with that Pastor Thomas."

"Mathis!" Priscilla stands up at her seat.

"He's a grown man. He knows the facts of life."

My head is spinning. Entirely too much information. I don't care how grown I get, I don't ever want to know about my mother doing something like that. I don't even want to think of her having sex with my father. Prefer to believe I was left on the doorstep.

"Your father is lying. I have never had any inappropriate relationship with *any* man, much less my pastor."

For the sake of my sanity, I choose to believe my mother.

Mathis laughs and shakes his head. I know him well, but for some reason, I can't interpret this body language.

"You know what, son? I'm going to fund this trip. It's about time somebody exposed some of these rotten hypocrites."

Okay . . . this is a victory, but somehow it doesn't feel like one. I feel guilty about the tears forming in my mother's eyes and the glee dancing in my father's.

"But," continues my father, "this is the last time you're getting money from me. If this doesn't work out, you're getting a real job. It doesn't have to be at Bainbridge Transports, but I'm not taking care of you anymore."

I think my heart stopped. Big Mathis has raised the stakes, and I don't know if I want to bet my easy life on a could-be crooked pastor.

"Dad, sometimes it takes a while for this kind of thing to materialize." I try to sidestep, give myself some time to form a backup plan.

"You've got until the end of the year."

I protest, "But it's already September."

Mathis clears his throat. "Then you had better get moving."

"It's on and popping," I tell my best friend, Leon, as I put the finishing touches on our submarine sandwiches.

"What's on and popping? And when did you say the fight was coming on?"

"Pops is fronting me the money for Atlanta, and the fight doesn't come on until eleven."

"Seriously! All right, now. Atlanta is the home to lots of fine, thick black women! As soon as I get a chance, I'm visiting."

I laugh as I watch Leon rub his hands together hungrily. He is obsessed with what he calls "thick" women, but he and I have totally different ideas on our definitions of thick. To me, thick is no larger than a size twelve, but to Leon, thick begins at size sixteen. It doesn't help matters that Leon is all of one hundred fifty pounds on a six-feet frame. The brotha has a Jack Sprat complex.

"You are not coming down to my crib and filling it up with all of your big girlfriends."

"Don't hate just because I want me a girl who can fry chicken and make a sweet-potato pie."

"Thin girls can't cook?"

Leon raises an eyebrow. "How many do you know who can?"

He always wins this argument, because he's right. Out of all the model types I've ever dated, not one of them has even been able to boil a hot dog. Shayna is probably the worst. I knew she was a lost cause when she tried to bake a can of Pillsbury biscuits in the microwave.

I take a bite of my sandwich. It's perfect. "So Priscilla is going to find an apartment for me and have it all decked out when I get there."

"Must be nice, man."

Leon always finds a way to make me feel uncomfortable talking about my family's money. He grew up in a single-parent household with his mother working two jobs to be able to save enough money for his college education. Every time I mention anything about my parents giving me money, Leon's quiet contemplation makes me feel materialistic.

Leon asks, "So what are you going to do about Shayna when you leave? She's making wedding plans, you know."

"Man, listen! I don't know how many different ways I can say 'Baby, let's slow down.' She ain't hearing it."

"I told you to stop cooking for these women, man. That's what gets you in trouble. All that cooking and sweet-talking, and you're right out of every black woman's fantasy."

"Here you go."

"Man, I'm serious. How many women do we know who grew up with a bunch of women and not one man in sight? To them, the ideal man is the one who is going to cater to their every whim while they sit up and eat that pasta stuff you be fixing."

"Man, you are a fool!" I can't help but laugh, even though I've heard this all before.

"I speak the truth, man."

My doorbell rings, and I jump up to answer it. I'm not expecting anyone; tonight is fight night. Usually me and Leon kicking it in an estrogen-free environment. I look out the peephole.

Speak of the devil and she'll appear. My head starts pounding with a frustration headache. This woman insists on making our bedroom romps permanent, and I'm not there yet. Don't know if I'll ever be there.

I hesitate before opening the door, but she ain't having that. "Darrin, you better quit playing!"

"Shayna . . . what's up?" I ask with the fakest smile ever.

She kisses my lips like she doesn't see my boy and our grub. She knows this is the "no ladies" night. She purrs, "Baby, I was just thinking about you, and I had to see you. I haven't heard from you all day."

She hadn't heard from me, since I hadn't called. I'd spent the whole day packing for my Atlanta trip. I hadn't even thought to call. And I don't feel like being smothered with her 'love talk.'

"I know. I've just been busy."

"Hey, Leon," she says to my friend. He grumbles under his breath.

She glances over at three boxes in the corner, then

looks at me for an explanation. "You giving some stuff away to the Purple Heart veterans?" she asks.

Okay . . . trying to think quickly. I don't want to tell her about Atlanta yet. Want to wait until the day before I leave.

"No . . . not exactly," I reply as I nervously shift my weight from leg to leg.

She notices my jitters and is immediately suspicious. She hits me with rapid fire, her red curls bouncing like flames. "Looks to me like you're moving. Or is someone moving in with you? You cheating on me, Darrin? Who is she?"

How did we get from Purple Hearts veterans to cheating? I will never, ever understand this woman's thought process.

Might as well tell the truth and get it over with. "My father is giving me the money to go to Atlanta."

"I can't believe you are still on that. You're really going to write a story on Bishop Prentiss?"

"Yes, I am, and I cannot wait to get started."

"So when do we leave?" Shayna asks timidly.

"We?"

I knew this was coming; that's why I didn't want to tell her. But Shayna can go on somewhere with that noise. The only word I'm feeling for her is lust, so there is no way I'm bringing her to Atlanta with me.

"Yes, we! As in you and me," she replies indignantly.

"You are not going to Atlanta with me."

I say this slowly, calmly, deliberately. Don't want her to have a scene in front of my boy. I want to end the conversation without any casualties, but the deep frown on her face is telling me that battle wounds are on the way.

"Baby, did you forget you have a job?" I ask, "baby" slipping off my tongue like I really mean it. "I have no idea how long I'll be gone."

"No, I didn't forget about my job, but you're rich. I shouldn't have to worry about working if we're together." Shayna's bottom lip protrudes in a juvenile-looking pout. I hate when she does this.

"My father is rich. I am not."

Leon rolls his eyes and sucks his teeth. Shayna glances at him with much attitude and continues, "Same difference. I don't know if I can do a long-distance relationship, Darrin."

I wince like she's stabbed me with a knife. "There you go with that word again."

"What word? 'Relationship'?"

I wince again and clutch my side. Leon snickers and takes a giant bite from his sandwich.

"If we don't have a relationship, Darrin," asks Shayna, "then what do we have?"

"Why do you have to define everything all the time? Why can't we ride things out and see how they go?"

With a burst of angry energy, Shayna spins on her heels and heads for the door. I half want to let her go and forget we ever met, but the view of Shayna leaving is too much for a brotha like me. I can't let that fine woman walk away hating me. As wrong as I do them, most of the women I lust and leave still want me. Shayna won't be any different.

"Don't you even want to know when I'm leaving?" I ask, trying to stall her while I think of something good.

Shayna takes a pause but doesn't reply. I know she's

thinking about it. She doesn't want to let me go so easily, either.

"Baby, why don't you come over here and give me a hug? I am going on the road, remember? You don't want me to be all love-deprived when I get to Atlanta, do you?"

I watch her anger subside and the frown melt away from her face. I've still got it.

She turns and hugs me, punctuating the action with a slow grind. I almost want to tell Leon to scram so we can finish what Shayna is trying to start. But that would be counterproductive. Plus, I really want to see this fight.

I try to reassure her. "Look, girl, I'm not going to Atlanta to hook up with another woman, I'm going there to work."

"I know you, Darrin," she replies.

"If you knew me, then you'd know this is not about finding a woman, Shayna. It's about my career."

Convinced, she wraps her arms around my neck and squeezes me again in a tight embrace. This time her exclamation mark is a deep tongue kiss that weakens my knees.

She says, "Don't forget about all this while you're in ATL."

"How could I?" I respond truthfully. "I'll call you from Atlanta."

Shayna walks out of my door, maybe out of my life. I will call her once or twice while I'm in Atlanta, to smooth the transition and keep her from doing anything nutty. But I'm cooling this down. I'm not trying to be anyone's husband or, worse, baby's daddy, and Shayna is getting way too serious for my comfort.

Leon shakes his head.

"What?" I ask.

"Told you, man . . . all that French toast and pasta. You be having them chicks feening over you."

"It's not just the food, my man. I have many talents."

Chapter Four

DIARY OF A MAD BLACK BLOGGER

Guess what, yo? I'm on location. Can't tell y'all where, but this whole bling-bling-but-I'm-a-man-of-God thing has got me bugging. So, I'm going Malik Yoba (NY undercover, for the televisionally challenged) on this megachurch pastor. I'm gonna get the goods and see if this one particular shepherd is for real. Don't worry, though, I'm gonna keep y'all posted on all the developments. And if I find out some dirt, I'm gonna help "shine the light of heaven" all up in that piece. Real talk. Maybe, in the meantime, I'll meet a nice church girl and settle on down. Let me quit playing. I'm out, y'all. Hit me up in the comments section.

Chapter Five

Emoni

I am not a pretty girl. I'm saved, sanctified, and filled with the Holy Ghost . . . but I'm not pretty.

I stand back from my full-length mirror and squint. Every Sunday morning I do the same self-appraisal, and every Sunday I come to the same conclusion. I'm not a pretty girl.

Wait, let me qualify that statement. I'm not some low-self-esteem-having, fishing-for-compliments basket case. I just know what I see in the mirror.

Daddy says I'm cute, and my mother calls me handsome, as in "Emoni, you are a handsome woman." But handsome is not pretty. It might actually be the opposite of pretty.

The state of my looks is relevant information because as of right now I am the president of the singles' ministry at my church, but I'd much rather be the president of the married couples' ministry. I'm ready for the Lord to bless me with a husband, but obviously, He and almost all of the eligible brothers at my church feel otherwise. And we've got a big congregation, too. I just can't understand how, out of ten thousand members—three thousand of those being men—the bishop's oldest daughter can't seem to find a man.

Must be my looks, because everything else in the package is right.

I look like my father. I have the same close-set brown eyes and short lashes, same short stature. I'm twenty-four, with a teenager's acne and thick hair that looks good in a roller set or bone-straight. My skin is the color of coffee with a little bit of cream, but not enough to make me high yellow, like my sister, Sascha.

Sascha is the pretty one. And my brother, Tyler, is the pretty boy.

The youngest two Prentiss children can stop traffic with their looks. Nineteen-year-old Sascha is the spitting image of our mother's Creole ancestors, with long, wavy jet-black hair set against skin the color of a porcelain doll. Tyler is twenty-two and has the same complexion as Sascha but wears his curls cut close to his head. His thick eyebrows and lashes accentuate the green eyes that I call a blessing and he calls a curse.

Even though I'm not pretty, I have my own set of blessings. My tiny waist and pop-out behind can stop a little traffic, too. I turn around in the mirror and view myself from behind to confirm that fact. And to top it all off, I have great teeth. Don't think great teeth are a blessing? Well, wait until you see a cute girl smile with teeth like a shark's.

Plus, I'm smart. Honestly, my intelligence wasn'

something I really valued until recently. I'd always tried to dumb down when I met men, but that gets old quickly.

I know my daddy, Bishop Kumal Prentiss, values my brainpower. I work full-time for his ministry, and truth be told, I'm the one who keeps everything operating smoothly. I'm the planner of conferences, the queen of damage control, and the go-to person for all questions and complaints.

I have time to do all of this because I don't have a man.

Sascha swings my door open, like she always does. "Emoni! We are about to be late for Sunday school! How long are you going to stand in front of that mirror?"

Right. Like she really wants to go to Sunday school. She's just in a rush to see her tacky little boyfriend, Kevin. Not even Sunday is sacred for those two fornicators. They sneak off in between services to park in a borrowed car and do whatever it is they do that leaves passion marks all over Sascha's neck.

Am I just a little bit jealous of them? No. I'm really jealous. More like seven-deadly-sins kind of envious.

I take one last look in the mirror, let out a sigh, and give up on waiting for my reflection to transform into a pretty one. "I'm ready."

"Well, then, let's roll," calls Tyler from the hallway.

The three of us walk downstairs single file to meet with our parents in the foyer. Even though we don't ride together, Daddy likes us to leave the house as a family.

My sister and I are wearing standard church apparel. I have on a tailored navy blue suit, and Sascha is wearing a cream-colored dress. Tyler, on the other hand, has on baggy jeans and a Karl Kani button-down shirt.

After appraising his outfit, I comment, "You could've at least put on a tie."

Tyler rolls his eyes. "Don't start, Emoni."

"Don't start what?" I ask. "I'm just trying to remind you that we're going to church and not the bowling alley."

I can't help being a little judgmental. I wouldn't be a big sister if I weren't.

Daddy and Mother finally join us in the foyer. Their outfits are color-coordinated, as they always are. A taupe suit for Daddy with an olive-green patterned tie. Mother is wearing an olive-green suit with hat, shoes, and purse to match. They complement each other perfectly.

Our mother, Diana, is a tiny woman, not even five feet tall. Her round face is the same porcelain shade as that of her two youngest children, and her eyes are greener than Tyler's. She wears her hair in a chin-length roller set and never ever goes a Sunday without wearing one of her pretty hats.

Bishop tries to mediate. "It's all right, Emoni. Your brother is fine."

"She's right, Bishop, he should put on a suit. He looks like a hip-hop hooligan," retorts Diana.

"We are not having that conversation this morning. I'm just blessed to have all of my children worshipping with me, even though they're grown."

People always find it funny that Mother never calls Daddy by his first name in public or even in front of us. After he'd started preaching, she didn't think it respectful for her to call him Kumal in anyone's hearing. Sascha and Tyler have taken her lead. They don't call him Daddy anymore—only I do that.

Daddy assesses us all and smiles. "So are we ready to go?"

"One second," says Diana.

One of the couch pillows is uneven, and the other is falling to the floor. If Mother doesn't fix that before she walks out the door, she's going to be thinking about it all day at church. She's really weird with her neat-freak thing. I can remember her combing and recombing my ponytails until they were perfectly symmetrical. Sometimes it took hours to get them the way she wanted. I was so glad when she started letting me go to the beauty salon.

Sascha laughs. "Mommy, just leave that."

Mother ignores Sascha and continues straightening until she feels satisfied. One thing about Mother: She takes great pride in this house, even though it's modest by mega-church-preacher standards. For a while she pressed Daddy to get her a new home with six bedrooms, four bathrooms, and a finished recreation room. He staunchly refused and used the poverty of many of the members as an excuse. Daddy couldn't in good conscience live in excess while his members suffered. Mother did not agree, but Daddy wouldn't budge.

When she's satisfied with the state of her home, Mother finally says, "Okay, now I'm ready."

We walk outside to our separate vehicles, Daddy and Mother to their ten-year-old Cadillac, Tyler to his used Ford F-150, and me and Sascha to my used Toyota Corolla. If you ask me, Daddy takes this living-modestly thing to a ridiculous extreme. He refuses to buy any of us a new car, not even a Hyundai or something cheap. True enough that the Cadillac runs well and is still in great condition, but it should've been traded in a long time ago.

It's not that I'm all for pastors living high off anybody's hog while the rest of the church resides in slave quarters. I'm disgusted by that. But Daddy deserves more! He works tirelessly, never has a vacation, and is always at the beck and call of every member at Freedom of Life. I don't think anyone would be mad if he upgraded a little bit.

Anytime I bring it up, though, Daddy always quotes the Scripture at Romans 14:16: "'Let not then your good be evil spoken of . . .'" He doesn't want anything to take away from all the good he does preaching the Gospel. That's why I'm watching him and Mother roll their windows down on this muggy September morning instead of blasting the AC.

Sascha jumps in on the passenger side of my car. Why didn't she ride with Tyler? "I know you're driving today," she says, "but can I use your car later this evening? I'm going out."

"Why can't Kevin drive?"

"If you must know, his fuel pump went out. His car is not running right now."

I'm smirking because I can't stand Kevin. "So it looks like you two are stranded, because y'all won't be using my car as the hotel room on wheels."

"You are so evil, Emoni. I wish Daddy would buy me my own car."

"He will when you graduate from college. Oh, wait! You dropped out. Looks like you're going to be hoofing it."

Sascha rolls her eyes at me and slumps back in her seat. Ask me if I care. Daddy probably will buy her a car, even though she has no intentions of finishing her classes at Clark Atlanta. She's spoiled rotten.

We ride in silence, which is a blessing, because I like to meditate on God before I walk through the church doors. Since Sascha's in the car, I can't talk to Him out loud like I usually do, but I send up a silent prayer.

Sascha and I part ways as soon as we get to the church parking lot. Her friends Gina and Alissa are waiting for her, looking like those two crows from the old Looney Tunes cartoons. They both look at me with disdain, and I return the favor; the feeling is definitely mutual.

Oscar is also waiting, right at the edge of my assigned parking spot. "Praise God this morning," he says with a smile that is way too big and unnatural. That's his church smile. He gets on my last nerve.

"Hi, Oscar," I say as I go to close my car door.

Oscar jumps in front of me, nearly pushing me over. "No. Let me get that for you."

"It's just a car door. I am capable of doing that myself."

Oscar smiles and takes my Bible, purse, and gym bag. I snatch my purse back and give him an evil glare as he gets ready to protest. There is no reason why a man should carry a woman's purse. Not even if he thinks he's in love with her and wants to marry her.

That thought makes me shudder. I can't see myself walking down anybody's aisle with Oscar, but he is intent on making it happen. I don't totally brush him off, because even though I'm not feeling him, I don't see any other brothers stumbling over themselves to get with me. Who knows, maybe the older I get, the better he'll look.

We step into Daddy's office, where he has already started the preparations for morning worship. He's drinking a cup of tea prepared by Sister Ophelia Moore, head nurse and president of Freedom of Life's gossip ministry. She's the only one who makes Daddy's tea the way he likes it—cool enough to drink straight down but still warm enough to open his vocal cords.

"Praise the Lord, Emoni," says Sister Ophelia.

Without cracking a smile, I reply, "He's worthy."

Daddy should've replaced Sister Ophelia when she started that vicious rumor about Sascha and her grandson, Kevin. She'd caught the two of them in his bedroom, half naked, and then proceeded to tell everybody in our church family who would listen. If they'd let her, she would've made it a church announcement.

For the life of me, I couldn't understand why she wasn't embarrassed to drag her own grandson's name through the mud. Maybe she was happy she could point the finger at someone else's child for a change.

Daddy was furious, of course, but not at Sister Ophelia. I had never seen him tear into Sascha the way he did. He gave her a lecture that ran the gamut from being displeasing to God to embarrassing our family. I remember feeling sorry for Sascha, but not sorry enough to comfort her. She and Tyler don't care one bit about the impact of their actions on Daddy's ministry.

Anyway, Daddy forgave Sister Ophelia and allowed her to remain in her post as head nurse. Mother and I tiptoe around the woman, wondering when she will drop another bomb on our family.

Daddy is just about ready to go out in front of the congregation. He's singing "Something About the Name

Jesus" in a low tone, giving honor to God and warming up his voice.

Daddy is known for the way he can minister the preached word of God and especially for his ministry in song. I've personally witnessed God use him to cause people to come to repentance after hearing a song that he wrote and sang.

As spiritually powerful as Daddy is, he doesn't have a very memorable physical appearance. He's around five feet seven and not over one hundred and eighty-five pounds. His salt-and-pepper hair is brushed to the back in waves, and dark-rimmed glasses cover his compassionate brown eyes. When he's not preaching, Daddy is a meek and soft-spoken man, but when the Spirit of God takes over, Daddy is transformed. Under the anointing of God, Daddy is an amazing orator and singer.

To say that I'm proud of my father is an understatement.

Oscar, who besides being my pest, is also Bishop's armor bearer, asks, "Is there anything else you need, Bishop?"

"Did you tell the sound people to add extra bass when I start?"

"Yes, Bishop, everything is in order."

"Good."

After quickly swallowing the tea, Daddy stands up from his desk and holds out his arms. Oscar rushes over to adjust his cuff links and then gingerly places a freshly dry-cleaned and pressed preaching robe over Daddy's shoulders. When Oscar is done, Daddy nods and motions toward the door. Oscar responds immediately and opens the door to Daddy's office, allowing three ministers dressed in clergy attire to enter.

One of the ministers takes oil from a bottle on Daddy's desk and rubs a little on the head of everyone in the room. When he finishes, we join hands and bow our heads for the prayer.

We can all hear the worship service from inside Daddy's office. The congregation seems to be in an uproar. I can feel the spirit of the Lord as well.

Daddy prays, "Lord, I ask that you use me, your humble servant, this morning. Tell me what to say to your people, Lord. Make me the messenger of your will. Lord, God, I decrease so that you may increase. Let your congregation not see me this morning, but let them see your spirit operating in me. Lord, touch each and every one of them with a word for their situations. Cause souls to be saved and deliverance and healing to take place. I ask these things in the mighty name of Jesus. Let every heart say amen."

"Amen" comes from everyone in the room.

Daddy smiles and says, "All right, y'all. Let's go."

Oscar opens the door, and the ministers exit first. Daddy is next, with Oscar on his heels. I use the other entrance and slip into the congregation unnoticed. Everyone is too busy applauding Daddy to pay any attention to me sitting in a row at the back of the sanctuary.

Daddy takes the microphone from its cradle and says, "I feel the presence of God in this place."

The congregation responds with more applause and shouts of "amen" and "hallelujah."

"I can *feel* him in the atmosphere!" Daddy continues. "Lord, you are welcome today. Let's give God some praise right now. Give God a *high* praise!"

I clap fiercely as the congregations' applause grows

louder and the excitement reaches a fever pitch. One woman gets up from her seat and runs down the aisle, rejoicing and shouting.

"That's right, sis! Bless Him!" Daddy implores. "Bless Him! Don't look at her funny. You don't know what the Lord has brought her through."

The woman stops running and starts into another phase of her praise. She jerks and stomps her way into a spontaneous dance. The people sitting near her start to clap in time to the music, which is playing faster and faster.

To the right of me is a young man I've never seen before. The sight of him snaps me right out of my praise break, and instantly, I picture him as my boyfriend. I dismiss the thought almost as quickly. He's the type of guy who dates Sascha.

He seems out of place, with a notepad and a brand-new Bible on his lap. I'm talking brand-new, like he just ripped the shrink wrap off on his way into the sanctuary. He's scribbling furiously in that little notepad even though Daddy hasn't started preaching yet.

He must feel me staring at him, because he looks over at me. He smiles, and it takes my breath away. Boldly, he looks me up and down, his eyes resting on my behind. My God, that brother is fine. Where has he been hiding, because I'm sure he's never been to Freedom of Life.

After service is over, I do my pastor's-daughter duty and go over to introduce myself to our visitor. Okay, so I'm not usually in a rush to fulfill that particular task, but the fineness of this brother is so exceptional that it's making me want to step outside the box.

Just as I'm about to unleash all of this Emoni charm

on that tall milk-chocolate black man's answer to the Greek Adonis, I'm cut off at the pass. Dorcas, Mother's armor bearer and basic irritant, has made it there first. I have never seen Dorcas fellowshipping at the back of the church, where the latecomers usually congregate. Her hungry self must've sniffed out fresh man meat from her seat up in the front of the church.

I stand close enough to listen to their conversation without being too obvious.

"Is this your first visit to Freedom of Life?" she asks.

"Yes, it is."

"Are your wife and family with you this morning?"

"I'm not married."

I feel my heart jump. Okay, he's fine and single. Keep it moving, Dorcas, keep it moving.

Okay, she's not moving. She's still talking, and she's working my nerves. "Did you enjoy the service?" Dorcas asks, trying to make her voice sound deep and throaty, like some kind of Eartha Kitt wannabe.

"I did. Thank you for asking."

His voice is rich, deep, and smooth—exactly how it should sound. I hate to see a fine brother open his mouth and sound like Pee-wee Herman.

"I'm Dorcas. If you need anything, let me know. We want you to come back and visit us again."

We? Us? Who are these pluralities? That heifer knows she wants this brother not only to come back to church but to scoop her up out of her lonely little existence. She's so thirsty.

I can't stand her.

Speaking of thirsty people, here comes Oscar, pressing his way through the crowd and trying to make it to me.

Looks like I'll have to meet Mr. Adonis some other time, because I'm not about to let him think Oscar and I are a couple. I slip out of my aisle and out the church doors into the parking lot. Oscar, of course, gives chase.

"Emoni . . . wait up," he gasps.

"What is it, Oscar?"

"I was wondering if you'd like to have lunch with me. My treat."

I smile at him. I'm not totally heartless. "Not today, Oscar. I've got to finish up some articles for the church newsletter. I'll eat something at home."

"Do you want some company?"

Why does he have to be so relentless? "Thank you for thinking of me, but I'll be fine."

I leave him standing there looking lonely and walk over to the other side of the parking lot, where Sascha and her little friends are congregated. The loser Kevin Moore is there with his arm wrapped around Sascha's waist. Obviously, neither of them is going to go out of his or her way to dispel Sister Ophelia's gossip; it's like they *want* everyone to know they are sleeping together. Sascha looks up and sees me, then pushes Kevin away. I don't know why she's trying to hide her mess from me. Everyone else knows.

Sascha's best friend, Gina, asks, "Sascha, you driving tonight?"

"I don't know, y'all," she replies loudly enough for me to hear. "Emoni is tripping, and she just snitched on me and Kevin the other night."

"I'll drive, then," states Alissa, the third member of Sascha's crew.

"Ain't nobody getting in that hooptie. Sascha, when is your father going to get you a car?"

I snicker to myself, because I know the deal. Daddy told each of us that we would get a car the day of our college graduation. But Sascha started dating Kevin her freshman year and failed all but one of her classes. She dropped out after one semester.

"Here's a thought," I offer when I get close enough to join the conversation. "Why doesn't Kevin get himself a decent car? He's a grown man, right? Grown enough to take my little sister to bed, but he can't even drive her to the movies?"

Kevin looks at me with pure hatred in his eyes. Whatever. Somebody around here has to speak the truth.

Just as Kevin is fixing his mouth to say something foul, Tyler walks up and interrupts his flow. Gina and Alissa shamelessly flirt with my brother, who doesn't really take them seriously. They are too ghetto for his tastes, but they still try. It's sickening, but me and Sascha are used to it. The only son of a mega-church pastor is a good catch.

Tyler asks, "Sascha, what did I tell you about hanging with these two?"

"You know you love us," says Gina, using an almost unrecognizable sexy tone.

Tyler smiles seductively. "Where y'all kicking it to?"

"You want to kick it with us, big brother?" Sascha asks, breaking up the flirtation between Tyler and Gina.

Kevin glares at me and pulls Sascha into a tight embrace, practically molding his body with hers. Again she pushes him away. I feel my anger rising at his brazenness.

"Kevin, we're still at church—"

Kevin rolls his eyes. "Right, right. I keep forgetting about that 'Holy Ground' thing."

Tyler seems to notice my blood boiling and walks over to me. He gives me a big bear hug, lifting me off my feet. I can't contain my smile, even though I still want to spit fire at Kevin.

"Sorry about this morning, sis," says Tyler. "Next week I'll wear a tie for you."

"Yeah, right."

Sascha pleads her case again. "Come on, Emoni. Let us use your car. Oscar will take you home."

"No."

"It's not like you have any plans."

"You don't know whether I have any plans or not."

"What?" asks Kevin. "Is there a prayer meeting tonight?"

I am lost without a comeback for that raggedy Kevin, so I turn away. I mean, I'm a normal God-fearing single woman. I'm not out here acting like Jezebel, but I'm no Bible thumper, either. It annoys me how some people try to make me feel bad about living right.

I leave them to their plans and walk over to my car. I don't care to know what they're up to, anyway. I just want to go home, have a bowl of ice cream, and watch the newest episode of *Grey's Anatomy* that I Tivo'ed.

Under my breath, I'm muttering curses at Kevin as I click the automatic lock on my car. I'm so engrossed in my irritation that I don't notice Mr. Adonis standing right in front of me. He scares the living daylights out of me when he steps up to open my car door.

"So, chivalry is not dead! Thank you," I say.

Oh my God, that sounded so stupid, but I had a brain freeze and couldn't think of anything better. My hand goes to my hair. I want to make sure my little swoop bang is still covering that majestic-size pimple on my forehead.

Mr. Adonis smiles again. Again I have to fight for my next breath. "My mother raised me well," he says.

It makes absolutely no sense how fine this man is. His complexion is a smooth chocolate. He has slightly slanted eyes and a nose that boasts an Indian ancestor or two. And the waves on his low haircut did not come out of a box. Makes no sense at all.

"So . . . did you enjoy the service?" I ask.

"Yes, that's exactly what I told Sister Dorcas."

Dang. So he knew I was eavesdropping. Have to think quickly.

"Oh, I'm surprised that's all. You were staring so hard at my booty when I walked past that I'm shocked you even heard the message."

Mr. Adonis throws his head back and lets out a loud and unhindered laugh. Like he's never heard something so funny in his life. I can't tell if this is a good thing or a bad thing. He holds his hand out for me to shake. "I'm Darrin Bainbridge. And you are?"

"Emoni Prentiss."

"Bishop Prentiss's daughter?"

"Yes, one of them. Welcome to Freedom of Life. I hope you visit again."

"I will."

I step into my car, hoping Darrin doesn't see my hands trembling as a result of his unreasonable good looks. His eyes are following my every move, which does nothing but make me more nervous.

"Are you going to join the church?" I ask after Darrin closes my door.

"I am seriously considering it."

"We have a great . . . singles' ministry."

Darrin's smile turns into another laugh. "So I've heard."

Dang that Dorcas. She beat me to the punch again. "Well, I'll see you around."

"Count on it."

"Have a blessed week," I say as I pull out of the parking spot.

I glance into the rearview mirror as I drive away. Darrin smiles and waves. How had he known I would even look back? Am I that transparent? I wave back, my heart filling with hope. Maybe I'll have my first romance with Mr. Black Adonis.

Chapter Six

Darrin

Hush my mouth and call me a believer. Well, not exactly, but I am most definitely impressed. Seeing Freedom of Life in person is worlds different from seeing it on television. They must've spent a grip decorating that church. And when I say a grip, I mean add up the building funds of about one thousand little storefront churches and then work your way up.

Bishop Prentiss can hang in the preaching department, too. He didn't preach on anything new—I've heard the Prodigal Son message dozens of times—but his manner left me with a pleasant feeling. Bishop Prentiss didn't hoop and holler like the old-school Baptist preacher at Priscilla's church. He just intellectually broke down the Scriptures, and the crowd went wild.

After the service started, I was honestly trying to pay attention to the message when one of the juiciest booties I'd ever seen sashayed past me in a snug navy blue skirt.

I have never seen the likes of that in Cleveland. That behind must've been nurtured on biscuits and gravy and sweet tea.

Now I know that the booty belongs to Emoni Prentiss, Bishop's daughter, which makes her off-limits. Totally off-limits. Even if she is funny and sassy. Even though she has a tiny waist to match that behind. I don't need any emotional attachments compromising my story. And a brotha could get emotional over a booty like that.

Just thinking about Emoni is making me restless, so I decide to take a swim in the gym. Priscilla followed through and hooked a brotha up with a sharp two-bedroom apartment in Lithonia, where a lot of the up-and-coming black folk live. I would've preferred Buckhead, but since I'm not paying the bills, I'm not complaining.

Before I can make it out the door, the telephone rings. "Hello?"

"Hey, boo. How's Atlanta?" Shayna says in her raspy and sexy tone.

I feel the frown form on my face. I did not give her my new phone number. "Shayna. I was going to call you later."

"Don't lie, boy. I had to get your number from your mother. Plus, you didn't answer your cell phone."

I make a mental note to inform Priscilla when I break it off with a woman. "That's cool. I thought you were mad at me."

"I might be. A little."

"Don't be. I'll buy you something really nice when I get home." Here I go making promises I have no intentions of keeping. Just want this conversation to end on a high note. It's not good to have a woman somewhere hating you or hating on you.

Shayna giggles. "Of course you will. Have you met Bishop Prentiss yet?"

"No. I went to my first service today, though."

"What did you think?" Shayna's excitement travels across the telephone lines.

"Well . . . it was different."

"Are you having second thoughts about trying to destroy a man of God?"

I reply honestly. "I'm not here to destroy anyone who doesn't deserve destroying. Anyway, so far I haven't seen anything unusual, so this may be a waste of time."

I watched Bishop Prentiss exit the church. Bishop and his wife got into a nice but not extravagant Cadillac. The son drove a used but well-kept pickup truck, and Emoni drove a used Toyota Corolla. It was not at all what I had expected from a man who was fleecing his flock. Maybe he keeps his fleet of cars at the house.

"I told you," states Shayna matter-of-factly.

"His church seems to love him. They have nothing but good things to say about him."

"I *told* you."

"Yes, you did. But you didn't tell me how well he can preach. I have to say, I was impressed."

Shayna laughs. "Uh-oh! Watch out now. You just might mess around and catch the Holy Ghost up in there."

"Baby, I am in *no* danger of that."

"Mmm-hmm."

"Well, I was on my way out when you called."

"Got a date already?" Shayna sounds irritated.

I'm irritated that she's irritated. "No . . . going to work out. I'll call you sometime next week, okay?"

"Uh, okay." And now she's hurt.

I place the receiver back in its cradle and make another mental note to buy a new phone that's equipped with caller ID. Don't want any more distracting conversations with Shayna.

The fitness room is virtually abandoned when I enter, and most of the equipment looks brand-new. I pass by the weight benches, treadmills, and stair-stepper machines and open the door to the indoor Olympic-size pool. I can't wait to get into the refreshing water.

I've stripped down to my trunks and am about to dive into the pool when someone else walks into the fitness center. It's a female who looks familiar, and on closer inspection, I see that it's Dorcas.

She'd looked nice at church, even though she was pretty plain, but she looks much more appealing in her workout clothes. She has her long hair pulled up into a ponytail on the top of her head, showing pretty skin the color of a caramel apple and dotted with freckles. Her eyes are clearly the focal point of her face: large, brown, and framed by thick dark eyelashes. Her spandex workout clothing gives me a much better view of another sweet-tea-and-biscuits body.

She looks over at me and frowns like she can read my mind. She pushes open the door to the pool room. "Do I know you?"

I pull off my swim goggles so she can see my face. "I'm sorry. We met at church this morning."

Her frown softens immediately upon recognition.

"Oh, Brother Darrin. I'm sorry. I thought you were some stranger ogling me."

"Was I ogling? I thought I was simply admiring."

She blushes. I'm in there like swimwear.

"Do you live here?" she asks.

"I just moved in a week ago. I'm from Cleveland."

"Ohio? You're a long way from home," replies Dorcas. "Do you mind if I join you?"

"Not at all."

She snatches off her spandex shorts and walks over to the pool in a one-piece Speedo. Now I *am* ogling.

She dives into the water and swims a quick freestyle lap, her arms slicing the water and her legs propelling her like a fish. She pops out of the water when she finishes and smiles at me.

"So what made you come to Freedom of Life?" she asks.

I ease into the warm water and reply, "A friend of mine at home is a partner. She suggested that I check it out."

Dorcas nods. "Well, what did you think?"

"I'll be back again, that's for sure."

She cracks her neck and stretches. "Wanna race?"

"Sure."

"On your mark . . . get set . . ."

Dorcas takes off before she says "go," leaving me to catch up on her head start. Easily, I pass her by. Her swimming skills are nothing compared to mine. I have muscular legs and toned arms, and I swam on the teams in high school and college and for a hot minute considered training for the Olympic team.

I'm waiting at the edge of the pool with a slick smile when she emerges from the water.

"You cheated," I say.

She shrugs. "But you still won."

"Do you want to get something to eat later?"

"Not today. Maybe another time."

She jumps out of the pool and starts to dry herself off. I'm still ogling and trying to figure out how this girl just turned me down. I'm not too familiar with being rejected.

She continues, "I don't want to keep you from your workout. It was nice seeing you again."

"Same here. Perhaps we'll run into each other again."

Dorcas cracks a faint smile. "Perhaps. Bible study is on Wednesday, and the singles have a meeting on Saturday evening."

Sounds like if I want a date with this girl, it's going to be at church.

Chapter Seven

DIARY OF A MAD BLACK BLOGGER

*What up, my cyberspace homies and homettes? So, I told
y'all I was on location, right? Trying to see what I can see
about this "Mand of Gawd."*

Check this.

*The church is slamming . . . I've never seen such a
thing. Of course, I grew up in the land of storefronts.
Oh, you ain't know? Cleveland is known for having
a tiny storefront church on just about every corner.
I'm talkin' 'bout a Baptist, Pentecostal, Holiness,
Church of God in Christ, AME, and Reformed-Baptist-
Fire-Baptized-Holiness-Church-of-the-Lord-Our-King
all in one neighborhood.*

*So this whole mega-church thing is new to me. The
carpeted sanctuary with padded stadium seats is ridiculous, and the shuttle bus from the parking lot (because it's
a ten-minute walk if you're late) is all brand-spanking-
new. When I walked in and saw television screens on*

*every wall, I got ready to hear about how I could name
and claim my victory, deliverance, healing, salvation, and
financial blessings all by sowing a seed.*

*BUT I DIDN'T HEAR IT!!!! That's right. Bishop
So-and-so (can't give all the details yet) didn't even have
an offering. This dude has little slots in the lobby for people
to place their freewill offering. And I'm gone say this real
quietly. He actually preached about something real. I left
feeling uplifted.*

Yeah.

*So I'm thinking this dude might be on the up-and-up
when it comes to the money. BUT! And I should probably say BUTT.*

*He's got a daughter that is hella fine. Well, fine in that
girl-next-door-your-mama-want-you-to-marry kind of
way. Anyhoo, sweetie was feelin' me. She couldn't help
herself.*

*And y'all know . . . it ain't nothin' more scandalous
than a PK (preacher's kid, for the short-bus people).*

*Still on a mission, yo. And by the way, tell somebody
about my blog! Gotta get my hit count up so I can get that
long advertiser dough. Y'all know how I do.*

Hit me up in the comments section!

COMMENTS

Jia 8:59 p.m.

MBB, you dead wrong for lusting after the bishop's
daughter. All PKs are not the same! I should know. My
daddy was a pastor, and I didn't do anything to embarrass him. I kept my dirt on the low, you know what I'm
sayin'?

Tyrone 9:14 p.m.

Yeah, that's real talk, bro. Them pastors' daughters be off the chizzain! Keep us posted.

Chapter Eight

Darrin

Let's say that Dorcas's little rejection has interested me enough that I'm eager to see her again. Eager enough, in fact, that I'm sitting at one of the front tables in Freedom of Life's Bible study class. Plus, I want to meet Bishop Prentiss face-to-face, and I figure that it'll happen in a more intimate setting.

The first person I see is Emoni Prentiss. She's wearing a long jean skirt and a sleeveless blouse and has her hair in curls. She's smiling at me, and I feel myself shift in my seat as she walks over.

"You're here early," she comments as she takes the seat next to me.

I nod slowly. "Yep. I'm an early bird."

"Me, too."

Her perfume is nice. It has floral undertones and a hint of spice. Yeah, I know what a floral undertone is. It has an intoxicating effect, as do the singing silver bangles on her arm.

I'm searching my brain for a word to describe Emoni. She's attractive, though not pretty. Not in that traditional way that makes brothas like me swoon. But there is something . . . intriguing about her. Her deep eye contact makes our small talk feel like pillow talk.

She smiles. "I'm glad you decided to visit again—"

Before she finishes her sentence, Dorcas walks up to the table, grinning from ear to ear. She's wearing sunglasses and a sundress, looking very young, very casual, and hot to death. I can't help but grin right back at her. Emoni stands to leave, obviously unwilling to share our conversation with another female.

I touch Emoni's hand. "Don't go. We're not done talking."

I don't know what made me do that. I *need* her to go, to keep it moving. Because even though I don't mind us getting more personal, I don't like to deal with too many women in the same location. That can get messy. Although I definitely plan to investigate Emoni territory, I'm gonna deal with Dorcas first. First come, first served.

"Hey, Emoni," says Dorcas in a tone that is friendly only on the surface.

Emoni nods a hello and cringes a bit when Dorcas pulls a chair from another table in front of us.

Dorcas continues, "So I see you've met Darrin. He's coming to us by way of Cleveland."

Emoni nods, her shine extinguished. She notices someone across the room and rolls her eyes. I follow her gaze and see a corny-looking guy in a sport coat and slacks making a beeline for our table. He pats his small Afro and strokes his goatee as he approaches. Dude looks like he used to work out back in the day, but now he's soft, with a middle-aged man's gut.

He thrusts his hand into my face. I take it and give it a rough shake. "I'm Darrin Bainbridge."

"Trustee Oscar Williams," he replies.

Trustee? I guess it's not the middle-aged-man gut. It's the let's-go-to-the-all-you-can-eat-buffet-spot-after-church gut.

He looks at Emoni and frowns. "Your father needs you in the back," he says.

Emoni glances at me and reluctantly stands. Looks like she wants to sock the dude in his soft belly. "Darrin, we'll have to finish our discussion some other time."

"Right . . . of course."

Oscar and Dorcas both seem pleased as Emoni strides away. Dorcas moves to Emoni's seat, and Oscar turns on his heel, chasing after Emoni.

Dorcas says, "Those two are a couple."

"Are they?" I'm shocked, because Emoni definitely strikes me as available.

"They might as well be. Oscar is with her twenty-four/seven, and he's basically a part of the family. He's been in love with her for years."

Don't know why, but I'm jealous. Don't know anything about the girl except her name and the scent of her perfume, but I'm jealous. Even with a beautiful woman at my side who is clearly trying to get with me, I'm still jealous.

After a few moments of idle chitchat, a praise team assembles at the front of the classroom. They sing a medley of upbeat old-school gospel cuts like "Jesus on the Mainline" and "He's All Right." Dorcas leaves my side and takes her seat next to Bishop Prentiss's wife.

Bishop Prentiss emerges from a closed door and goes directly into his message. "Praise the Lord, saints of God. This evening we are going to continue our study on Christian living. Turn in your Bibles to Second Timothy, Chapter Two, and we're going to start reading at Verse Twenty."

Everyone stands to his or her feet and reads in unison.

But in a great house there are not only vessels of gold and of silver, but also of wood and of earth; and some to honour, and some to dishonour.

If a man therefore purge himself from these, he shall be a vessel unto honour, sanctified, and meet for the master's use, and prepared unto every good work.

Flee also youthful lusts: but follow righteousness, faith, charity, peace, with them that call on the Lord out of a pure heart.

Bishop continues, "The topic tonight, y'all, is 'Fleeing Youthful Lusts.'"

Great. I meet two of the most intriguing women in this church, and Bishop Prentiss wants to preach on lust. That's not even right.

"Saints of God," preaches Bishop Prentiss, "I get a lot of prayer requests from singles trying to live holy and from courting couples trying to have a chaste courtship. They always ask me how they can successfully remain pure and pleasing to God."

Here we go. I used to get my hopes up when visiting

churches with my various girlfriends. I'd hope that at least one preacher could tell me how to live for God and not chase tail.

"I'm going to start by saying that as long as you live, you will battle your flesh. That sexual drive is real. It's necessary for the survival of the human race. The flesh is drawn to that which is sexually attractive, and there is nothing you can do to alter what the flesh wants. The flesh wants what it wants."

All right, now. Get real with it, Bishop. I feel myself scooting to the edge of my seat, wanting to hear more.

"But yet as Christians, lovers of God, we are compelled to battle this flesh. Paul said that he died daily. What does it say in John Three verse Seven? You must be born again.

"Saints, when we are born again, our flesh doesn't disappear. We've got to kill it, starve it, battle it with the help of the Holy Spirit. Now, I know what y'all are thinking. Y'all want to know how to really do that. How to practically apply these words to your everyday life. You can say 'I die daily' all day and all night, but if you get your lonely self in a predicament with a fine sista or brotha, how are you really going to say no?"

That's *exactly* what I'm talking about.

"Biologically, saints, our bodies are made to respond to sexual stimuli. Our bodies are wonderfully made by the Lord to do this. But when you choose to serve God, you choose to place that flesh in subjection to the will of the Holy Spirit that lives inside you. Now, listen close, y'all. If you want to serve God with sexual purity, you're going to have to do some things most of y'all don't like to do."

A collective groan rises from the audience. Bishop must be about to give us some tough love.

"Like having chaperoned dates and not watching those late-night movies on Skinemax." Laughter fills the room. "Y'all think I don't know about that mess, but I do. When you find someone you like and might want as a mate, get to know each other from a distance or in the presence of trusted friends. Be creative and write letters or even e-mails. Choose Christ and don't give the devil room."

I'm really feeling this message. Operating in the realm of my reality, if I get a woman alone and have the opportunity, I don't know if I can resist what my flesh wants.

Bishop continues, "I know what y'all still out there thinking about. How can I get to know my future mate if we never get a chance to be alone? Well, some of you have fed your spirit enough and fortified it enough that you can spend limited amounts of time alone with the opposite sex. But most of y'all got starving spirits and gluttonous flesh that gets fed all day, every day, by the media. Look, if you don't want to get mugged, what do you do? You stay out of dark alleys. And if you don't want to get struck by lightning, you go inside when it rains. Let's not put ourselves in situations where our flesh might win."

I see Emoni out of the corner of my eye. She's grinning at me. That girl ain't nothing but a rainstorm in a dark alley.

"We, as Christians, on this Christian walk, need to pray every day. And you don't have to pray long for it to be strong. I said more than a few 'Jesus help me's' when I was courting First Lady Diana."

Everyone laughs, including me. I can't imagine this man getting hemmed up in a car or a hotel room and having to pray his way out. But his realness strikes a chord with me. Makes me want to see if I can live right. Makes me want to give God a chance in my life.

I find myself walking down for the altar call, nodding when they ask me if I want to be baptized. This time I'm doing it because I really want to and not because I'm afraid of hellfire. Emoni and Dorcas are both on their feet, clapping with the rest of the congregation while I'm making silent promises to God.

In a little changing room, I'm putting on baptism clothes with tears streaming down my face when a small twinge of something pierces my penitent prayers.

It's a very small thought, but it's there nonetheless. It's me telling myself: Darrin, you're here to write a story.

Chapter Nine

Emoni

It's Friday night. The first night of the weekend and two nights before church. And I'm doing what I always do on Friday nights. I'm curled up in my bedroom on my pink beanbag chair, reading a book, sipping Pepsi, and eating microwave popcorn. And although I hate to admit it, I'm feeling lonely.

Actually, tonight I've got two books. One is entitled *Serving the Lord with Your Whole Heart*, and the other is a romance novel I ordered from Black Expressions called *Someone to Love Me*. I'm really interested in the spiritual subject matter, of course, but since I met Darrin Bainbridge, I'd also like to read about something steamy.

He was feeling me at Bible study. I know he was. When he asked me not to leave the table, I couldn't have gone anywhere if I wanted to. I'm getting butterflies just thinking about his hand on mine. I can't believe how weak he makes me feel, and I don't even know the brother. And now that he's baptized, he's going to have to beat off these desperate heifers with a stick.

Like Dorcas. She straight bogarted her way into our conversation, swinging that ponytail on top of her high-yellow head. I wanted to smack her. But she's my sister in Christ . . . yeah, okay, so I still wanted to smack her.

If Dorcas wasn't enough, here comes Oscar, trying his best to lay a claim on me when I for darn sure don't belong to him. He needs to quit tripping, because if I haven't gotten with him in all these years, it's not going to happen. Anyway, he only wants me so he can be Daddy's assistant pastor and maybe even the senior pastor one day.

It's not that I haven't given Oscar a chance. He's not bad-looking, and he keeps a job. I've even gone out on a few dates with him. It's just that his past is way too checkered for me, and he still carries some emotional baggage around with him. On one of our dates, he blew up on me because I wouldn't give a dollar to a homeless man on the street.

I said, "I am not going to support anyone's habit."

"Did you ever think that maybe he's just trying to live? Everyone on the street isn't an addict," he replied angrily.

But Oscar was an addict. When he joined Freedom of Life, he was a hot stinking mess, unemployed and strung out on crack cocaine. He walked up to that altar, and Daddy embraced him and prayed for him on the spot, not caring what he might catch or if the stink would ruin his good suit.

That was six years ago. I was only eighteen then. By the time I came home from college, Oscar was a new man in Christ. He was clean and working on Freedom of Life's staff as the head armor bearer and security chief. He thought that when I accepted a full-time job at the church, a relationship with me was inevitable.

Thinking about Oscar's testimony makes me open my Christian book and toss the romance novel across the room. I know that God will send me my husband, hopefully, one day soon. The way Darrin looks at me, I'm praying it's him.

I start reading, but I can't concentrate. This house is too quiet. Mother and Daddy are already asleep, Tyler's out at a youth revival, and Sascha is running the streets with Kevin. It's nearly one in the morning, and Sascha still hasn't brought herself on home. She is going to mess around and get in trouble with Kevin.

I'm concerned about Tyler, too. Ever since he met this new up-and-coming preacher Pastor David Maxwell, he's been missing in action around here and at Freedom of Life. Tyler used to be the president of the Youth Council, teach the junior Sunday school, and lead the evangelism department, but now he barely makes it to Sunday-morning service.

At one point Daddy seemed to be grooming Tyler to be his successor, but they started disagreeing on how to reach people and bring them to Christ. Tyler thinks that the church should embrace youthful expressions like gospel hip-hop and relax the strict dress code. Daddy, on the other hand, is old school. He wants people to experience freedom in Christ, but within the rules of the church. We've got folk at Freedom of Life who would have a conniption if a woman stepped into the sanctuary wearing—gasp—pants. Tyler calls our church name, Freedom of Life, an oxymoron. In some ways, he's right.

I get up to refill my glass of Pepsi and hear Sascha trying to sneak in the house through the kitchen doors. I leave the lights off so she doesn't see me.

"You're going to end up pregnant," I say as she tries to tiptoe upstairs.

She jumps. "Emoni. You scared me. Why are you standing in here in the dark?"

"Waiting on you to come in. It could've been Mother or, worse, Daddy."

Sascha rolls her eyes. "No. You're the only one who waits up late looking for something to snitch about."

"I'm not trying to snitch on you. I just think you should be careful. Kevin only wants one thing."

"What do you know about that?" Sascha asks sarcastically. "You don't know anything about what men want. You've never even had a man."

She goes upstairs, leaving me standing there speechless. I hate when she gets out on me like that, but it is the truth. I've never had a boyfriend, not a real one, only Oscar. He doesn't even really count, because we never kissed or shared anything sweet.

I feel hot tears stinging the corners of my eyes. Why do I have to be the sensible one? The homely one? Why can't I be the one all the men want?

I go back to my bedroom and slam the door. I pick up my discarded romance novel and plop down in my beanbag chair. I open it up and read the fiery words and take in all of the heaving chests and ripped bodices. All the while, tears are making little hot rivers on my face.

Mother says it's a blessing that I don't have to worry about my chastity.

What kind of backhanded compliment is that?

Chapter Ten

Emoni

If it's not bad enough that I spend every Friday night chilling at home reading a book, I add insult to injury and attend the singles' ministry meeting every other Saturday evening. We're supposed to be here encouraging one another on a night that's tough for the lonesome, but most of us are just trying to hook up with somebody on the sly.

After thinking about Darrin all last night, I decided to go to the salon this morning and get a fresh new haircut. It's short in the back and on the sides, and the front swoops down in a drastic bang that covers one of my eyes. I went all out with the eyebrow arching and facial and got a manicure and pedicure and all new accessories to go with a sharp red pantsuit.

I've never looked better.

I see Sister Ophelia walking across the room, looking me up and down, probably trying to think of something smart to say. Technically, she is a single, but come on! She's pushing sixty-five, and I believe that she caused her late husband's heart attack with her unbearable nagging. She just comes to the singles meetings to tell us all how sinful we are.

"Praise the Lord, Sister Emoni," says Ophelia.

I give her a one-armed hug. "He's worthy, Sister Ophelia. How are you this evening?"

"Blessed in the city," she responds. "Honey, what is going on with you and all that red? Did your mama see you walk out the house? You look like your name should be Babylon."

I bite down on my tongue so hard that I draw blood. "I bought it new for tonight. Do you like it?"

"No, I most certainly do not. And I also do not care for that man's hairstyle you have. A woman's hair is her crowning glory, and you done cut all yours off. Honey, you should've kept that hair. It was all you had going for you."

I think I might explode and take Sister Ophelia with me. She has got to be the meanest woman on the planet. I calm down a little when I notice Darrin walking in to the meeting. Sister Ophelia notices him, too.

"Look at those desperate heifers," says Ophelia while pointing to the small crowd of women that has formed around Darrin. "I mean, can they let the man get saved good before they start tossing their panties at him?"

I let out a giggle. That's the thing about Sister Ophelia. She's funny as all get out as long as she's talking about someone else. And since that thirsty Dorcas is the ringleader of the crowd, I'm not going to disagree.

"Sister Ophelia! You are wrong for that."

"Yes, I said it. And it's the truth, too. I even saw you

grinning up in his face at Bible study. You need to quit, girl. Go on and marry that Oscar. He the one that wants you."

"Oscar and I are only friends."

Sister Ophelia crosses her arms. "Humph! That's only 'cause you ain't got good sense. Oscar is a good man, but you'd rather stand next to the baptism pool looking for a husband. Don't you know some of them men go down dry devils and come up wet devils?"

When I don't reply to her question, Sister Ophelia walks across the room, probably looking for a more willing ear. I consider the possibility that she might be right about Darrin. He sure seems to be enjoying all of the attention from the ladies.

I peer across the room, trying to get Darrin's attention. He's one of only a few men here, so he is thoroughly occupied with all the vultures vying for a conversation. On one side of the room, Oscar is standing with a plate of chicken wings and a cup of punch. He's glaring at Darrin as if they're mortal enemies.

Finally, I make eye contact with Darrin. His slow smile is making me nervous, but I hope he can't tell. He starts walking toward me, and I'm fidgeting with my hands, trying to wipe the sweat off my palms and maintain what little composure I have left.

"Brother Darrin! I'm so glad that you could make it out," I blurt with a tight smile.

"Thank you for inviting me."

He's close enough that I can inhale his cologne. I close my eyes and breathe deeply, allowing his scent to fill my nostrils. When I open my eyes, he's grinning, and his eyes are dancing. He knows he's got me open.

"You cut your hair," he comments.

Self-consciously, I move my hand to my hairdo. "Do you like it?"

"I love it."

He says that like he really means it, and I feel butterflies. I'm so glad I took the extra time to do everything, because he's taking me all in, from hairdo to toe rings. He's drinking in my look like a cold glass of red Kool-Aid on a ninety-degree afternoon.

Dorcas breaks up our moment. She shoves a notebook in Darrin's face so forcefully that he has to take a step back. "You need to *register*."

"Thanks, Dorcas," I answer, and grab the notebook. "I can handle it from here."

"Well, he's my guest," Dorcas spits angrily.

I look at Darrin and note his response. This brother is enjoying this. He must be used to women acting stupid over him. Fighting over him. He's got me messed up.

He smiles and takes the notebook from my hand. "Well, it seems like you've both invited me. I'm so grateful that everyone is making me feel so welcome."

Oh, I am not about to sweat him. I don't care how fine he is. That is not my style. At all. Well, technically, I don't have a style, but if I did have one, it wouldn't be this. I glance around the room for an escape route, and even though it kills me to do it, I leave Darrin with his number one fan, Dorcas, and walk over to chat with my number one fan.

Oscar immediately accosts me with "We don't know anything about him."

"Who are you talking about?" I ask, even though I know he means Darrin.

"This Darrin person. We don't know anything about him. I want you to be careful."

I roll my eyes. "I'm grown, Oscar."

"He comes from another city and immediately tries to get close to you and Dorcas?"

"I think he's just being friendly. Plus, it looks like Dorcas is the one trying to get close to him. Now what?"

Oscar frowns. "I still don't trust him. I'm watching him."

"Why don't you watch me walk right back over there and give our new member the welcome he deserves?"

Dorcas has obviously marked her territory, because all of the other single women have gone back to talking among themselves. I've never seen this side of Dorcas. She's tossing her hair back and forth, and dare I say, her freckled skin looks radiant.

"Emoni," says Darrin as I approach them, "Sister Dorcas tells me that you are the editor in chief of the church newsletter. Are you looking for any additional writers? I'd love to join the staff."

"Yes, we're always looking for new writers. You can bring me a writing sample on Sunday, and we'll take it from there."

"Great. I'll come up with something riveting for you."

"I'm sure you will." I hope there was a hidden meaning to his statement. I raise one of my eyebrows and squint, thinking maybe his gesture is coquettish. I admit, I'm not an expert on flirting. I twist my body a little bit to make sure Darrin has a good view of my . . . blessings.

Dorcas looks about ready to breathe fire, so I decide

to back down. For now. "I'll let you two finish your conversation. Darrin, we'll talk more about the newsletter on Sunday?"

"Absolutely. Thank you again for the welcome. I don't know anyone in town, so it really helps."

"The pleasure was all mine."

Chapter Eleven

DIARY OF A MAD BLACK BLOGGER

So, I turned my life over to Christ, y'all . . . Had to say that all casual, though, 'cause I don't want to lose any more cool points. Yeah, I lost a whole lot of them standing up at the altar crying like a bi . . . Well, I'm not gonna use that word, because honestly, I did just give my life over to Christ.

But I'm afraid.

Why, you ask? Because I don't know how to be saved. I mean, I've been around saved people my whole life. I could probably speak in ten unknown tongues, and I know all the steps to cast out a demon. But I don't know how to live saved.

I'm trying it out, though. So . . . um . . . those of you who know the words of prayer . . . keep me lifted up.

But back to my story about Bishop So-and-so and his daughter. Well . . . the plot thickens. Let's add to the mix *a fine redbone that is ALSO feeling me and don't have no problem telling it on the mountain.*

I can mos def see this scenario getting all out of control, like one of those Street Fiction titles. Don't trip like y'all don't be reading that stuff! My title could be Fornicating Behind the Pews. *Don't play. It would go all the way to number one on the* Essence *best-seller list.*

But anyway, don't forget about the prayers, 'cause right about now, I'm a WIP Christian. Work in Progress for the unchurched.

Hit me up in the comments section.

COMMENTS

Tyrone 11:01 p.m.

Naw, dawg. Say it ain't so! You can't be trying to get righteous on us. We need you to still bust your story wide open. My mama's pastor just got caught with an illegitimate baby by one of the nurses. Dude. You the voice for the people, bro. Don't get caught up.

Jia 11:15 p.m.

Shut up, Tyrone! I'm glad MBB has given his life to Christ. But I still think you're obligated to speak up if there's a scandal. Maybe that's what God is calling you to do.

Sister Mary 1:01 a.m.

The Lord ain't playing with you boy. You giong strait to hell for trying to find dirt on a Bishp.

Lee-Lee 2:32 a.m.

Sister Mary . . . spell check is a beautiful thing. MBB, I'm proud of you! I'm praying for you. When you gone show us a photo? 'Cause I bet you fine . . .

Chapter Twelve

Darrin

This afternoon is a first for me. Well, it's a first date with Dorcas, but that's not the first that I'm referring to. Since I've entered adulthood and taken part in the human mating ritual, I have never met a woman at our date destination. It has always been me picking her up, or if I wanted to get straight to business, I'd invite her to my apartment.

But I'm here, in Atlanta of all places, finally trying to live right. So I'm taking Bishop Prentiss's advice. We're meeting at a coffeehouse in the afternoon for tea and dessert. The unsaved Darrin would've meant for dessert to be a double entendre, but the new me actually means Heath-bar cheesecake.

Dorcas is already here, and she waves at me to come and join her. She looks nice and casual in a jean skirt and tank top. Her hair is in some kind of grandma bun, but her sexy hoop earrings make up for it.

This is going to sound weird, but part of me wishes I was meeting Emoni and not Dorcas. A huge part of me. Made me want to lose my salvation when she showed up at the singles' ministry meeting in that red pantsuit and fly haircut. I almost asked her out.

But the truth is, I'm still looking for a story. Bishop Prentiss might preach a message to call a sinner like me to repentance, but that doesn't mean he doesn't have a skeleton or two of his own. If God could use a donkey to send a blessing, then He can surely use a crooked preacher.

Seriously, though, I wouldn't be mad if there were no story. Bishop Prentiss is growing on me like moss on the shady side of a building. I want to be able to refer to Bishop as my father in the gospel. Wow, did I just say that?

Father. In. The. Gospel.

Wow. I'm already using the church terminology and whatnot.

But right now I'm thinking about my natural father and his not so idle threat of taking away my source of income—his wallet. I've got to come up with something to keep him off my back. A brotha's got to eat, right?

"Dorcas . . . you look stunning," I say.

She laughs. "Boy, you better quit playing and sit down."

"I mean that, Dorcas. You look great. Sometimes less is more."

She looks down at herself and shrugs. "Whatever floats your boat."

"What are you drinking?" I motion to her half-empty teacup.

"Passionfruit green tea and vodka."

"What?"

She bursts into laughter. "I'm playing! It's just passionfruit green tea."

I exhale loudly and laugh a little. Her joke wasn't funny, but it definitely broke the ice. I don't know why I'm so uptight.

"So what did you think of our singles' ministry meeting?" Dorcas asks.

I answer as honestly as possible. "It was . . . interesting."

She frowns. "You didn't like it?"

"Let's just say I felt like a T-bone steak at a pit bull's feeding time."

"It wasn't that bad."

"Tell that to the steak."

We both laugh, and I feel more relaxed. I order a cup of tea from the waitress.

"Okay," I acquiesce, "it wasn't that bad. It's just that I would've rather been a spectator for my first meeting. I don't know the Christian dating rules yet."

"What rules?" she asks with a highly skeptical look.

"Like, is it okay to date more than one saved lady at a time? I don't know. Is it okay to get someone's phone number at the singles' ministry meeting? Is it okay to fornicate on Saturday if I repent on Sunday? I just don't know."

Dorcas picks up her purse and sunglasses and stands. She is ready to go.

"Sit down, girl," I say with a laugh. "I'm joking."

Dorcas chuckles. "It seems like neither one of us is funny."

"I think you might be right!"

She sits back down and leans forward. "But while you're talking about it, I do think you have another admirer at Freedom of Life."

"Who?" Of course I know she means Emoni.

"The bishop's daughter. I think she wants to get with you."

She's fishing. Smart girl.

"I thought you said she was digging that trustee dude." My tone gives her absolutely nothing to work with. Game recognizes game.

"Sometimes I don't know about her and Oscar, because he's asked her to marry him so many times."

"Seriously? She keeps turning bro man down, huh?"

Dorcas nods slowly. "Yep."

"I think she's just being hospitable to me."

"I know Emoni, and she doesn't get that excited about most new members. You've been to three services, and already you've got the bishop's daughter smitten."

"And what about you? Are you smitten?" I ask playfully.

Dorcas pretends to ignore my question. "So, you're from Cleveland. What brings you all the way to Atlanta?"

"Well . . ." I should've thought of an answer to this question before I left home. It's not like I can tell her that I'm writing a story about Bishop. "I'm pursuing my writing career. I'm afraid there weren't many opportunities in Cleveland."

"What do you write?"

"Freelance essays and editorials, mostly. One day I plan to write a novel."

Dorcas seems truly interested. "You'd definitely be

good for our church newsletter. It's not huge, but it has at least ten thousand readers monthly."

"I know. I showed Emoni a writing sample yesterday, and she was excited to have me volunteer."

"Well, well, well. It pays to have crushes in high places."

"The heavens have smiled upon me."

"So it would seem." Dorcas's eyes dance flirtatiously, accentuating her mascaraed eyelashes.

I venture again. "You didn't answer my question."

"What question?"

"Are you smitten?"

"I don't know yet. You haven't given me enough to be smitten about."

"What else do you want to know about me?"

"Hmm . . . Where are you working in between your freelance gigs? Our apartment building isn't cheap. And I peeped that Hummer you're driving."

This is too easy. Well, almost too easy.

"Are you serious? You want to know if I'm paid, huh? You a gold digger?"

Dorcas purses her lips and frowns. "Why can't a woman ask about a guy's financial status these days without being classified as a gold digger?"

I comically wipe my brow. "Whew! I'm glad you're not a gold digger, because I'm broke."

"You are?" She looks disappointed.

"Seriously, I am. But my parents are rich."

"Oh, so you're a trust-fund brat?"

She says it with such disdain that it sounds like an insult. "I guess so. For now, anyway. I'm about to blow up."

"Really?"

"Yes. I'm only doing these freelance gigs until I get my book deal. I'm thinking I can pull a five- or six-figure advance, like Omar Tyree or Eric Jerome Dickey."

"Wow. No one can say you aren't ambitious."

Do I detect a hint of sarcasm? "I'm just trying to chase a dream. What about you? What do you dream about?"

"What I really want to do," says Dorcas as a wistful look comes over her face, "is open a school for physically challenged kids."

I don't even know how to respond. She's got noble plans and ideas. I want to land a book deal. She must think I'm shallow.

"Wow. That's great."

She smiles. "I didn't mean to get all 'save the world' on you. It's just that my sister had cerebral palsy. She died when we were teenagers, and I'd like to do something to honor her."

"That's a beautiful thing, Dorcas. I'm an only child."

"I have five brothers, and I had one sister. I always wanted to be an only child."

I put my hands up in feigned fearfulness. "Five brothers? Oh, I cannot holler at you."

"They're harmless."

I wave for the waitress. "Unh-uh. I don't believe it. Girl, I'm paying this check right now. Forget you ever met me."

Dorcas is cracking up and holding on to my arm, trying to keep me at the table. After a couple of moments, I stop struggling and really look at Dorcas. She's grinning playfully, blinking up at me with those big, beautiful brown eyes.

I think I might be the one who's smitten.

Chapter Thirteen

DIARY OF A MAD BLACK BLOGGER

What's cracking, cyber homies and homettes? I'm sending out a bat signal to some of you saved folks, 'cause a brotha's got a dilemma. Here's my question: If you're kicking it wit a church girl, how soon is too soon to pop the question?

Whoa! Not that question! A brotha ain't going out like that. I'm talking about how soon can I invite her for a sleepover? Aw, don't act like y'all don't know. Saved women talk a good game, but they be giving up the panties, too.

I see all y'all super saints talking about me. I can see y'all through my computer screen. Well, I just got baptized! I'm not all the way saved yet.

Dang. Writing that just convicted me in my spirit. Literally. Y'all forget I asked that, and please keep me in your prayers.

COMMENTS

Sister Mary 11:03 p.m.

The blood of Jesus is against you. I'm gone pray for that girl you trying to coreupt.

Tyrone 1:00 a.m.

Keep the real talk coming. I be seeing girls from the club in the choir stand every Sunday!

Jia 2:14 a.m.

Oh for heaven's sake, Sister Mary. You are hurting my eyes with all that bad spelling. And if you hate this blog so much why do you keep coming back?

Chapter Fourteen

Emoni

For Darrin's first assignment on the Freedom of Life newsletter, I've invited him to cover a fund-raiser dinner for the community recreation center. Daddy is speaking, and it should be an easy way for Darrin to showcase his writing skills.

It also gives me another chance to show him what he's missing out on by not getting with me. I overheard Dorcas telling one of her friends that she and Darrin had gone out for tea one afternoon. Supposedly, it was their first date.

If I have anything to do with it, it'll be their last.

Even Daddy brought up the new couple. He said at the dinner table, "I hear Dorcas is dating that young man who got baptized at Bible study."

"Is she? Wow, that was fast," Sascha replied with a laugh.

"Well, he seems like a decent young man" was Daddy's judgment.

Sascha added, "Emoni, I thought you wanted him, or somebody else, what with this new look you got goin'."

"What? I haven't paid him any attention. I can't even tell you what he looks like."

Everyone sat at the table giving me a blank stare. They can go on with that. I'm not that obvious.

I've picked out a black and silver gown to wear to the fund-raiser; it accentuates all of my curves and cinches in at my waist.

"Whoa," says Tyler as he peeks into my room. "That dress is nice. What's gotten into you lately?"

"Nothing. Just trying to step my game up a little bit. What about you? Aren't you going to the fund-raiser?"

"Nah. I gave my ticket away to one of the deacons."

"But you go every year."

He nods slowly. "I know. But Pastor David asked me to go with him to speak to troubled youths at a detention center."

"Pastor David?" I flinch at the informal title for a supposed man of God.

"That's what he likes to be called. He says it makes him more approachable."

It hurts me to hear my brother speak about this Pastor David with the same respect and reverence that he used to have for our father.

"You really like Pastor David, huh?"

A smile spreads across my brother's face. "Sis, you have no idea. His vision is my vision. We are on the same page."

"You and Daddy aren't?"

"We aren't even in the same book."

Tyler kisses me on the cheek and leaves my bedroom. I can hear him bouncing down the stairs, taking three at a time like he used to do when we were little.

My next visitor is Sascha. She's wearing a skintight pink suit and has her hair in an updo. Against everyone's wishes, she's going to tonight's festivities with Kevin.

"Are you going to wear a scarf to cover up that sucker bite on your neck?" I ask.

Sascha pushes me out of the mirror. "I thought that faded." She inspects her neck closely. "There's nothing here, Emoni. You get on my nerves."

"Scared you, didn't I? You need to be more careful."

Sascha rolls her eyes at me and goes downstairs. I follow her, and the entire family, minus Tyler, piles into Daddy's Cadillac.

After a twenty-minute drive through little to no traffic, we make our entrance into the ballroom. Immediately, I scan the room for Darrin, who is already seated at our reserved table. He and Dorcas are having an animated conversation. I feel my temperature start to rise.

I stride confidently over to them. "Darrin, aren't you supposed to be reporting on this event?"

"Wow . . . uh, good evening to you, too, boss."

I don't crack even a hint of a smile. "Good evening, Brother Darrin. I hope you're taking notes."

He pulls a little notebook from the inside jacket pocket of his tuxedo. "I've got it covered."

"Good."

A little embarrassed over my outburst, I take my seat at the table and pretend to read the program. They look great sitting there at the table, like one of those candid photos that magazines take for marketing campaigns. Dorcas is wearing a stunning sleeveless off-white gown, and her hair is styled in a French roll, accentuating her long yet graceful neck. Darrin can't seem to take his eyes off her. My stomach drops when I can't see myself anywhere in that picture. What was I thinking?

They continue their conversation where they left off. "So, you think you can handle hiking on Stone Mountain?" Dorcas asks.

"Puh-leeze. Girl, I used to sled down a bigger hill than Stone Mountain."

She laughs. "You did not."

"I did so. We called it Grandpappy Hill."

I feel like a desperate intruder. The worst part is that they sound really good together, like their meeting was destiny or something. Oscar spots me and hurries across the room, and for a change, I'm actually happy to see him coming.

Oscar takes a seat next to me and whispers in my ear, "What is he doing here?" The hairs on the back of my neck stand up from Oscar's hot breath. It takes every bit of Holy Ghost in me not to cringe. I ignore the question in favor of making brief eye contact with Darrin. He smiles at me and winks.

"Sister Emoni, you look beautiful tonight. That dress really looks good on you," Darrin comments while Dorcas nods in agreement. I don't need her to cosign Darrin's compliment, though. She can go on with that.

"Thank you, Brother Darrin," I say.

Oscar clears his throat as if nobody saw him sit down. Darrin says, "Brother Oscar." He extends his hand for Oscar to shake.

Oscar ignores this and replies, "It's Trustee Williams."

"Oh . . . my bad, Trustee." Darrin lowers his hand slowly, seeming to notice the negative vibe that Oscar is putting out there.

Oblivious to all of the bad blood, Daddy and Mother sit down at the table. Daddy says, "Brother Darrin! Good to see you. Emoni has been raving about you all week."

"Daddy!" I feel like hiding under a rock. Could I be any more embarrassed? No. I think not.

"Good evening, Bishop and First Lady," says Darrin with a smile. "First Lady, you look lovely."

Mother looks from Darrin to Dorcas and raises an eyebrow. "Thank you, Brother Darrin."

Darrin grins and winks at me again. He turns his attention to Dorcas and teases, "Have you been raving about me, too, Sister Dorcas?"

This is not going well. He is not supposed to be using my embarrassment to flirt with that heifer.

Dorcas does not respond. Maybe it's because I'm looking half past evil, or maybe she's embarrassed, too. Mother gives me a consoling look that is not helping matters at all. What a nightmare.

Oscar asks, "Dorcas says that you're a writer. Have you published anything?"

Darrin says to Dorcas, "So you *have* been raving about me." He then answers Oscar's question. "I frequently write editorials for our local newspaper. I've also had several of my essays published in small magazines."

"Doesn't sound too lucrative," notes Oscar. "How can you afford to relocate? And you drive a Hummer, too, right?"

Darrin replies, "You've done your research. My parents are quite wealthy. They're footing the bill."

"What does your father do?" I ask, trying to muscle my way into the conversation. Plus, I really am curious.

"He's in the transportation business. He has a fleet of vans that pick up people for their doctors' appointments, shopping, whatever," Darrin explains. "He's got three major contracts with the city."

"Maybe I'll get to meet your father and talk to him. I'd like the church to have a transportation service," Bishop responds with much interest.

Darrin turns to Oscar. "Does that answer all of your questions?"

"For now."

The waitstaff brings the first course of the meal around to the table. It's a hearty lobster bisque.

"This is really good," says Mother after tasting her soup.

Darrin replies, "Mine is better."

"You cook?" Dorcas and I exclaim simultaneously. Um . . . I'm going to need that to never happen again.

Darrin nods slowly. "I would've added more paprika and a smidge of garlic."

"What's so special about that? Anyone can cook if they can follow a recipe," scoffs Oscar.

"A recipe is only part of it. A really good cook adds flair to every dish," responds Darrin. He grins at the glaring Oscar as the event's emcee walks up to the podium.

The emcee says, "We'd like to thank everyone for coming out tonight in support of building a new recreation center for our youth."

A round of applause rises from the audience. I try to get Darrin's attention again, but I'm unsuccessful. He's got his notebook out and is looking straight ahead, intent on covering his story sufficiently.

"The price of your tickets for this event will cover about forty percent of the cost," continues the emcee. "We'd like to invite to the podium our speaker of the hour, Bishop Kumal Prentiss, to come and convince you to dig deep in your pocketbooks for that other sixty percent."

After the laughter dies down, the emcee concludes with "But seriously, without any further ado, let us receive Bishop Prentiss with a round of applause."

Bishop takes the microphone from the young emcee and gives her a bear hug. "Good evening, everyone! I am truly happy to be here tonight. I never pass up an opportunity to do something good for young people, so when I received the invitation, there was no way I'd say no."

Darrin takes a few notes on his pad and then whispers something to Dorcas. A flirty smile crosses her face, and she bites her bottom lip. Darrin scoots his chair closer to Dorcas, and she leans in closer still. I'm watching this whole scene helplessly, wishing I stayed home and didn't fuss over getting myself ready.

And no, this fool Oscar didn't just put his arm around my chair. I knock it off so quickly and so severely that it catches Darrin's attention. For a moment confusion flashes across his face. He leans over to me and whispers, "That's no way to treat your date, Sister Emoni."

I hiss back, "He is *not* my date."

"I'm sorry," he replies, "Dorcas told me that you two are a couple."

"Did she?"

Ooh, that girl better be glad I'm saved. I should've known there was a reason Darrin was steering clear of me. Dorcas has him thinking that me and Oscar are together? Now that I see she's playing dirty, my gloves are coming off, too.

"Will you two be quiet?" says Oscar indignantly. "I am trying to hear the man of God."

Darrin places a finger to his lips and shushes me. The smile that I'm trying hard to suppress blossoms across my face. Darrin smiles back and winks again, like we have a secret.

Oh, how I would love for us to have a secret.

Chapter Fifteen

Darrin

After Bishop Prentiss's speech is over, I am not ready to end the evening. I ask Dorcas to join me at the coffee shop again. This time for coffee and not tea, and dessert is still dessert. Carrot cake for me and a man-sized cherry torte for her.

There's a different ambience for the late-night coffeehouse crowd. The lights are dimmed, and the tables have been shifted to leave a little space for dancing. Dorcas and I have chosen two large recliners, separated by an end table where we place our goodies.

For some reason, I'm filled with a sense of urgency. Maybe it's because Mathis called me today for a status report. I had nothing to report except that I'd met two fine women and Bishop Prentiss is on his way to sainthood. Then my father started talking about the new furniture he was ordering for my corner office. I've got to start on my story, even though I don't have a clue where to begin.

I start the conversation with Dorcas. "Bishop's message about the youth was really inspiring. He's a dynamic speaker."

"It was. He always gets really passionate about young people. I think it has something to do with how he was raised."

"And how was that?"

"No man in the house, only his mother and grandmother. He left home when he was sixteen."

"He's come a long way."

"Yes, he has."

This gives me a start. Dig through Bishop's past, and maybe I'll find something. There's no way he left home at sixteen and stayed clean.

Dorcas says, "You should read Bishop's book, *From the World to the Word*. He talks all about his testimony. About how he used to sell drugs and then how he started using his own supply. Then he tells how God saved him."

I nod thoughtfully. Of course he has a book. A testimony. Preachers turn their skeletons into testimonies.

I inhale the rich Jamaican coffee in front of me. A cup of this will keep me awake for a week. It's a good thing, too, because I'm going to be up for days trying to dream up a story.

Dorcas sips her coffee, too, and takes a bite of cherry torte. She sits the pastry down and winces.

"It's not good?" I ask. "I can get you something else."

"No . . . it's fine. Just let me . . ." She reaches down and takes off her shoes. "Ah, that's better."

I laugh. "Your feet hurt?"

"Oh, yes! You don't know how long I've been waiting to get out of these shoes."

"Why do women wear shoes that hurt their feet?"

"The only shoes that don't hurt my feet are sneakers," she responds, "and I don't think they'd really go with this dress."

"By sneakers, you mean tennis shoes?"

"That's right, northern boy."

"Give me your feet."

Dorcas scrunches her nose suspiciously. "For what?"

"'Cause this northern boy knows how to give a foot rub." I can see her hesitation. "Come on, girl. You can trust me."

"I don't know about that," Dorcas counters while placing her feet across my lap.

"Now lean back and close your eyes. Relax."

Dorcas obediently follows my instructions. Closes her eyes and breathes deeply while my hands knowingly rub all of the soreness out of her tiny feet. I'm kneading muscles and cracking joints left and right, hitting every possible pressure point. When she lets out a moan, I drop her feet like they're hot. Can't hear her moan if I'm going to stay saved.

"Wow."

"It was good?" I ask, but the glazed expression of pleasure on her face tells the story.

Dorcas answers, "Too good. You do that for all the girls, right?"

"Not at all. Mostly, my foot rubs are reserved for one very special lady."

"And who is that? Some girl you left at home in Cleveland?"

"Yeah. My mama."

"Okay, then," Dorcas replies.

I feel the mood intensifying so I had better steer this conversation back to safer territory. "How long have you been a member at Freedom of Life?"

"About eight years. I started coming here during my freshman year of college. I feel so blessed to have Bishop Prentiss as my pastor and to know him personally."

"I'm looking forward to getting to know him better as well. His family, too."

"Bishop and First Lady have some great kids," Dorcas gushes, her entire face becoming animated. "Emoni is so smart and talented, although she doesn't realize how attractive she can be. Tyler has a call on his life. I guarantee you he'll be in the ministry one day."

"And what about the youngest girl? Her name is Sascha, right?"

"I think she's trying to figure out the type of woman she wants to be. She's the youngest, and she doesn't really seem to care about succeeding."

I ask, "Is she in college?"

"She was for a minute, but she dropped out for what was supposed to be a semester, then turned into a year. I think she'll go back, though."

I'm mentally recording this conversation with Dorcas. Maybe the pastor is blameless, but it sounds like his children might be another issue. I feel the story forming in my head as we speak. The title: "Mega-Church Pastor Fails at Home."

"So tell me," Dorcas asks, "what do you really think of Freedom of Life?"

I'm caught off guard by the question and have to think

for a moment before replying. "I can honestly say that Freedom of Life is the best church I've ever been to."

"Have you been to many churches?"

"No . . . so I guess that doesn't say much."

"It's okay. Freedom of Life is the first church I've ever attended."

"Seriously?" I could've sworn she was a church girl from birth. "What about when you were a little girl?"

"Let's just say that my family members aren't church folk," answers Dorcas with a weak chuckle.

"My mom made me go to church every week. I was a junior everything! Junior usher, junior deacon, junior choir director . . . and then I discovered girls."

Dorcas throws her head back and laughs. "And that was the end of church, huh?"

"Until now."

"Well, everyone seems to think highly of you."

"Everyone except Oscar—I mean Trustee Williams."

"Don't mind him. He's got some major control issues."

"I think it's more than control. He's probably got a thing for you."

"I don't even think so! He and Emoni are together."

"So you say, but Emoni says she's not with the brother."

Dorcas shifts nervously. "Well, maybe not officially, but inevitably."

I'm still trying to figure out what's up with this whole scenario. More than likely, Dorcas is being a typical female and blocking on Emoni. Because Emoni is clearly not feeling that dude.

I instigate further. "No, no. I'm pretty sure I was sensing some jealous vibes from him."

Dorcas responds adamantly, "He is like a brother to me."

I sit back in my recliner and cross one arm over my chest and rest the other hand under my chin, trying to look like an elderly British professor. "I've seen the way he looks at you, and it's not brotherly."

"That's all your imagination, Darrin."

I lean forward and smile. "I hope so, because honestly, I don't want to have to fight him."

Dorcas blinks rapidly. I can tell her heart is racing. The chemistry is undeniable. But oddly enough, I'm cool. I don't feel the need to trick her into spending the night with me. Bishop Prentiss would say that it's the Holy Spirit transforming me. I'd have to agree, because it sure isn't me. My flesh wants what it wants.

Chapter Sixteen

Emoni

I'm sitting here in Daddy's office, watching him read the article Darrin wrote about the fund-raiser dinner. Darrin looks nervous, like he's on line for a fraternity or interviewing for a six-figure job. It's only going to be in our church newsletter—not that serious.

Maybe I'm still angry about how that whole dinner thing went down. I wanted to bum-rush Dorcas in the parking lot when I overheard her make plans with Darrin for a little after-party at the coffee shop. I don't know how I got so far behind in this race. Seems like I just looked up, and that heifer had lapped me.

And then Oscar had the audacity to say, "The Word says 'he that findeth a wife,' not 'she that findeth a husband.' You need to back off of Darrin, Emoni."

I don't know if he had himself confused with my daddy, my big brother, or my man, but on all accounts, he was wrong. Wrong, wrong, WRONG!

I answered him ignorantly, "I'm going to do what the Word says and let my no mean NO. You need to back off of me."

I left him there, picking his face up off the ground. I was trying to be nice, but I can't have my future husband thinking that me and Oscar are together. That wouldn't be prudent at all.

"Darrin, I'm impressed," Daddy says after finishing the article.

Darrin seems to relax. "Thank you, Bishop Prentiss."

"I'd like for you to cover all of my events."

"For the newsletter?" Darrin asks, sounding delighted.

"Not necessarily. I would like to have a written record of my ministry activities."

Darrin's eyes light up. "I am definitely the man for the job."

Now, this is a shock. Daddy must feel something good in his spirit about Darrin, because he doesn't usually bring people close to him this soon after meeting them. Maybe the Lord told Daddy that Darrin is his future son-in-law. Ooh . . . that makes me want to speak in tongues. Hah! Glory!

Daddy hands me the article. "You've got to read this. Brother Darrin is an exceptional writer. You were right to recommend him for the newsletter."

I quickly scan the article. "This is good. There are a few changes that I'd make, but for the most part, it's good."

"Changes?" asks Darrin, both his eyebrows raised in defense.

"Nothing major," I say with a bit of an attitude. "There are some areas that could flow better. That's all."

"You know, Emoni used to write in college," Daddy says with a look of pride.

"Daddy—"

"And she's good, too! She does most of the writing for the newsletter."

"I do *some* of the writing."

Darrin laughs. "Let your father brag about you, girl!"

I crack a tiny smile but drop my head to prevent Darrin from seeing it. After all that clownish jocking of Dorcas last night, he's on punishment from any niceties from me. He's got to earn my smiles.

Oscar swings the office door open and strides in as if trying to make an entrance. I almost burst out laughing because he looks more than ridiculous. He has this stern look that reminds me of the Buckingham Palace guards who aren't supposed to move a muscle even if touched.

"Bishop, I'm sorry I'm late. My mother needed—" Oscar stops midsentence when he notices Darrin seated in front of Bishop's desk. "Brother Darrin," he says, making the greeting sound like an insult.

Darrin responds in kind. "Trustee Williams."

This is interesting. There is some tension between these brothers, and I think I like it. Well, I'm loving Darrin's tension, but I can do without Oscar's.

Just like he did at the banquet, Daddy is ignoring their antics. He says, "Brother Darrin, I've got another assignment for you. I'm speaking in Savannah next Saturday, and I want you to document it. I feel there's going to be a tremendous move of God on that day."

"I'd be honored, Bishop." Darrin smirks in Oscar's direction.

"Bishop," Oscar says, smirking right back at Darrin, "may I speak with you in private?"

"Of course."

Darrin and I take this as a cue to leave the office, but he takes his time. I think he's deliberately trying to rile Oscar, which puts him that much closer to earning a smile from me.

We're standing in the hallway outside of Daddy's office, and suddenly, I'm nervous. Alone with Darrin, and I'm equipped with nothing but wisecracks and insults. I don't have any idea how to let this man know how appealing he is to me, or how I wish he'd forget all about Dorcas. I don't even know what to do with my hands. I smooth my hair, play with my skirt, and smooth my hair again. He just keeps grinning at me, which is doing absolutely nothing for my frazzled nerves.

"So, do you like Atlanta so far?" I ask. I'm praying that he doesn't notice the tremble in my voice.

Darrin responds lightheartedly, "I love it here! At home, I'd be pulling out my winter wardrobe."

"But it's only the beginning of October."

"My point exactly."

"Well, we're glad to have you here."

"You are?" His sly smile lets me know he's teasing me.

Now I'm all flustered. "F-freedom of Life is glad to have you, I'm sure."

"Oh . . . I thought you meant—"

"Why are you flirting with me?" I ask angrily. "Don't you like Sister Dorcas?" Might as well put it all out on the table. I need to know what's really going on.

"Whoa!" Darrin exclaims. "Can you and I be friends?"

"Of course we can. I'm sorry." So I see he's going to avoid the Dorcas discussion.

"It's cool."

"But what I meant was that you came to our church and hit the ground running. Daddy loves hard workers."

Darrin takes a bow. "I aim to please."

"Really? Is that what you're doing with Dorcas? Aiming to please?"

He puts his hands up in surrender. I've won this round—I think.

"Dorcas and I are only friends, too, Emoni. I'm not in Atlanta to find a woman."

"Right, right. You're here to launch your career."

He nods. "That's correct."

"But chasing a little tail in the meantime won't hurt nothing."

Darrin's eyes widen. Guess he's shocked that the bishop's daughter knows anything about chasing tail. Actually, I don't. And I'm coming pretty close to exhausting all of my scant knowledge of men. I hope he doesn't see right through me.

"Girl, don't start nothing, it won't be nothing."

Darrin's warning sounds like a challenge, and I'm totally up for it. "What if I want there to be something?"

Darrin looks relieved when Daddy's office door opens, saving him from answering that question. I'm relieved, too!

"All right, son," Daddy says to Darrin. "Looks like it's going to be the four of us this weekend."

"Four of us, sir?" Darrin asks.

"Yes. Emoni and Oscar will accompany us to Savannah. It should be a great time."

Darrin nods and smiles at me. "That sounds perfect."

"Oscar will pick you up around eight in the morning."

Oscar adds, "Be ready. I hate tardiness."

"How about I drive my truck and meet you there?" Darrin says with a hint of irritation.

Oscar responds in kind: "That is an excellent idea."

Daddy shuts them both down. "No sense wasting gas money. There's no reason why four children of God can't put up with each other for a few hours."

"Of course," replies Darrin through clenched teeth.

I leave the hallway with a wave, almost certain that at least one set of eyeballs is following my every move. I can see that Darrin is not going to make this easy. Obviously, he's used to women falling all over him.

So, I'm standing in the doorway to Sascha's bedroom, watching her read a magazine and trying to get up the courage to ask for help. I'm in over my head with this Darrin thing, but I do know that I want him, and not just in the holy way that a woman of God would want a husband. I *want him* want him, which completely and utterly terrifies me.

"Sascha, can I talk to you for a minute?" I ask, trying to sound as agreeable as possible.

Sascha finally looks up from her magazine. "What is it?"

I peek down the hallway like a criminal on the lookout. When I'm sure the coast is clear, I close Sascha's door. She seems shocked when I sit down on the edge of her bed.

"I need your help," I admit.

Sascha is suspicious. "With what?"

I take a deep breath. "I want Brother Darrin to notice me instead of Dorcas."

"I can't believe you're asking me to help you."

"I don't have much time. I'm going with Bishop to Savannah on Saturday, and Darrin's going, too."

"Is Dorcas coming?" Sascha asks.

"No. That's why I want to look really nice."

Sascha taps her finger on her chin, deep in thought. "Wait a minute. How is Oscar going to feel about all of this?"

"Who cares? He's not my boyfriend."

"But Emoni, you know that he likes you. He's *always* liked you."

I am not going to allow her to make me feel guilty about Oscar. Why does everyone think I should settle for him? No one ever tells pretty girls to settle for the only man who might ever want them.

"But I don't like him that way," I reply quickly, dismissing any further conversation about Oscar. "Are you going to help me or not?"

Sascha folds her arms and lowers her eyebrows in what looks to be a serious expression. "I don't know if I should. You haven't exactly been the best sister lately, with all of your tattling and whatnot. What's in it for me?"

"How about the fact that if Darrin becomes my man, then I won't have any time to pay any attention to you and Mr. Kevin?" I reply with a grin.

"Good enough!" exclaims Sascha. "The first thing we need to do is get you to the spa for a facial. That acne is not the business."

"Okay, then what?"

"Um . . . let's see. Straight to the MAC counter. You need some good foundation and lip gloss."

"I don't do makeup."

Sascha stands up from her bed and places both hands on her hips, looking exactly like Mother. "Do you want my help or not?"

"Yes, but why does it have to involve slathering makeup all over my face?"

"Because your face is pretty, but you're always hiding it under some bangs."

I lift the bangs. "Umm . . . did you forget my acne problem?"

"No, I did not! The only reason it's a problem is because you've always got those greasy bangs hanging in your eyes. I'm going to get you a deep-cleansing facial and some good makeup. Don't worry."

"Okay." She sits back down on the bed. A serious expression has come over her face.

"What's wrong?" I ask.

"Nothing, really. It's just that . . . Well, now that we're sharing things . . . Can I share something with you?"

"Sure."

Sascha reaches under her pillow and pulls out a small jewelry box. She opens it to show me an engagement ring with what looks like a half-carat marquis-shaped diamond.

"Nice ring. Whose is it?" I ask.

"Mine. Kevin gave it to me last night."

My eyes are about to pop right out of my head. "Where did Kevin get the money to buy this? He asked you to marry him?"

"This ring is the reason he hasn't gotten his car fixed. And yes, he asked me to marry him."

"Wow . . . but why aren't you wearing the ring?"

"Because I haven't said yes yet."

Now, this is shocking. First of all, the fact that Kevin even opened his mouth to say "marry me" has me really twisted. How about what Mother always says—why would men buy the cow if they're already getting the milk? And second of all, the fact that Sascha hasn't said yes is throwing me for a loop.

"Wait," I say, hoping the answer to my next question is no. "You're not pregnant, are you?"

Sascha lowers her eyes and nods. "Yeah. Only a couple of weeks, though."

I can't even find the words in the English language that will convey my feelings. "You . . . How could . . . My God, Sascha . . . What are you going to do?"

"I don't know, Emoni, but please don't tell anyone."

"Have you told Mother? Daddy?"

"No, I haven't told either of them, and I don't plan to anytime soon." She seems irritated, like I'm the one dropping bombs.

"Well, soon you won't have to tell them. It'll be obvious."

A tear forms in Sascha's eye. "Maybe not."

"Don't tell me you're thinking of getting rid of your baby!" I gasp for air.

Sascha is crying now. "I don't know. It seems like the best option for everybody."

I grab both of Sascha's hands in mine. "I know we don't do this very often, but please, Sascha, let's pray about this."

She nods, so I continue, "Lord God, we come to you right now. We ask forgiveness of our sins. We ask that you wash us clean with your blood. Oh Lord, please help Sascha to see that no matter how this child came to be in her womb, the baby is not a mistake. Father God, help her through this tough time, and let her know that your strength is made perfect in her weakness. Lord, allow her to know that I am there for her as a sister, confidante, and friend. Lord, we thank you and we love you. In Jesus' name."

Sascha says amen, and we sit on her bed. I'm embracing my younger sister and stroking her hair. Somehow it doesn't seem the right time to talk about makeovers and new boyfriends.

Chapter Seventeen

Darrin

I'm used to women falling all over me.

Not trying to sound cocky or anything, but it's been the story of my life. It started in the first grade, with Melissa Sanford trying to sharpen my pencils for me and then wanting to give me the snack cake from her lunch.

Most of the time women make it easy for me. Too easy. Even saved and sanctified Dorcas is easy as pie. If it weren't for me trying to live right, we'd already be on the altar begging the Lord to forgive our fornicating ways.

But Emoni is different.

I don't think she even knows what she's doing, which is the pure beauty of it all. I know she digs me, that is without question. But she has been challenging me ever since that first day at church, when she caught me admiring her behind.

I wouldn't be a man if I weren't thrilled by the prospect of a challenge. But how would she feel about me if she really knew me? If she knew my whole purpose for being in this city was to bring the bishop to shame?

And about the whole shaming the bishop thing . . . I don't know about that, either. It's starting to bother me. Maybe it's because I'm taking a liking to Bishop Prentiss and his ministry. He shows more interest in my talents than my own father.

Anyway, I'm in my kitchen preparing dinner on a Friday night. I'm making my creamy shrimp pasta with freshly baked garlic bread and a tossed Caesar salad. It's a good thing I work out on the regular, because if I didn't, my stomach would be looking like Oscar's.

I don't think anyone from back home would believe that I'm cool with being at home alone in my apartment, cooking dinner and watching television. Friday used to be the start of my weekend. Friday would be the first night of dates and booty calls that lasted through Monday.

But I've been doing what Bishop Prentiss laid out for us in Bible study. I've been reading my Bible. Didn't really know what to read, so I just started at Genesis, giving myself a refresher course on everything. I'm praying a lot, too. I've never prayed this much in my life.

The water for my angel hair pasta is beginning to boil when the telephone rings. I read my parents' number from the caller ID.

"Hi, Mom."

"How did you know it wasn't your father?" Priscilla asks.

"Dad doesn't call."

"And apparently, neither do you. Why is it that I had to hear from Shayna that you got baptized?"

"I was going to tell you. Why are you still talking to Shayna? We broke up, you know."

Priscilla replies, "Nonsense. She says that you two are reevaluating your relationship. That doesn't sound like a breakup to me."

"Trust me, Mom. I'm done evaluating with her."

"Don't be so hasty. She's a lovely girl and from a good family. She'd make a wonderful wife."

Usually, I don't mind Priscilla dabbling in my business, but she is getting very close to crossing the line over Shayna. And why is she calling my mother? I'm going to have to handle her the hard way, and I've been trying to avoid that.

"So you've gotten quiet," says Priscilla, "and just when I was about to ask you about your story. How is that coming?"

"Honestly, I have no idea what I'm going to write about. If Bishop has any flaws, they are not apparent on the surface."

"Your father is not going to be happy about that," responds Priscilla. I can hear her frown from her tone.

"But I am getting very close to the family. I'm writing for the church newsletter, and I've made friends with the oldest daughter."

"Ah! Now I see why poor Shayna has been discarded. You've met another woman."

"You're wrong, Mom. Shayna was history before I even came down here. She just refuses to accept that."

"Well, you know what they say—persistence breaks down resistance."

Who says that? "Mom, persistence will lead her to stalker charges."

There's a knock at my door. "I've got to go. Someone's at the door."

I hang up the phone and go over to the door, my

stomach growling after I've taken a whiff of the baked bread. After the conversation about Shayna, I'm almost afraid to look through the peephole.

I let out a huge sigh of relief when I open the door to Dorcas. "To what do I owe this visit?"

"Oh, I don't know. I was home and didn't have anything to do. I thought you'd like some company if you were home, too."

"Your instincts were right. Come on in."

Why did I invite her in? What am I thinking? I don't know if I'm strong enough to have her pheromones all up in my personal space. She's wearing loose-fitting sweats and her infamous ponytail.

She's glancing around my spotless apartment; I see her taking it all in. I hope she doesn't think I'm a neat freak or a freak in general. See, I'm already slipping— referring to myself as a freak.

"Have you eaten?" I ask as I start a new pot of angel hair pasta. Between phone calls and opening doors, I've overcooked the first one.

Dorcas shakes her head. "No, I haven't. I thought we could order some takeout, but what you're cooking over there smells delicious. What is it?"

"It's my creamy shrimp pasta. I perfected the recipe about three years ago," I declare proudly.

"What's in the sauce?"

"You want to know my secret recipe?"

Dorcas laughs. "You don't have to worry about me stealing it. I'm afraid I've never tried to cook something so complex. I'm a steak-and-potatoes girl myself."

"I guess I can tell you, then. I use fresh cream, shallots, garlic, Parmesan cheese, and a little white wine."

"Wow! Where did you learn to cook like that?"

"Don't sing my praises yet!" I lift a wooden spoon full of sauce to Dorcas's lips. "Here, taste this, and then tell me what you think."

Dorcas sips a small amount of the sauce and squeezes her eyes shut. "Mmm" is all that she can say.

"You like?"

"Oh, yes! It's wonderful."

I lead Dorcas over to the table. "Sit here and get ready to give your taste buds a treat."

She takes a seat and grins up at me. I grin back and then head back to the kitchen to complete my masterpiece.

Breaking my concentration, Dorcas asks, "Are you always this prepared for company?"

"I eat like this every night."

"Why?"

"You know, it's funny that every woman I've ever entertained has thought it's strange, the way I prepare for my meals, but you are the first one to ask why."

"I just think when someone takes this much care to do something," she explains, "then it must mean a lot to that person."

"I don't know why, really, or even how it started. It probably has something to do with my mother."

"Your mother is a homemaker?" Dorcas asked.

"If you call instructing the staff being a homemaker, then yes."

"Staff? I heard you say your family was wealthy. I didn't know you meant *staff* wealthy."

"I don't talk about it much. It's not my money, it's my father's," I say as I place our plates on the table.

"But it will be yours one day."

I tilt my head back and laugh. "My father is probably taking some youth serum so that he'll live forever, to spite me."

Dorcas tries to laugh at my joke, but she has just eaten a mouthful of pasta. She smiles with pleasure as she chews. "If you ever get married, your wife is going to be a butterball if you feed her like this," she comments.

"I'll make sure she's on a fitness plan. You can eat whatever you want as long as you work it off."

"Sometimes women need more than exercise. Especially after we hit twenty-five."

"You're fine, Dorcas. Here, have some garlic bread."

She looks like she's having second thoughts about taking the crusty, gooey bread. But after some cajoling on my part, she takes it and greedily chomps a huge bite. She leans back in the chair and sighs, her carb craving satisfied.

"Don't get too comfortable. I've got to get to bed early tonight."

"Why is that?"

"I'm traveling with Bishop, Oscar, and Emoni to Savannah tomorrow. Bishop wants me to report on the event."

"I'm surprised Emoni is going. She usually doesn't go to Bishop's speaking engagements."

I sense her irritation, but I choose to ignore it. "I'm thinking we'll have a great time."

"You're probably right. I even think that once Emoni gets over her little crush on you, you'll end up being great friends."

Ouch. Can somebody spell h-a-t-e-r-a-t-i-o-n?

"Yeah, I could see us being friends. She's cool."

"You don't sound too convinced about that."

"Let's say that I don't have too much success with making friends out of former admirers."

I guess Dorcas doesn't know how to respond to this, because she stuffs a huge forkful of pasta in her mouth. I hate to admit it, but my track record in the friends-who-are-women category is pitifully weak. Probably has something to do with the fact that I've ended up sleeping with all of my *friends*. Maybe the new me will fare better.

"So, what really made you come up here tonight? Did you follow the aroma of my pasta sauce?" I ask.

Dorcas blushes and replies, "I don't know. I've never done anything like this before."

"Anything like what?"

"I guess . . . I've never made the first move."

I can't stop the smile from spreading across my face. "It's obvious to me that you are inexperienced in first-move making."

"What?"

"I actually thought that I made the first move when I rubbed your little feet. That was a much better first move than coming to my apartment unannounced and eating up my dinner."

Dorcas laughs. "You're right! I'm a first-move rookie."

"It's quite all right. I accept your feeble attempt at a first move, because it's been a long time since a woman even tried. Thank you."

"You're welcome."

Chapter Eighteen

Darrin

Have I mentioned that I'm not a morning person? I'm that guy who presses the Snooze button thirty times and wakes up late anyway, because my body won't move until it's good and ready. And please don't think I'm rising before the sun. That is the purpose of the sunrise—to be the harbinger of the new day.

But here I am at the crack of dawn, sitting on my couch, fully dressed with notepad and briefcase ready to go. Incoherent as all get out, because why? It is the crack of cotton-picking dawn.

And where is the ever so punctual Oscar, who is already a half hour late? I'm getting ready to dial his cell phone when I hear a banging on my door that sounds like a bounty hunter looking for a felon on the run.

I open the door, ready to greet Oscar with a friendly hello, but he is already walking back down the hall to the elevator. And how did he get upstairs? I know I'm sleepy, but I didn't hear the buzzer.

I grab my briefcase and lock my door before dashing down the hall to catch Oscar. "Good morning," I say when I reach him.

"You should've been outside waiting."

I crack my knuckles, trying to calm my nerves. "You didn't say that before."

"I guess everybody wasn't born with common sense."

I give up. I'm not going to get into an altercation with this dude, though it's obvious that he's trying me. Maybe he thinks I'm some pampered rich kid who can't defend himself. Well, my father's money paid for ten years of tae kwon do lessons.

We get off the elevator, and Oscar rushes to the door. Instead of holding it for me, he lets it slam in my face. If Dorcas weren't standing next to Oscar's car, grinning at me, I would've stole on the brotha.

"Good morning!" Dorcas sings. She shocks me by giving me a more than sisterly hug and a soft kiss on the cheek that stirs me on the inside. And I don't mean in the spirit.

"Well, good morning to you. I'm glad to see that someone is in a good mood," I say. I jerk my head in Oscar's direction, and Dorcas nods knowingly. She hands me a greasy-looking brown paper bag.

"What's this?" I ask, although I can smell the corned beef through the bag.

"I thought you all might get hungry on the road, so I bought some corned-beef sandwiches from the deli up the street. They are the best in town."

"Now, I didn't think I'd be able to find a good corned-beef sandwich in Atlanta."

"Trust me! This will rival any of the ones you've had in Cleveland."

Oscar seems irritated with our chatting, so since I have to be in the car with him for four hours, I'm going to make one more attempt at peace and try to bring him into the conversation. "What does a woman know about a sandwich, anyway? Right?"

Oscar grunts a reply and gets into the car. He motions for me to get in on the other side.

Dorcas says, "Enjoy the trip, Darrin. You can thank me properly for the sandwich when you get back." She shocks me again by giving me another hug. She stands in my arms with her lips deliciously parted. I can't help but kiss her inviting mouth, and I feel her go a little limp. Our tender moment is cut short by honking. Apparently, she's shocked Oscar, too, because he looks as if he's ready to go into convulsions. "Let's go," he barks.

I take a deep breath and let it out slowly, trying to calm my rage. Finally, I release Dorcas from our embrace and grab the car handle. "We can finish this when I get back."

Dorcas's face lights up, which tells me she's game. I get in the car and close the door. Anticipating the finishing with Dorcas has got me whistling to myself.

"Can you chill with that whistling? I'm trying to hear from the Lord."

Okay, I can't take it anymore. "Man, what is your thing with me?"

"I don't know what you're talking about," he replies smugly.

"What is it? Did you try to get at Dorcas and she turned you down? I can't believe you'd try to get with

Emoni, but that could also be the case." I watch his scowl deepen. I must've hit a nerve. "So it is Emoni? You're in love with your pastor's daughter? Wow. She probably doesn't even think of you like that."

Oscar's hands clench the steering wheel until his knuckles are white, but still he remains silent. I continue, "Then a suave, handsome, and debonair brother like me comes along, and your little boo is about to lose her mind. Actually, now I understand why you don't like me. It's cool."

Oscar swerves the car angrily and hisses, "You keep their names out of your mouth. I know that you're up to no good, and when I can prove it, I'm going to send your suave, handsome, and debonair self running back up north where you belong."

"Is that a threat, brotha? You are really killing me with all this Christian hospitality."

Oscar glares at me but turns his attention back to the road. After a short drive, we pull into a development of moderate-sized homes with meticulously manicured lawns and at least two cars in every driveway. It's a community of upwardly mobile African Americans who, through hard work and two or three incomes, have been able to purchase their own slice of the American-dream pie.

We stop at the Prentiss's home, which is located on the corner of a cul-de-sac. Their lawn is as beautiful as the others. Oscar eases the car into the driveway, gets out, and slams the door without giving me any further instructions. I get out of the car, too, and stand next to the door, waiting to see what will happen next.

Emoni comes outside first, wearing a perfectly fitted

tan two-piece suit. She's styled her haircut differently. She looks too good to be going to church.

She sashays up to me and asks, "Aren't you going to open my car door?"

"Of course. Are you sitting in the backseat?"

"If you are."

I chuckle as I open the back door for Emoni. She slides into the car, keeping eye contact with me the entire time. Someone has obviously been schooling her, because she has stepped her game way up. I'm impressed, but I don't know if I can deal with all this flirting without breaking somebody off.

Bishop Prentiss emerges from the garage with Oscar right on his heels. I open the front passenger door for Bishop as he gets close to the car. When Oscar sees Emoni sitting in the backseat, he opens his mouth, probably to object, but quickly closes it again.

Bishop gives me a hearty handshake. "How's everything going?"

"Good, Bishop! I'm happy to be accompanying you today."

Oscar interjects, "Bishop, are you sure you don't want to sit in the backseat with Emoni so you can stretch your legs and relax?"

"The front is fine. Besides, I have some last-minute instructions for you."

Oscar scowls at me and gets in the car. It takes every bit of my self-control to suppress my laughter. I also get in the car, and Oscar barely lets me get the door closed before he pulls off.

As we speed down the road, Emoni comments, "It smells like meat in here. What is that?"

Oscar replies, although Emoni was clearly directing the question to me. "Oh, that's just the sandwiches that Sister Dorcas bought for Darrin to eat on the road."

"Oh," responds Emoni in a whisper.

I'm touched by Emoni's disappointment, so I try to clean up Oscar's comment. "Actually, Dorcas bought corned beef for everyone."

"Well, wasn't that thoughtful?" says Emoni with one of the fakest smiles I've ever seen.

"It sure was," continues Oscar. "Emoni, did you know that they live in the same apartment building? What a coincidence, right?"

Score one for the haters, because there is no way for me to recover from that low blow.

"I didn't know that," states Emoni sadly.

Bishop interjects, "Give me a hunk of one of those sandwiches, because I'm famished."

I pass the bag up to Bishop and slump back in my seat. I do not want to travel an uncomfortable four hours with a scowling girl sitting next to me. She's looking out of the window, blowing little frost circles on the windows and scribbling them away.

For lack of a better idea, I pull out a piece of paper and a pen and draw a tic-tac-toe board. I make the first move—an X in the upper-left corner—and then tap Emoni's shoulder. When she glares over in my direction, I hand her the folded-up game board. She asks quietly, "What is this?"

I hold one finger up to my lips to shush her and motion for her to open the paper, which she does. I don't want Oscar to know about our game. A huge smile spreads across her face and she quickly marks her move on the tic-tac-toe board and passes it back. We keep passing the little paper until Emoni has won four times in a row.

In a last-ditch, desperate effort to win, I try to cheat by making two moves at once. Emoni's mouth opens wide when she sees the obvious, and she bursts into laughter. I start laughing, too, the kind of laughter that makes my stomach muscles tighten and tears form in the corners of my eyes.

Oscar clears his throat. "You two are having way too much fun back there. Why don't you all try to reflect on the move of God that we're about to witness in Savannah?"

Emoni and I lock eyes, and we laugh even harder. Oscar looks at Bishop, possibly searching for an ally, but Bishop shrugs, smiles, and takes another huge bite of his corned-beef sandwich.

Chapter Nineteen

Emoni

I am utterly confused. I want to say that I know for certain Darrin has been flirting with me all the way to Savannah. But what if I'm overreacting? What if he's just being nice? It's hard to tell with him lunching on sandwiches from that heifer Dorcas. Isn't buying food for a man a girlfriend type of thing to do?

I'm trying not to think of Dorcas, because I'm absolutely not in competition with her. No matter what she has going on with Darrin, until he discourages me from flirting, I'm not going to stop. I mean, if they're getting serious, he wouldn't be flirting with me.

He sits next to me in church, and I don't know how I'm going to pay attention to the sermon. He smells so good that I just want to hug him and never let him go. But that would be more than desperate, so I'll keep my hugs to myself.

Determined to concentrate, I turn my attention to

Daddy, as he's entered the pulpit area. He's wearing a simple black suit and his minister's collar. He never wears the robes when we go on the road; those are for Sunday mornings at home.

He stands at the podium, ready to deliver the Word of God. The congregation here at New Bethany Baptist is the opposite of our congregation in sheer numbers and worship style. At Freedom of Life, it is customary to see people standing with uplifted arms, waving flags or even kneeling at the altar at any given time during the service. But New Bethany Baptist has a program, and they are sticking to it. The deacons have done devotion, the choir has sung two hymns, and now the congregation is sitting with folded hands, waiting for the message.

Daddy starts, "I want to bless God for bringing me here this afternoon. I truly believe that there is a revival going on in the body of Christ, and I'm just ecstatic beyond words to be a part of that. Some of you know me, and you know of my Pentecostal background."

Heads solemnly nod in the audience. Darrin scribbles furiously on his notepad. I try to peek over to see what he's writing, but he catches me in the act and hides his paper.

"So, y'all probably think that I'm going to preach a holiness-or-hell message, right? A get-right-church-and-let's-go-home message, right?" The deacons and church mothers all clap and nod in agreement.

Daddy continues, "Well, I'm sorry. I'm not going to preach that message today. I'm not saying that it's a wrong message, because the Lord says, 'Be ye holy'; for I am holy.'"

One of the mothers shouts, "That's right, Bishop! That's what He say!"

"But I feel the Lord leading me down another road today. He's been leading me to preach a message of love and restoration. Because only through the love of Christ and the restoration into covenant with Him can holiness be accomplished in a sinner."

Darrin sits on the edge of his seat with a look of anticipation. He seems so eager to hear what Daddy is going to say next.

"Open up your Bibles to the gospel of John, the eighth chapter, and read with me starting in Verse Three and ending in Verse Eleven."

Everyone stands and reads along with Daddy. When he's finished, Daddy shakes his head as if the mere reading of the verses has been enough. "Verse Three says that the Scribes and Pharisees brought to Jesus a woman who was caught in the act of adultery.

"Imagine the shame of this unnamed woman to be exposed by the very shepherds of her faith. There was no hiding her sin and no explaining her way out of it. She was caught red-handed, so to speak. But come on, somebody—each and every one of us is that woman! The church is that woman!"

Several people are standing, including Darrin. Daddy's tone is dripping with passion for the Scriptures.

"We've all got a laundry list of dastardly deeds and dirty little secrets. Though the person sharing the pew with you may look and dress fine, they've got a secret box, locked away so deeply that no earthly man can see it . . . but it's there.

"Oh, but I serve an awesome God! The devil, like

the Scribes and Pharisees, wants to lay our secret boxes bare. He wants to tell the world that this brother has a lust issue and looks at pornography in secret or that this woman had six abortions while singing in the choir every Sunday . . . Oh, but I serve an awesome God!

"He quietly waited while the devil accuses the ones He loves. He was silent when the Pharisees brought Him the woman. Was it because He had no defense of her? No! He knew that in a short time, His blood would be shed to cover the woman's sins. He knew that she would be able to walk in the newness of life and be washed as white as snow, even though her sins were crimson red."

A young woman breaks down in tears at her seat, sobbing, "Jesus, Jesus . . ." For some reason, I feel led to go to her. I take her hand and whisper a prayer in her ear, and the young woman sobs on my shoulder. I can feel the weight of her pain, and I pray for her strength.

Daddy continues his sermon. "What did Jesus ask the woman? He asked, 'Where are those thine accusers?' The Pharisees, convicted by Jesus' words, had scattered. Their evil intentions could not flourish while the grace of God abounded. The devil may accuse you and betray you after leading you into sin, but he must flee—I said he must *flee*—when the glory of God is present.

"Then finally, Jesus told the woman, 'Neither do I condemn thee . . . go and sin no more.' Did he give her an impossible task? How could this woman go the rest of her life and sin no more? The fact of the matter is that we, like the woman, need Christ daily—we need His blood daily. When we live a life surrendered to Him, He gives us power to resist sin, and yet when we do fall, His innocent, uncontaminated blood erases our debt.

"Emoni, come up here and sing this song for me."

I stand and walk down the center aisle with tears in my eyes. I always cry when the spirit of God is present. It's involuntary. When I get to the front of the church, I take a microphone from the organ player and start singing Daddy's favorite worship song, Donnie McClurkin's "Great Is Your Mercy."

Daddy starts the altar call. "Come on down and surrender yourself to Jesus. Let His blood cover you all the days of your life."

The prayer line extends to the rear of the church, with nearly a hundred people wanting or needing something from God. Even Darrin comes up for prayer.

Last in the prayer line is a woman who looks a hot and utter mess. Her clothes are dirty and crusty, and her hair weave looks like it could get up and walk off of her head. She staggers slowly down the aisle, holding on to a young man with her. I can smell her from the pulpit, but Daddy doesn't seem to mind; he's holding out both arms.

"Come on down to the altar, daughter. The Lord wants to bring a healing in your life."

The woman looks up from the floor, and her eyes lock with Daddy's. A strange expression of fear and guilt comes over Daddy's face. Now the woman is smiling. So many of her teeth are missing that her smile looks like a sneer.

When the woman gets to the front of the aisle, she thrusts the young man in front of Daddy. He jumps back as if the boy has the plague.

In a low, scratchy growl, the woman asks, "Why don't you lay hands on your son, Kumal?"

Daddy places one hand on the young man's head and says a brief prayer. Only me and Oscar are close enough to see that Daddy's hand is trembling. A queasy feeling grips my midsection.

When Daddy finishes the prayer, Oscar rushes forward and whisks Daddy out of the sanctuary. The congregation doesn't see that anything is wrong. They all think that Daddy is spent in the spirit.

I have just one question. How does that disgusting woman know my father's first name?

Darrin and I follow closely behind Oscar and Daddy. As we approach the car, I notice the young man standing next to the vehicle. Even though he seems harmless and is holding a Bible in his hand, I feel a horrible sense of apprehension.

"Is everything cool?" Darrin whispers to me.

I shrug. "I don't know."

Oscar goes completely into security mode and strides ahead of us, making sure he'll reach the man first. He says in an ignorantly loud voice, "Can I help you with something?"

The young man replies, "N-no. I just n-need to speak with the bishop, if that's all right."

Oscar looks skeptical, but Daddy intervenes. "What is it that you need?"

The young man says, "I thought our reunion would be a lot more joyful than this. I've been waiting for this moment my entire life."

A dark frown has come across Daddy's face, like a shadow. "Young man, I don't know you. I think you've got me mistaken for someone else."

"Is it okay if we speak in private, sir?"

Why does he need to talk to my father in private? Looks like Darrin and Oscar have the same question, because the two of them circle in like vultures.

Daddy replies, "There's no need for that, son. Go ahead and tell me what's on your mind."

"Well . . . there's no easy way to say this, so I'm just going to spit it out. Bishop . . . you . . . you're my father."

"I'm afraid you're mistaken," repeats Daddy confidently. "I don't know you or the woman who was with you."

"Sir, I'm not mistaken. You remember my mother, although she was a lot prettier when you knew her. Her name is Genevieve."

Daddy's gaze jerks from the car door back to the young man. "Did you say Genevieve?"

"Yes, sir. Genevieve Walters. You and her used to get high together. She says you're my father."

Daddy wipes his face with his handkerchief, but he can't wipe away the guilty expression. "She looks like death warmed over."

"So you do remember her! You got clean, but she never did. She drinks, too, got a bad case of cirrhosis, but she can't get on the transplant list because she's got that crack cocaine in her system."

"That's a shame. What's your name?"

"Kumal. She named me after you. Said you was the only one who ever cared about her."

I get over my loss of words when he says this. "Are you trying to say that you are my father's son?"

Kumal Jr. lights up and reaches out to hug me. "You're my sister?"

Darrin stands between us. "Hold up, brotha. This ain't a family reunion yet."

Kumal says to Daddy, "Look, I don't want anything from you. I was just hoping you'd talk to my mother and try to convince her to get off drugs."

"I will pray for your mother, but you are not my son. That's impossible. Let her know that I'm praying for her."

Tears are in young Kumal's eyes. "Sir, I promise, I don't want nothin'. Can I just get to know you? It's been hard growing up not knowing you."

Daddy takes one last look at the young man and then gets in the car. I want to say something to Kumal, anything that will make that look on his face disappear. I want to tell him that he looks exactly like my daddy and that I believe him, but the thoughts never become words.

I feel Darrin's strong grip pulling me over to the car, but I can't move. The tears running down Kumal's face are the saddest thing I've ever seen. I break away from Darrin and hug Kumal. I whisper a prayer in his ear, like I did for the young lady in the church.

He seems better when I'm done. His tears are still flowing, but he looks hopeful. Now I allow Darrin to lead me to the car, where Oscar and Daddy are waiting for us.

The car ride home is silent. Darrin and I don't share any jokes or games of tic-tac-toe. No one even makes eye contact. Every breath Daddy exhales sounds like a forlorn sigh.

All of this is entirely too much to comprehend. I think of the strangest things under pressure. Like I probably should be asking Daddy all about Kumal's mother, but I'm a little bit thrilled that I have a sibling who looks like me.

I've got a big brother. And he's named after my daddy.

Chapter Twenty

DIARY OF A MAD BLACK BLOGGER

What's up, cyber homies and homettes? I know, I know. It's been a minute since I last wrote. That's because I've been busy. I've been doing what my mama calls "running for Jesus."

Seriously.

I've been working hard—real hard—trying to live right and helping out in the ministry. I've been touched by the Bible in so many areas of my life, and I've been able to successfully fight some powerful man urges.

But.

And this is a big ole but.

Let me just give y'all a hypothetical situation. What if a pastor—a bishop—is a great preacher and teacher? What if he leads people to deliverance every week? What if he lives modestly, gives to the poor, and does great things in the community?

What if he has a secret illegitimate son?

I may have the scoop of a lifetime, but I'm gonna get back with y'all when I get facts and details.

I really, really need y'all to pray for me . . . Y'all can hit me up in the comments section, but put me on the prayer list, too.

COMMENTS

Sister Mary 10:13 p.m.

The blood of Jesus is against you, MBB. Touch not my profet. That's what the Word say.

Angie 11:00 p.m.

Wow . . . MBB, I'm praying for you. That's a tough situation. Did you get the girl though?

Single black churchgoer 12:19 a.m.

Yeah, MBB, which of those hot girls did you choose? The bishop's daughter or his wife's armor bearer? Don't nobody wanna hear about the pastor's illegitimate child! They all doing some kind of dirt anyway. Follow Christ, and you ain't got to worry about all that.

Chapter Twenty-one

Darrin

I'm sitting cross-legged on my couch, deep in thought, the evening's weirdness still feeling fresh. Got a notebook full of good notes from Bishop's message. It was a good message, but I can't even think about that right now. I'm thinking about a story.

More specifically, I'm thinking about *the* story. The one that I came all the way to Atlanta to uncover. The exposé that's going to put me on the map and get my father off my back. *That* story. In my gut, I know I've found it, but now that I've found it, I have no idea what to do with it.

My choices are clear. Write the story or don't. Writing the story involves my finding that woman in Savannah and compelling her to spill the beans. Not writing the story means that I turn a blind eye to the scandal staring me in the face. The journalist in me can't allow that to happen.

And since the scenario in Savannah, I'm starting to feel like it's useless trying to do the Christian thing. Bishop stared his possible son in the face and basically said, "See ya!" And right after he preached a good message and prayed for people.

It's late, after eleven p.m., when I hear a knock on my door. Does anyone in Atlanta call first? But I know before answering the door that it's Dorcas. More than likely, she wants to know how the day went.

"Hello, Dorcas. I wasn't expecting you," I say dryly as I open the door.

"Hi! I know it's late, but I wanted to see how things went in Savannah."

I sit back down on the couch and close my eyes. It is entirely too late for her to be this bubbly.

"That bad?" she asks.

"Worse."

Dorcas sits down on the couch next to me. "Do you want to talk about it?"

I shock Dorcas by bursting into spontaneous laughter. It has occurred to me that this saved woman is visiting me at my apartment late at night. A month ago we would have already been in the bedroom. It's funny to me that taking her virtue hasn't even crossed my mind.

"Sister Dorcas, are you here with good intentions? Because back in the day, when a woman visited me at this hour—"

Dorcas laughs. "This is *not* a booty call."

"Okay. I just wanted clarity."

"What I really want to know is what happened with Emoni. Did you two hit it off?" asks Dorcas with a nervous chuckle.

Yeah, we hit it off. Thinking about our jokes brings a smile to my face. I can't remember the last time I laughed that hard. Instead of making her seem immature, Emoni's youthfulness is innocent and attractive. And then she earned my respect when I watched her pray for that girl in the church and the man who might be her brother.

But I don't say any of this to Dorcas. "We actually had a lot of fun, mostly cracking jokes on Oscar."

"See, I told you. Emoni is a great girl."

"You've made a believer out of me."

Dorcas stands. "I guess I'll get going, then. I don't want to keep you up. Besides, we've got church in the morning."

"You sure? I could pop some popcorn, and we could watch a movie." I need the distraction. I'm not ready to be left alone with my thoughts about Bishop.

Before Dorcas can reply, I'm on my feet and getting the microwave popcorn out of the cabinet. Dorcas smiles and sits on one end of the couch with her feet stretched clear to the other side, leaving a small area for me to sit.

When I'm done, I walk back over, holding a bowl of buttery popcorn. "Where am I supposed to sit?"

"Down there," answers Dorcas as she points to the opposite end of the couch.

I laugh. "All the way down there?"

"I think that's the wise thing to do," Dorcas replies, her face serious and her arms crossed.

"What if I want to make a comment about the movie?"

"Write me a note."

I sit down slowly and rub my hands on my jeans. My heavy exhale shows my frustration.

A rush of thoughts floods my brain. I'm remembering Dorcas's lips on mine. I'm feeling like if Bishop Prentiss can't walk the straight and narrow, then how can I?

Whatever the reason, I slide across the couch in one fluid motion. Before Dorcas can object, our lips are locked in a deep, deep kiss. It's the kind of kiss that can end only one way. At first she doesn't resist. I can feel her heart racing and her breathing becoming ragged. But when I place my hand in the warm spot between her legs, she jumps up like I've gotten out of pocket.

"D-Darrin! What are you doing?"

"Baby, what did you come here for?"

Dorcas frowns and hisses, "Not this."

"Wow. I thought this was what you wanted."

Dorcas's chest heaves in and out. "What I want is someone who respects himself enough to wait until he's married. I want a saved man."

I'm embarrassed and confused. I've never been in this situation. It feels like I should be apologizing, but the words won't come.

"I guess I'm not him, huh?" I ask with a sigh.

Tears fill Dorcas's eyes. "You could be, Darrin."

She goes to the door and sees herself out. I don't even try to stop her because I know that I've blown it.

I sit back on the couch and take in what Dorcas said. She told me that I don't respect myself. Wow.

I whip out my laptop and open up my blog page. Right about now I feel the need for strangers to tell me that everything is cool in my world.

DIARY OF A MAD BLACK BLOGGER

Why am I up at the midnight hour blogging? Real talk. I just went through something brand-new in my life of dating. I just had a woman tell me no.

Now, I've spit game to women before and been shot down—so that's not what I mean. I'm talking about a woman who's feeling me and has been dating me. I tried to take it to the next level. The sexual level. Y'all know what I'm talking about.

Anyway, she turned me down; told me that I don't respect myself.

Most women hit you with that "You don't respect me" line. But she told me that I don't respect myself. I gotta say, that cut me deeper than any curse words or blows that could've been thrown my way.

I. Don't. Respect. Myself.

And the really scary part is: I think she's right.

Here I am, trying to be a Christian, and at the first sign of trouble, I'm ready to throw it all away and jump in the sack with a woman I like but don't love. Maybe I'm a lost cause.

I'm closing the comments on this post, because I'm not sure I'm ready to hear your replies. Mad Black Blogger signing off . . .

Chapter Twenty-two

Emoni

It's Sunday morning. The Lord's day. We should be rejoicing and being glad, but our house is in an uproar.

Daddy came home last night and apparently told Mother everything that happened in Savannah. They argued late into the night. I've never, ever heard them yell at each other. But Mother unleashed a fury no one in this house knew she had.

I'm standing before my mirror, playing with my feathered bangs and feeling anxious. I'm thinking about my brother Kumal and how I wish we'd gotten a chance to talk more. Also, I can't help but consider how well Darrin and I got along. I just hate that the evening ended on a low, low note.

I hear a light knock on my door. Must be Tyler, because Sascha never knocks.

"Emoni, what in the world is going on?" asks Tyler nervously.

"I don't know, Ty."

Tyler comes into my room and closes the door behind him. I sit down on the edge of my bed, trying to wrap my arms around this situation.

Tyler questions, "Did something go down in Savannah? Did Oscar flip out on that Darrin guy?"

"Why would Oscar be going off on Darrin?"

Tyler raises his hands apologetically. "No reason. Forget I asked."

"Actually, some man confronted Daddy."

Tyler's eyes widen. "Confronted Bishop how?"

"He says he's Daddy's son, by a drug abuser named Genevieve."

"You don't think Bishop could be—"

"No. Oh, I don't know. His name is Kumal, and he looks just like Daddy."

"Well . . . Daddy is a man, and he has a past that we don't really know anything about."

"Tyler, I'm not about to sit up here and speak anything wrong against Daddy. I'm sure he'll explain this to us in due time. And we know all about Daddy's past. He testifies about it all the time." I say this with conviction, hoping that it's the truth.

"I'm just saying that it's possible. That's all. Everybody's got skeletons."

I need to dismiss this conversation immediately. "Tyler, I can't hear this right now. You want something to eat?"

"Nah, I'm good."

"Well, I'm getting something in my stomach."

I leave Tyler sitting on my bed and go downstairs to the kitchen to make breakfast. I guess that's only if you consider a piece of toast and bottled water breakfast. I'm not sure my stomach can handle anything else.

The doorbell rings. Strange for a Sunday morning, but Oscar is prone to checking in on Daddy personally when something is wrong.

I open the door, but it's not Oscar, it's Sister Ophelia. "Sister Ophelia. What a *lovely* surprise."

"Gal, don't lie on the Lord's day. You ain't happy to see me." She rolls her eyes and purses her lips tightly, looking like she sucked a lemon.

"I'm being polite, Sister Ophelia."

"I value truthfulness over politeness."

"Obviously."

"Honey, I need to speak to your mama. In private."

"Is everything okay?"

"Did I stutter or whisper when I said *private?*"

This is not good. First of all, Ophelia never comes to our house. And she wants to talk to Mother in private? She must know about Sascha and Kevin. For half a second I debate on whether or not I should get Mother. This is so not the day for any other revelations.

But I don't have the chance to make the choice myself, because Mother is already walking into the room. Her eyes are puffy from crying all night long, but she is still wearing her "greet the saints" smile. Even though Ophelia asked for privacy, I'm not leaving until Mother asks me to.

Ophelia stands from the couch. "Hello, Diana. You know, you really ought to put some plastic on this sofa if you want it to last."

"Praise the Lord, Sister Ophelia. Is there something troubling you?"

"Yes, there most certainly is."

"You couldn't have called?" asks Mother while raising one eyebrow.

Ophelia responds, "Ain't I welcome in your house?"

"It's not that at all. It's just that it must be important for you to drive all the way over here, on a Sunday morning, no less."

Ophelia takes a deep breath. "Your daughter has seduced my grandson. Right now they are laid up in a hotel together. Fornicating."

Mother pauses before replying. She blinks rapidly, as if waiting for Ophelia to recant her story. Ophelia crosses her arms and sits back on the couch.

"Sascha spent the weekend with her friend Gina. I have no reason to believe otherwise," mother says.

"You might not, but I do. I heard my grandson on the phone making hotel reservations for the two of them."

"Why didn't you say something to your grandson then, Ophelia?" Mother asks in an exasperated tone. "If they are together, you're partially to blame."

Ophelia stands again, nose to nose with Mother. It's on and poppin' now.

Ophelia screeches, "I'm to blame? No, you and Bishop are to blame for not keeping tabs on that hot-tailed heifer. A bishop's daughter is supposed to be holy."

"We're all supposed to be holy. Isn't that right, Ophelia? Anyway, I don't believe that Sascha would do something so stupid, holy or otherwise."

"Humph! You've got your beliefs, but what I've got is facts! You think that little hot-tailed heifer is better than my grandson? Well, she ain't. She as sinful as the devil himself!"

Mother smoothes her skirt. "Ophelia, I believe that our conversation is over."

"Turn a blind eye to it if you want," continues Ophelia as she stands to leave. "But I know the truth."

Mother places her couch pillows as they were before Ophelia moved them. "You have a blessed day, Sister Ophelia."

Ophelia narrows her eyes and fumes with anger. She marches over to our front door and slams it on her way out.

"Mother, are you all right?" I ask.

"Oh, yes." Mother beams through her puffy eyes. "Everything is right as rain."

Daddy comes downstairs still wearing his pajamas, even though it's almost time to leave for church. I follow him into the kitchen and watch him grab bacon and eggs from the refrigerator. Tyler joins us and starts toasting a bagel.

Daddy places eight slices of bacon on the hot pancake griddle and hums a gospel hymn.

I ask, "Daddy, are you going to get ready for church?"

"Not going," he replies curtly.

"Are you okay, Daddy? Do you want to talk about Savannah?"

"I'm fine. Your mother and I are taking a day off, that's all."

Daddy taking a Sunday morning off is the opposite of fine. He never misses a Sunday. Not even when we go on vacation. We always make sure to be home on Sunday. Once Daddy was so sick with a stomach virus that he could hardly stand, and he had to let one of the associate ministers preach. But he was right there in the pulpit, doubled over and giving God the praise.

"Good morning, Tyler," says Daddy, even though they've been standing in the same room for several minutes.

"Hey, Bishop," says Tyler.

"Where are you off to? A football game?" No doubt Daddy is making reference to Tyler's jeans and tennis shoes.

"I'm going to church with Kevin this morning."

Right, like Kevin is actually going to church. He and Sascha are probably still curled up in their Super 8 Motel room.

"Kevin's not attending Freedom of Life anymore?" Daddy asks incredulously.

Tyler takes his time responding. "Well, he visits Love Outreach sometimes. We're going there today."

Daddy nods slowly as he turns the browned bacon. A good number of our members have defected over to Love Outreach and Pastor David Maxwell. Most of the defectors are under twenty-five and borderline backslidden, like Kevin. I wish Tyler would just tell Daddy that he wants to worship there instead of making up excuses every Sunday.

Daddy asks Tyler, "What do you think of Love Outreach?"

Again Tyler pauses before replying, as if he's choosing his words carefully. "If I hadn't grown up in church, I would definitely prefer Love Outreach to Freedom of Life."

"Why is that?"

"It's almost like when you go into a normal church, there's an expectation. You're expected to lift up your hands, clap as the choir sings, and shout hallelujah in the appropriate places. But at Love Outreach, you can just come and listen, and no one looks at you strange."

I interject, "That's because most of the people there *are* strange."

"Shut up, Emoni," Tyler retorts.

Daddy places his crispy bacon on a plate lined with a paper towel. "How is that any different than Freedom of Life? We also invite people to come as they are."

"That's what we say." Tyler chuckles. "But there are a lot of folk sitting up in Freedom of Life who don't really aspire to that philosophy."

"We have a very loving church," Daddy counters.

"Yeah, as long as you look and smell nice; as long as your children are well behaved and you have a nice car."

Daddy shakes his head. "I don't know what you're talking about."

"Don't you remember when Oscar first came to Freedom of Life?"

"Yes, of course I remember. But that was a special circumstance. Oscar was a mess," Daddy says.

Tyler replies, "But that didn't stop you from embracing him and welcoming him to Jesus. Bishop, you might be the only one at Freedom of Life who has that kind of love for people."

Daddy bites into a piece of bacon. I wonder if he's going to admit that Tyler is right. Because Tyler is . . . right. Folk at Freedom of Life are as hung up on appearance as people at any other church; as people in general.

Tyler continues, "Over at Love Outreach, you don't have to look or dress a certain way or drive a nice car. You get treated the same if you ride the bus or pull up in a Caddy. And the pastor is so young. He knows what the youth are going through."

"If I didn't know any better," says Daddy suspiciously, "I'd think that you were a member of Love Outreach."

"No. But honestly, I've been considering a change."

"What?" Daddy is visibly stunned. It's as if Tyler has taken a ton of bricks and dropped them on his chest.

"I didn't say I was leaving for sure. I just said I was considering it."

I know, and Daddy probably knows, too, that Tyler has already made up his mind about Love Outreach. Maybe if Daddy hadn't been confronted with drama in Savannah, he would've offered more objections. Instead, he nods, takes his plate of bacon, and heads back upstairs to the sanctuary of the bedroom.

"Did you really have to do this today, Tyler?" I ask my brother.

"Do what? Speak the truth?"

"Daddy didn't need this today. With what happened in Savannah and Sascha being pregnant—"

"Sascha is pregnant?"

Oh . . . my . . . God. I didn't mean to say that. Tyler doesn't know— Well, didn't know, because now he does.

"Don't say anything, Ty. Mother and Daddy don't know yet, but Sister Ophelia was just here and told Mother about them sleeping together."

Tyler is breathing heavily. I can feel the heat from his blood boiling. Kevin is his best friend, but Sascha is his baby sister.

"Kevin . . . is sleeping with . . . Sascha," he says. "I was hoping that I was wrong."

Before I can answer, Daddy comes rushing back down

the stairs in his pajamas still, though with shoes and a jacket on. Mother is two steps behind him.

"Kumal! You don't even know where you're going!"

Daddy stops for a half second, clarity seeming to come over his face. But another half second later, he's grabbing his keys and heading for the door.

When he's gone, Tyler and I look at Mother for an explanation. She says, "I told him what Ophelia said."

"Are you going to go after him?" I ask.

"Your father is a grown man. He doesn't need me to help him handle this."

I don't think the this she's talking about is Sascha and Kevin. She's referring to Daddy's blast from his past. My brother . . . his son.

Chapter Twenty-three

Darrin

The ministers are in an uproar. The entire Prentiss family is missing from church, and no one knows why. Even Oscar is in the dark and scrambling to keep a sense of order and decorum, but the rumors have already started.

"Bishop had a heart attack."

"I heard Tyler left to start his own church."

"Bishop got in a car accident on the way back from Savannah."

I see Dorcas trying to fend off the entire missionary board. Seeing her immediately makes me uncomfortable. But I do want to apologize, since I didn't do it last night.

I tap her on the shoulder and say the first thing that comes to mind. "Trustee Oscar needs you in the pastor's study."

Dorcas looks visibly shaken when she turns to face me.

She takes a long swallow. "Do you know what's going on? Have you talked to Emoni?" she asks in a timid voice.

"I was just about to ask you that same question."

We step into Bishop's study almost unnoticed, due to the commotion. The ministers are arguing about who's going to preach the morning message. Oscar is trying to calm everyone down, but he's not doing a good job of it.

Oscar says, "Deacon Bagley, will you go and start service? The praise team has been singing for nearly an hour, and they're getting tired."

Deacon replies, "Why don't you have the other deacons do it?"

Elder Brookins interjects, "Trustee Williams, you are not calling any shots here. We'll start service when I say so. I am the assistant pastor."

"Respectfully, Elder Brookins," says Oscar in an exasperated tone, "service should've started half an hour ago."

"Trustee, why don't you try to go and locate Bishop Prentiss?"

I ask the obvious: "Has anyone checked their house?"

The ministers all look at Oscar.

Oscar throws his arms up and leaves the office with Dorcas and me following close behind. We follow Oscar as he flees to the church parking lot. A thought comes to mind: I wish I had my notebook. I quickly push it away. This is a crisis, and I'm thinking about a story. But I can't help it. It's a darn good story.

Dorcas marches up to Oscar and fusses, "When are you going to tell me what's going on? I haven't been able to reach First Lady or Emoni on their cell phones this morning."

"What does *he* have to do with anything?" asked Oscar, obviously referring to me.

Dorcas hisses, "He's fine. Why don't you tell me something?"

"I don't know anything! I haven't been able to reach Bishop, either," Oscar says. He tries to threaten me with his expression, as if I shouldn't tell Dorcas what happened in Savannah. He then jumps in his car and speeds off. It's almost funny that he thinks he intimidates me. Funny because in the real world, Oscar is nobody. An ex–drug abuser who probably has a record full of felonies. But here at Freedom of Life, this brotha is the man. Funny.

Dorcas looks at me with questions in her eyes as we hear one of the elders praying over the loudspeakers.

"Looks like they decided to get started," I remark.

Dorcas looks at the ground, apparently avoiding eye contact with me. "Guess so."

"Look, Dorcas, I'm sorry. I didn't mean—"

She interjects, "No, Darrin, don't. It's not necessary."

"But I think—"

"Nope," she interrupts again. "Don't say anything. You were just a tool of the adversary."

This woman is finding new and innovative ways to insult me. "Come again?"

"You are on assignment, brotha," Dorcas says with resignation. "You tried to make me backslide. And that's straight from the pits of hell."

Dorcas turns and runs back toward the church. Okay, first of all, she tried to make *me* backslide. I was doing everything in my newly saved power to keep her from backsliding until she showed up at my apartment late at night.

I can't even bring myself to go back in the sanctuary for morning service. I need to think. And I can't do that on an empty stomach. I've got a decision to make, maybe a story to write.

On the way to my truck, I see a distraught-looking Emoni trudging toward the church. Clearly, she's been crying, and if she walks into the sanctuary looking the way she does, the congregation will have a serious meltdown.

I walk into her path. "Emoni, are you all right?"

"No!" she sobs, and collapses into my arms.

"I'm going to suggest that you don't go in there. I promise you, it's not going to help."

"I don't know what to do."

I give her a sincere smile. "Why don't you come with me to my place and let me make you a good breakfast? You'll feel better after you eat."

"Okay," she responds with resignation and defeat in her voice.

Emoni follows me to my apartment building in her car. When we reach our destination, she emerges with a tear-streaked and puffy face. Normally, I'm not a sentimental type of guy, but the sadness in her eyes has me choked up.

I rush to Emoni and embrace her with a brotherly hug. "Everything is going to be all right, girl. Stop all that crying."

I lead her up to my apartment with conflicting feelings struggling inside me. My heart goes out to Emoni. I can't imagine how I would feel if I found out I had an older brother.

Emoni surveys my apartment and chuckles. "This is a real bachelor's pad."

"Not even. My mama picked out everything in here."

Emoni parks herself on my sofa. "She did? She has good taste."

"So what are you hungry for?"

"You know, I've really got a taste for Belgian waffles."

"Now, that's what I'm talking about."

Emoni takes off her church shoes and relaxes on my couch. Well, her body is relaxed, but her troubles are still etched all over her face.

"Aren't you going to help?" I ask playfully. "Does this look like a restaurant?"

Emoni looks down at her clothes. "I can't cook in this suit! I'd get batter all over it."

"That is a problem easily solved." I dash into my bedroom and come out with sweats for Emoni. "You can go in my bedroom and change."

She gets a nervous expression on her face, so I reassure her. "Girl, ain't nobody about to come in there on you! If you want something to eat, I suggest you get into those sweats."

Instead of changing out of my church clothes, I roll up my sleeves and put on my chef's jacket. After a few moments, Emoni comes out of my bedroom wearing my sweatsuit. She looks a lot better in it than I do. The flash of heat that rips through my body at the sight of her is hard to ignore. But I must. "It's about time. What took you so long? Were you snooping in my room?" I say.

"No. I was admiring how neat you are. Most men are slobs."

"Most men were not raised by Priscilla Bainbridge."

Emoni laughs. "Sounds like your mom is as bad as

mine. When we were kids, we couldn't play, eat, or do homework until our bedrooms were spotless."

"Yep. They sound like sisters."

Emoni continues, "I remember my mother going off on Daddy about some dirty socks. You would've thought he'd done something terrible."

I start to reply but remain quiet because Emoni's mood changed as soon as she mentioned her father. Her smile faded and her look of despair quickly resurfaced.

I hand her the bowl. "Here. Mix this. But not too much. We don't want to get a lot of air in the batter. I'll heat up the waffle iron."

Emoni points at my face. "You have flour on your cheek."

"Where?" I'm wiping but obviously not getting it, because she's still pointing.

Emoni steps closer to me. Dangerously close. "No. Right here."

Emoni stands on her tiptoes and brushes the flour from my cheek. She takes her time getting it all, and I know women well enough to know that she's doing this on purpose. I also know *me* well enough to know that if I don't escape soon, I'm going to be disrespecting myself again.

Then this stupid, naive girl takes my face in her hands and pulls it to her own. I have to suppress a moan when she places an innocent, unskilled kiss on my lips. It is the sweetest thing I've ever tasted.

Quickly, I pull away. I have to pull away. Seriously. "Don't do that. Don't start something that neither of us wants to finish."

"I just wanted to see what it felt like," Emoni explains as she drops her head in embarrassment.

"You mean that was your first kiss?" I'm so stunned I can hardly form the words.

Emoni nods, and I can do nothing but scratch my head in confusion. I don't even know how to proceed. What is the proper etiquette for first kisses? I can't even remember. I was eleven when I had mine. How can Emoni only now be having her first kiss and she's twenty-four years old?

"How was it?" I ask for lack of a better comment.

Emoni relaxes and smiles up at me. "It was great."

Okay, so I can't help but grin as I walk over to the waffle iron. Emoni's got me shook up, that's for sure. Even more than Dorcas, who now considers me the devil's spawn. But I cannot start this with Emoni. Not unless she knows why I'm in Atlanta.

While the waffles are cooking, I quickly set the table and fill a glass pitcher with juice. I also place freshly cut fruit, whipped cream, syrup, and butter in the center of the table. Then I motion for Emoni to sit down. "I'll take it from here," I tell her.

Emoni frowns when she looks at the table. She moves her place setting and chair so that it is adjacent to mine instead of safely on the other side of the table. She then smiles seductively as I serve her Belgian waffles and bacon. When I sit down, I bow my head, ready to offer my own silent prayer for my breakfast. This girl shocks me again by taking my hands.

She prays, "Lord, bless this food and make it fit for our nourishment. Bless the hands that prepared it. In Jesus' name."

"Amen." I snatch my hands away abruptly because her touch has me thinking thoughts that have no business in the context of a prayer. Forgive me, Lord.

Emoni takes a bite of her waffle. With her mouth full, she exclaims, "This is the best waffle I've ever eaten."

I smile with pride. "Thank you. Yet another satisfied customer."

"Why don't you cook for a living? It seems to suit you."

"I asked my father to send me to college to study culinary arts, and I think I literally saw his head fly off."

Emoni scoffs, "I can't believe that! Has your father ever tasted your food?"

"When I was seventeen, my mother let me prepare Thanksgiving dinner. I made roasted turkey, sausage dressing, seven-cheese macaroni and cheese—the works!"

"What did he think?"

"He was grubbing hard!" I say, fondly remembering the dinner. "Until my mother told him that I cooked it."

"Are you serious?"

"Serious as a heart attack. He started growling like a wounded bear and screaming at my mother that she was turning his only son into a punk."

"Oh no!"

I shake my head and laugh. "But I did catch him sneaking a plate of leftovers that night."

Emoni is tickled. "So that's how you became a writer?"

"Pretty much, but my dad hates this job, too. He calls it a hobby."

"Wow. You can't win, right?"

"I'm getting to the point where I don't care what my father thinks."

Emoni takes another bite, and her face becomes serious. As she chews, I can almost see the wheels in her brain spinning.

"Me, too. I'm tired of what Daddy thinks, Oscar, and everybody else. I'm sick to death of being boring, dependable Emoni."

I don't even know how to respond to this, but it sounds like an invitation. "So what are you going to do about it?"

Her eyes tell me what she's going to do before she moves a muscle. I offer absolutely no objection when she leans over and smothers me with another kiss. This one is less timid. She even has the audacity to bite my bottom lip, punctuating her maturity.

I want it to stop there. Don't mean for this to be happening. I'm trying to remember some of the tips from Bishop's Bible study, but my elevated hormone levels are drowning it all out.

"Emoni," I plead in a hoarse whisper, "don't do this. You don't really want this."

"Everybody thinks they know what I want."

She kisses me again, and as I'm about to push her away, her tiny manicured hands start groping where they have no business groping.

That's it. I give up.

With all my resistance gone, I start giving Emoni what she's giving me. She doesn't object. In fact, she's the one who stands from the table and leads me to my bedroom.

I don't need to give the details about what happened when we closed that door. But I will say that it wasn't just sex, or fornication for the church folk. It was more than that. I felt like after we both had our releases that

I was bound to this girl. Now I know what Priscilla is talking about when she says that I have soul ties to all of the women I've been with.

I wonder if Emoni feels the same way, because I can't tell what's going on in her head. I was expecting tears or worse, but she's strangely quiet.

"You all right, Moni?" I surprise myself by dropping the E off her name. It just comes naturally.

She nods slowly. "I can't believe we did this."

"I'm so sorry. I shouldn't have let it happen."

"We let it happen, Darrin. Not you."

I can't help thinking about what Dorcas said about me. She said I was on assignment and from the pits of hell. Looks like she was right.

A single tear runs down Emoni's cheek. "Darrin, can I ask you a question?"

"I am an open book." I can't help but note the dishonesty of my own statement. Actually, I'm a tightly shut book.

"Do you think that man in Savannah is really my father's son?"

So she's going to let me go here. Perfect. "Can I be completely honest with you?"

"Yes, of course. We're probably thinking the same thing."

"Honestly, I think he is your brother. I mean, looks-wise, the dude is a carbon copy of your father."

Emoni nods slowly. "You know, I've been thinking that exact thing, but I just can't believe that my daddy would turn him away like that without even finding out."

"Do you think your father wants to remember the life he had before Jesus?"

Emoni wraps my comforter around her body and stands up from the bed. She starts pacing the floor as I scramble to cover myself. I don't know why I feel *extra* naked.

"I don't guess he wants to remember. He never talks about it, unless he's testifying about God bringing him out," Emoni says.

She then walks out of the bedroom, dragging my blanket behind her. I wrap myself in the sheet and follow.

"Do you want me to help you find out the truth?"

Emoni grabs her glass from the table and sips her juice as if the entire conversation has depleted her energy. "I think I do. If I have another brother out there, I want to know who he is."

Emoni sobs into my chest, transforming my twinge of guilt into a stabbing pang. I can't write a story that's going to make her world even crazier. Something inside me fiercely wants to protect this woman. The feeling is more intense than the need to prove anything to my father.

Chapter Twenty-four

Emoni

We're having a family meeting.

Tyler, Sascha, and I are all sitting on Mother's favorite couch in the family room. The one she prefers we don't use. But since she and Daddy are pacing back and forth in front of the sectional, we have no choice except to use her favorite.

We do this only when serious stuff is about to hit the fan. The last time we had a family meeting was when Tyler stayed out all night as a teenager. The way Mother and Daddy are pacing and wringing their hands, I'm getting nervous.

That nervousness can't replace the other feeling I have, though. I am finally a woman! No one can tell me that I don't know anything now. I've known a man, and it was all the wonderful things that I've read in every romance novel.

And Darrin was so sweet to me afterward. I was afraid

he was going to push me out of his bed in disgust, but he didn't. Now that I think about it, he seemed to feel a little bit guilty. I'm guilty, too, though. I wish I could take it all back.

I know that sin does not come without consequences. I know that. And I'm sorry I didn't have enough confidence in God to wait until my wedding night. I regret my impatience and my lack of faith. And I am not going to continue down this path. Darrin's gotten all the tail from me that he's going to get unless he changes my last name. I just hope I've got Darrin thinking, Dorcas who?

Daddy clears his throat. I guess it's his signal that he's going to begin. He opens with a very brief word of prayer. Then he says, "I'm sure you all know that this family is under attack from the enemy right now. I can only hope all of this turmoil means that God is about to do something extraordinary in all of our lives."

Why is he talking to us like we're Freedom of Life? He is our bishop and everything, but right now I need him to be Daddy.

He continues, "I think I should share this with all of you, because it may soon be out in the open anyway. In Savannah a young man came up to me at church and accused me of being his father."

The only one of us who looks surprised is Sascha. She's been too caught up in her own secrets to notice anything going on around her. She was fortunate that Daddy didn't find her and Kevin in their love nest. Of course, her little raggedy friends covered for her.

"He *accused* you of being his father?" asks Tyler sarcastically. "Are you his father?"

"Not to my knowledge."

"What do you mean, 'Not to my knowledge,'" I say, the anger in my voice rising with each word. "You treated Kumal Jr. like he was a criminal when he just wanted you to acknowledge him."

Sascha's mouth is hanging open. "His name is Kumal Jr.? Does he look like us?"

"He looks exactly like Daddy."

Mother gasps when I say this. I suppose she's been holding out hope that this would all go away.

Daddy interjects, "Listen, we don't know anything for sure."

"Are you going to take a paternity test?" Tyler challenges.

"No. Your mother and I have decided that it would be best to give him and his mother a settlement that would help them live comfortably."

I cannot believe my ears. This cannot be my daddy talking about paying someone off to keep quiet. I'm stunned and hurt, but most of all, disappointed. My daddy, for the first time ever for me, has taken off his superhero costume. And now all I see is a man who's scared to death that his past is going to overshadow his future.

"What makes you think he wants money?" I ask. "He just seemed to want to get acquainted."

"His mother is a crack addict and probably hard up for cash. She's one of the most devious creatures I've ever known. The only reason she brought him to me is because she knew I'd pay to keep this quiet."

Sascha asks the question we're all thinking. "Why do you need to keep this quiet? You talk all about your former life in your testimony book. Everyone knows you have a past."

"It's one thing to have a pastor with a testimony," Daddy explains, "and quite another to have a pastor with a living, breathing reminder of his past."

Mother responds, "We need to all stick together and back Bishop up on this one. This is not the time for us to disagree."

Daddy takes Mother's hand and nods. "There is still, of course, the chance that this secret will be exposed, and we need to talk about how we'll handle that if it happens."

"Bishop, you're talking about damage control like we're some major corporation under siege. We're a family." This is Tyler, but Sascha and I cosign by nodding.

Bishop says, "I am, if nothing else, the head of this household. So, since our family is going to be under close scrutiny, if any of you have any secrets, I'd appreciate hearing about them now, instead of reading about them on the cover of the newspaper."

Tyler and I look at Sascha, and she frowns. "What y'all looking at me for?"

"Sascha," asks Daddy, "is there something you want to share?"

"No! I don't have anything to share."

Tyler rolls his eyes. "You might as well tell him, Sascha. It's not the type of thing you can hide for long."

Sascha's face reddens. "I know you not trying to front, Tyler! You've got a little secret, too!"

"Yours is worse—"

Mother interrupts the bickering. "I think you both need to come clean."

Daddy is sitting down and holding his head in his hands. He's obviously figured out Sascha's secret, but even I don't know what Tyler is hiding.

Tyler says, "I'll go first. I accepted an assistant pastor position at Love Outreach."

"You what?" I see Daddy squeeze Mother's hand tightly.

"I gave my first sermon before the church on Sunday evening, while you were here denying your oldest son."

Tyler's words hit Daddy hard. So much so that I want Sascha to be quiet.

But she's not. "I guess it's my turn. Me and Kevin are having a baby, and we're getting married."

Mother lunges across the room and grabs Sascha by the neck. "I knew it! Get out of my house."

"Mother!" I scream, and try to pull her off Sascha.

"This heifer has lost her mind. I'm not having some fornicating hussy living in my house. If she's grown enough to give it up, she's grown enough to get out!"

Daddy gathers his wits and pries Mother's hands from Sascha's throat. "She's made a mistake, Diana. If we put her out, she's going to run to her boyfriend."

"I don't care. Let her run to him."

"So." Daddy clears his throat, but his throat still quivers. "You and Kevin are getting married? Is that why Ophelia was here on Sunday morning?"

"She doesn't know yet," replies Sascha.

Mother asks, "Emoni, do you have anything to share?"

"Me? No, of course not."

Sascha narrows her eyes in anger. "Right. Of course not. What's going on with you and that guy Darrin?"

"Nothing! Don't try to drag me down with you and Tyler. I actually happen to care about Daddy's ministry," I say.

Tyler smirks. "You don't care about it more than

Bishop. He cares more about Freedom of Life than about his own son."

Tyler gets up to leave, even though we're not finished. We usually dismiss with a family prayer, each one of us sending a petition before the Lord. Sascha follows closely behind Tyler, leaving me feeling like a third wheel to my parents.

"Daddy, are we done?" I ask.

Daddy nods slowly and deliberately. His expression is defeated, and Mother's is unsure.

I venture to ask, "Are you really just going to forget all about Kumal Jr.?"

"His name is Kumal, but he's not a junior," replies Mother matter-of-factly.

Daddy's silence tells me that he isn't convinced. Neither am I.

Chapter Twenty-five

Darrin

Emoni is sitting in my living room, staring at the phone. It has been two days since we located Genevieve Walter's contact information on the Internet, and three days since our sin. Neither one of us has had the courage to discuss either.

"Do you want to call her?" I ask.

Emoni shakes her head. "Not yet. I need to build up the nerve first. Let's talk about something else."

"Okay," I reply. "You look nice today, and you did in Savannah, too. Did you, like, buy a whole new wardrobe?"

Emoni scrunches her nose. "Please tell me it's not that obvious."

"It is. But change isn't a bad thing. You look good."

"Thank you."

"Did you do all this for me?"

"No. What? *No!*" exclaims Emoni defensively. "I just wanted a change, that's all."

"It would be okay if you did it for me. I'd actually find it extremely attractive that you went to all that trouble."

"You would?" she asks.

"Of course, but that doesn't matter, because you didn't do this for me, right?"

"Uh . . . right."

I am the last person who needs to clarify or define relationships, but I'm not sure what's going on with Emoni. I'm calling it a thing because I don't know what else to call it. We're not dating, but we've warped past friendship. It's awkward.

But I'm really digging Moni. She reminds me of the first crush I ever had. Before I became a player and before the women in my life learned how to play games. When Emoni laughs at my jokes, the laughter is genuine. Everything about her is real.

Emoni sits gazing up at me with her inquisitive eyes, and I feel the sudden and overwhelming urge to kiss her. But I don't know if I should go there. We've already done the deed, so any type of foreplay is headed straight to the bedroom. And this whole "willful sinning" thing is not my cup of tea.

God must be listening to my thoughts, because there's a knock on my front door. I feel myself praying, even though I don't know what to pray for. *Lord, forgive me. For all of it. For accepting Emoni's virginity and not keeping my word about living right. I just don't know how to do this.*

I open the door and see Dorcas standing there, all

smiles, and carrying a grocery bag. I can't help but send up another short prayer. *God, are you trying to tell me something?*

Dorcas starts the conversation. "Hi. I just want to apologize for how I acted on Sunday."

"I forgive you."

"To complete my peace offering, I'd like to cook you dinner."

I start to object, but Dorcas doesn't wait for a response. She pushes me to the side and starts into my apartment. The countdown starts in my head. Five . . . four . . . three . . . two . . .

"Oh. Have I interrupted something?" Dorcas asks, her voice laced with attitude.

I reply, "No."

But Emoni simultaneously says, "Yes."

Dorcas looks at us both as if she's trying to decide whom to believe. I try to smooth things over. "We're doing a project for Bishop."

"What kind of project?" Dorcas asks.

I'm kind of shocked at her rudeness. It seems uncharacteristic, and it certainly isn't attractive. Emoni rises from her seat and walks over to Dorcas. "It's confidential, and we really need to get it finished," she says.

Okay, now we're having one of those uncomfortable silences. I hate those. Dorcas shifts her grocery bag from one hip to the other, glaring at Emoni the entire time. Emoni's smirk looks like a dare—an "I wish you would."

Dorcas says, "I won't be in your way at all."

It's time to end this. I'm not playing games, and I'm not going to lead anybody on. I'm making a decision right now. It's Emoni all day and all night.

I say, "Dorcas, our project really is important, but I appreciate your gesture."

Dorcas's expression goes dark. "Sure, Darrin. I'll call you."

Without another word, not even a goodbye to Emoni, Dorcas leaves the apartment. The fire in her eyes as she walks past tells me that I won't be redeeming that rain check anytime soon. It's cool.

Emoni asks as I close the door, "What is she apologizing for?"

"Nothing important. You've got a phone call to make, right?"

She takes a deep breath and picks up the cordless phone. Starts dialing the number that she has memorized from the frequency of dialing and hanging up. But she stops halfway through and hangs her head sadly. She's terrified of knowing the truth, but she can't go on not knowing the truth.

"Are you going to call anytime soon?" I ask. "Because I'm going to fix myself a snack if you're not."

Emoni sucks her teeth. "Did anyone ever tell you that you really stink at moral support?"

"I do support you! But why do I have to do it on an empty stomach?"

"Does your world revolve around food?"

I raise an eyebrow and hope she can read my mind. "Lately, yes."

Before Atlanta, before Bishop Prentiss and before Freedom of Life, my world revolved around my next bedroom episode. To be honest, I'm not totally cured, but I'm getting there. I just hope I'm not three hundred pounds before it happens.

"Is it good?" Emoni asks me as I smack on my tasty turkey sandwich.

"Yes, it is," I reply, and offer her the plate. "Do you want some?"

She takes a tiny bite. "It is good," she comments.

"Honey mustard instead of mayo. That's the secret."

"Did you have a girlfriend at home?" Emoni asks.

"Hey! Where did that come from? I thought we were talking about calling Genevieve."

"I will. In a second. Just answer the question. Did you or did you not have a girlfriend back home in Cleveland?"

I cock my head to one side and sigh. I suppose I'll tell her the truth, at least about this. "Do you want the long answer or the short answer?"

"The long answer, of course."

"I'm not going to lie. There was someone," I say, licking my lips nervously, "but it was only a casual fling to me."

"To her it was more?"

"I think so, even though I didn't give her any reason to think that."

I can see the alarm on her face. She's wondering if I'm feeling the same way about her.

I try to reassure her. "But I wasn't trying to live right back then. I feel totally different about you," I continue.

"How do you mean?"

"I think we have the potential for something long-term, not just a random date or two."

"Do you mean that? Did you say the same thing to Dorcas?"

She hits me with those rapid-fire questions like she thinks I'm running game. And she's right to do it. I *am* running game just a little bit. So is she.

"I was attracted to Dorcas, but she's pretty boring. Plus, I don't think she's feeling me anymore."

"That's the reason you're interested in me now? Because Dorcas kicked you to the curb?"

Man, I've got to get myself out of this corner. "Is that what you think?"

"I'm not stupid, Darrin. I hope that's not what *you* think."

"The truth is, I've been interested in you since day one. I just didn't want to get involved with the pastor's daughter."

"Why not?"

Now is the perfect time to tell her about my story, my blog—everything. Instead, I say, "You know what they say about preachers' kids."

"I know what they say," she says with a serious frown. "I hope I'm not proving them right."

I take her by the hand in an effort to reassure her. "You're not. Not at all. In fact, I think we have the potential for something special."

"Or the potential for you to get some more booty, right?"

I'm insulted. "I know you don't believe that. Girl, I've had enough booty for an entire lifetime. I want something more than that."

"I'm sorry. I don't know what to think, Darrin. I mean, we've done this thing backward, and now I'm thinking it was a bad move."

"It *was* a bad move."

She blinks rapidly, like she's trying to stop a waterfall of tears.

I need to clarify. "It was a bad move, because if God wants us to get together, I know He didn't want us to sin in the process."

"Wow." Emoni chuckles softly. "Doesn't it seem like I should be saying that? I am the bishop's daughter, right?"

"It's all right, girl. You just got caught up. I have that effect on women."

Emoni rolls her eyes and throws a couch pillow at me. We needed that joke. Needed to lighten up the atmosphere. I feel better now that we've got it out in the open.

Emoni picks up the phone. "This time I'm calling. For real," she says.

I say nothing, only watch her as she dials. She taps her foot nervously and exhales. This thing is deep for her.

"Hello," says Emoni. "May I speak to Genevieve?" She hits the speaker button so I can hear the conversation.

"Yes. Can I tell her who is calling?" says the male voice. It sounds like Kumal Jr.

The simplest of questions almost floors Emoni. "Um . . . yes. I'm Emoni Prentiss." There is a deafening silence on the other end. Emoni says, "Hello?"

"Yes. Hold on one minute."

Emoni trembles as she waits for Genevieve to come to the phone. I move closer to her and cover one of her shaking hands with my own.

Finally, a female voice answers. "Hello, this is Genevieve." It sounds like she's been sleeping or slumming or both. Kumal had told us she was sick, but she sounds near death.

"Hello! I'm Emoni Prentiss. I'm calling to ask if your son is really my brother."

There's more silence on the other end. Emoni looks worried. Maybe Genevieve won't answer. Maybe she'll hang up on us.

Emoni continues, "I believe that you and your son were at my father's preaching engagement in Savannah."

We hear a heavy, rattled sigh from Genevieve. "Why you calling me? What do it matter, anyway?"

"It matters because if I have a brother, I'd like to know him. I want him in our lives . . . at holidays . . . and weddings."

Genevieve laughs. "How's Diana?"

"My mother? She's fine. You know her?"

"Yeah, I know her. She's the reason why you don't know your brother."

"Oh." Emoni exhales.

"She didn't think the son of a crackhead would be good for yo' daddy's brand-new ministry."

I'm watching Emoni, trying to gauge her reaction. She's in shock, but she's listening to Genevieve, trying to believe her.

"Are you sure he is the father?" asks Emoni.

Again Genevieve laughs. "I'm a drug addict, sweetie, not a whore. Your father was my man. So, yes, I'm sure."

"Do you think Kumal Jr. will see me?"

"Ask him yourself."

Emoni looks at me with hope in her eyes. I just hope

that these two aren't out to use her or take advantage of the Prentiss family.

"Hello?" says Kumal Jr.

"Hi. It's your sister, Emoni."

"How are you, little sister?"

Emoni laughs out loud. There's joy behind that laugh. Not much, but it's there.

"Would you like to have lunch with me, big brother?"

Kumal Jr. laughs, too. "I'd love to. Here or Atlanta?"

"I'll come to you. There's a place on Tybee Island that I like called the Crab Shack."

"I know the place."

"How about Friday at two p.m.?"

"It's a date."

"Okay, then, let your mother know I'm praying for her health. I'll see you later."

"Bye, little sister."

Emoni presses the release button on the phone and beams up at me. "I'm going to lunch with my brother."

I nod with a tight smile. My mind is spinning. I'm suddenly feeling apprehension about this meeting. "I don't mean to sound negative, because I think this is a good thing, but what if he's not your brother?"

"He is. He looks just like my father."

"Stranger things have happened."

She ponders my words for a moment. "How will I know? Daddy won't take a paternity test."

I reach into the drawer under my coffee table and hand Emoni a package that I had shipped overnight.

"What is this?"

"Open it."

Emoni opens the unmarked brown box and gasps. "A DNA test? For me? You shouldn't have."

This is why I'm liking this girl. "I said I'd help you find out the truth."

"So what do I need? A hair? Blood?"

"Saliva."

"That's easy."

"It's easy to get someone's spit? How is that easy?"

"It's easy when the someone has a spit cup next to his side of the bed."

"That's nasty."

Emoni laughs. "Mother thinks so, too."

"So what if the test comes back negative?"

Emoni pauses before replying. "If he's not my brother, then I'll forget this ever happened."

"That's a plan. Do you want me to come with you to Savannah?"

"You would do that for me?"

"Of course."

Emoni wraps her arms around my neck and kisses me on the lips in one fluid motion. She's got to stop doing that. Catches my flesh off guard every time. I stand up and back away from her. "Emoni . . . don't."

"Don't what? Why don't you want to kiss me?"

She knows these are dangerous waters. "I didn't say that."

"So you do want to kiss me?"

"You're making this difficult, Emoni."

Her expression is one of irritation. "I don't get you. You say you think we can have something long-term, but you won't even kiss me."

"Let me break this down for you. You know how an

alcoholic who's trying to get sober won't even go in a bar?"

"Yes. What does that have to do with you?"

I take her hand and look her in the eyes. I want her to know how sincere I am. "If we start a fire, Emoni, I don't know if I'll be able to put it out. I'm not strong enough for that yet. And I don't want you to be just another one-night stand."

"I don't want that, either."

"So no matter how much I want to kiss you right now, I'm not going to."

"It's for the best. I don't want to end up pregnant, like my sister."

I feel my eyes widen with surprise. "Sascha's pregnant?"

"Yep. She and Kevin are getting married, too."

"Now, that should be interesting."

"I guess. I mean, why is all of this drama happening to my family? We go twenty-four years drama-free, and then all at once everyone goes crazy."

"Twenty-four years? You all are overdue," I say with a smile.

My moment of weakness over, I sit down next to Emoni on the sofa. She lays her head on my chest and sighs. "Is this okay?"

"I'm not just a walking sex drive. I do have some self-control."

"Good, because I need a hug."

I wrap my arms around Emoni and squeeze tightly. She relaxes in my embrace. Soon I start to feel the wetness of her tears as they soak through my shirt. I rock her back and forth in my arms, thinking that I wouldn't mind being here with her for the rest of my life.

Chapter Twenty-six

Emoni

You don't actually think you're dating him, do you?" asks Oscar.

"What's it to you?" I snap right back.

Oscar is waiting in our family room for Daddy to come downstairs. He's taking Daddy to a pastoral luncheon at one of our sister churches. After a few days of fasting and praying, Daddy's back to his usual church business, as if everything is roses. Just like Mother started planning Sascha's wedding after everything calmed down.

But everything is not roses. And Oscar gets on my nerves.

"I'm just surprised he picked you over Dorcas. I thought they were getting close."

"You thought wrong."

Oscar fumes, "What do you see in him, anyway? What did Dorcas see? And don't you women have some un-spoken code about not dating each other's boyfriends?"

"Darrin was never her man. They were just friends."

"And now he's your man?"

"Again I ask: What's it to you?"

"Everything that goes on in this family is important to me, Emoni. I care about you—y'all. I'm just doing my job."

"Oscar, I don't need an armor bearer. I'm cool."

"But you do need a man who wants more from you than sex." His tone has changed from fatherly to something I'm absolutely uncomfortable with.

"What are you talking about?"

Oscar sits down next to me on the sectional. Our legs touch, and it gives me the creeps. I hope he doesn't notice me scooting away from him.

"I'm talking about you and me."

I spring up from the couch. "Awww! Why'd you have to go and say that?"

"Because it's what I want. And it was what you wanted, too, until Darrin came along."

I don't get to respond because Daddy finally comes downstairs looking so fresh and clean. Not a care in the world. Especially not about Kumal Jr.

"Emoni, when you get a chance, will you run to the cleaners for me? I've got some robes in there that I need next week."

"Sure, Daddy."

"Oh, and I have a speaking engagement in Birmingham on Friday. A pastor's anniversary. Are you coming along?"

"I can't," I say flatly. "I have a lunch date in Savannah."

"With whom?"

"If you must know," I say, balking, "it's with my brother. Darrin's going to drive me."

"That man is not your brother," states Daddy with unnecessary roughness.

"You don't know that."

"He and his mother are just scam artists."

I roll my eyes. "Well, I would still like to get to know him. And Daddy, please don't try to stop me."

Daddy chuckles sadly. "I won't. Everyone seems to be doing their own thing around here. Come on, Oscar. I'm ready."

Mother walks in the room as soon as Daddy and Oscar leave. I'm so angry about my conversation with Daddy, as well as weirded out by my words with Oscar. I don't feel like talking anymore, but Mother seems to have conversation on her mind, too. What is this epidemic of everybody talking everything out? All of this communication is so unnecessary.

"Emoni, what is going on between you and Brother Darrin? Your father is concerned," says Mother bluntly.

"We're friends, Mother. It might turn into more. I don't know yet."

"Do you even know what that means?" she prods. "You've never been in this situation before."

"Mother, I'm not stupid."

"When it comes to men, you most certainly are. Has he tried to get you in bed yet?"

Now I'm offended. "I don't think that's any of your business."

"And what about Dorcas? Wasn't she interested in him?"

"So?"

"Emoni, I feel like I'm talking to a stranger right now. As a matter of fact, you, Sascha, and Tyler have all been acting strange lately. You're keeping secrets and backsliding! I don't even know my children."

"Mother, I know you aren't talking about someone keeping secrets."

"What do you mean?"

I stand toe to toe with my mother. "How about the fact that you've known about Daddy's son for years, but you didn't want him around messing up Daddy's ministry?"

"All I knew was that a drug addict was claiming to have a son with my husband. You don't understand, because you're not a wife."

"You didn't care that he might actually be Daddy's son?"

Mother sighs and slumps onto the couch. "Emoni, I was pregnant with you when we found out about that boy."

"His name is Kumal."

"Your father had just been installed as pastor at New Baptist Tabernacle, and we'd just bought this house. We were happy."

"But what about Kumal? Is it fair that he didn't get raised by his own father?"

"If that Genevieve would've given the boy to your father to raise, we would've done that. She just wanted to be in your father's life. She wanted him with her, holed up in a crack house somewhere."

"Mother, are you saying that you felt threatened by Genevieve? Did you actually think she could take Daddy from you?"

"No. Of course not. But when I met your father, it was after he'd gotten clean. I like to think of him that way and not as a recovering crack addict."

"Even if you don't care about my brother, I do. Darrin is taking me to see him on Friday."

"I don't think it's wise for you to be alone with Darrin."

"Why? We're two adults who enjoy each other's company immensely. I don't see anything wrong with it. We're not sleeping together."

A solemn look comes over Mother's face. "Just don't make the same mistake your sister made."

"You don't have to worry about me, Mother."

"I know, Emoni. I never have."

Chapter Twenty-seven

Darrin

Bishop stands before the Bible study class in his first appearance after Black Sunday. Everyone has questions, but the ones with answers aren't saying anything. I'm guessing he's about to give some explanation for his absence, because the entire church seems to be present. They had to move Bible study from the classroom to the main sanctuary.

He starts, "Praise the Lord, everybody. It is a blessing to be in the house of the Lord one more time. Before we start, I want to squash the rumor mill. No, I didn't have a heart attack; nor did I get into a car accident on the way home from Savannah. I did have a family emergency that needed my immediate attention. I apologize for any confusion that was encountered on Sunday morning. Now, I'm sure I can count on a few of you to get the word out to the congregation. You know who you are. I'm not going to call you gossips—I'm going to say the town criers." The congregation laughs.

Everyone looks relieved from what I can see, all except Sister Ophelia. She looks right angry, like she's ready to lead a blue-haired revolution. She's got her grandson, Kevin, stationed at her side, although he looks like he'd rather be anywhere but church.

Bishop continues to smile and scan the room. His eyes rest on me and Emoni. She's not sitting right next to me; she's left a seat between us. But it's a clear signal to everyone that we're "together." I'm okay with her sending out the signal, but I'm not sure I like Bishop glaring at me.

Bishop continues lightheartedly, "I'm not talking about you unless it's you."

Bishop goes on to give his study lesson on the fruits of the Holy Spirit. It's a good lesson; Bishop hasn't missed a beat, even with the turmoil going on in his household. I'm listening closely to the lesson when Emoni pokes me in the arm. When she has my attention, she passes me a note that says, "Look at Oscar."

My eyes go over in Oscar's direction, and to my chagrin, the brotha is staring me down. Hard. Like he wants to come lay me out with a two-piece.

Hope he's not feeling froggy tonight.

After Bible study is over, I walk up to greet Bishop. "That was a good lesson, Bishop. You bring out things from the Scriptures that I never would've gotten had I read them on my own."

Bishop pulls me to the side and asks bluntly, "Son, what are your intentions toward my daughter?"

I was not expecting this—at all. "Bishop?"

"She's never had a boyfriend before, and I'm worried that you might just be too experienced for her."

"Bishop, I have nothing but honorable intentions toward your daughter. I am very fond of her, and I think she feels the same way about me."

Bishop nods. "Are you still seeing Sister Dorcas?"

"Wow! Is nothing a secret around here?"

Bishop answers, "I'm just doing my job."

I choose my words very carefully. "I don't believe that Dorcas is the one God wants me to be with."

Bishop pulls me in real close and whispers in my ear, "Boy, ain't nobody stupid around here. I ain't been saved my whole life. If you even think of hurting my daughter, you gone regret ever setting foot in this church." Bishop releases the death grip he has on my arm. For the benefit of any onlookers, he says, "So you say you want to join the men's ministry?"

"Uh, yes, sir," I reply, feeling completely owned. It's almost like Big Mathis is here.

"That's a good choice, son. You can't go wrong with Jesus."

Bishop walks away, leaving me feeling like some kind of womanizer. I say a brief good night to Emoni and head out to my truck with my mind reeling. All of a sudden Bishop doesn't trust me? I know Oscar has something to do with that. I'm so engrossed in my thoughts that I walk right past Dorcas, who is standing in my path.

"Are we not speaking?" she asks.

Her voice startles me. "Oh. Hi, Dorcas. I wasn't sure you'd want to deal with someone on assignment from the devil."

"I'm sorry about that, Darrin. It was just a really intense situation. I didn't mean what I said."

"I think you did mean what you said, and honestly, it kind of hurt."

"Is that why you were sitting with Emoni tonight? Were you trying to hurt me back?"

"Emoni and I are dating now, Dorcas." Might as well put it out there with everybody.

"Wow. That was quick. Well, I just wanted to apologize again, Darrin."

"Mission accomplished."

She rushes away from me—a little embarrassed, I guess. Part of me wants to go after her and smooth things over. If I were in a better mood, I probably would. But seeing as my pastor thinks I'm a gigolo, and his right-hand man wants to thrash me, I'm going to let her go.

I'm about to pull off when I see Emoni running up to my truck. I roll down the window. "What are you doing out here? Oscar is going to have a nervous breakdown looking for you."

Emoni giggles. "I wanted to talk to you after Bible study, but you left so quickly."

"Yeah, your father was interrogating me, so I decided to make myself scarce."

"Interrogating you? About what?"

I decide to keep the content of the conversation to myself. "Never mind that. Get in the car. We'll go for a spin around the block."

Emoni jumps in on the passenger side of my truck. "Did you see Sister Ophelia?" she asks.

"Yes, and she was looking right salty. What is she so mad about?"

"She's mad because Mother won't announce Kevin and Sascha's engagement. Daddy doesn't think it's proper, since they've been blatantly sinning and all. But Sister Ophelia went off screaming and yelling obscenities at Daddy, and he made her resign from her post as head nurse."

"Are you serious? I bet she was furious about that."

Emoni laughs. "Yes, she was."

"Look at us gossiping like two biddies."

"I know! Daddy was talking about you tonight. You are the town crier!"

"I am not! I only know about five people's names in the whole church! *You* are the town crier."

Emoni laughs. "You're right. But it just felt good to share something about her when she's out here running Sascha's name into the ground."

I pull into a Krispy Kreme drive-through. "Do you want a doughnut?"

"No, thanks."

I order my doughnut and then ask, "Is that what you ran out to my car to talk about?"

Emoni shakes her head. "No. I just wanted to be near you."

See, I can't take it when she says things like that. "Wow."

"What does that mean?"

I park the truck in an available spot. "It means that I have absolutely no response to that. You have rendered me speechless."

"Is that a good thing?"

"That is indeed a good thing."

Emoni smiles. "I can't wait until Friday."

"Yeah, about that. Are your parents cool with me taking you to Savannah?"

Emoni crosses her arms defiantly. "I am a grown woman."

"All right, then. I'm not going to argue that point."

"Good."

Emoni is grinning at me with that mischievous look, raising the temperature in the vehicle about ten degrees. I crack the window so I can breathe.

"You warm?" she asks.

"Um . . . yeah."

"Me, too."

I take a deep breath and blurt out, "Emoni, will you be my lady?"

Emoni bursts into spontaneous laughter. "Yes, of course. I thought I already was."

"Just making it official. What in the world is so funny?"

Still laughing, Emoni explains. "Your *lady*? Who are you, Gerald Levert or somebody?"

"So, will you be my lady or not?"

Emoni holds her stomach like she's about to laugh herself to pieces. "Stop! Let me enjoy this moment."

"You are so silly!"

Emoni reaches over to hug me, and it feels so good. She says, "I don't know how all this relationship stuff works. You're going to have to help me."

"Not a problem." For the first time in my adult life, the R-word doesn't make me flinch.

I drive back to the church parking lot to drop Emoni off at her car. Oscar is standing next to the automobile, looking perturbed.

"See? I told you he would be looking for you," I say.

"Whatever," replies Emoni with a toss of her head.

"You're saying that now . . ."

"He's not my father."

I raise both hands in defeat. "Okay. You're the boss."

"I'll call you."

"All right."

Emoni gets out of my truck, comes to the window, and brushes a kiss across my lips. I smile and wave at Oscar. I'm not at all surprised that he doesn't wave back.

Chapter Twenty-eight

Emoni

Darrin—excuse me, my man—just pulled off and left me standing in the church parking lot, face-to-face with my "protector." Maybe if I ignore him and get in my car, he won't say anything to wreck my wonderful mood.

"What were you doing with him?"

Oh, well. So much for my mood. "Why wouldn't I be in my boyfriend's truck?"

"I thought you were just friends," says Oscar. The tremble in his voice tells me that he's affected by my news.

"We were, but now we're more than friends."

Oscar sneers. "Did you make it official?"

"If you're asking whether we had sex, it's none of your business one way or the other. Don't insult me like that again, or you'll be looking for some other pastor to smother."

I slam my car door and start the engine. Oscar knocks

on my window. The only reason I open it is because the fool has tears in his eyes. "What, Oscar?"

"Emoni . . . I—I love you. Darrin doesn't even know you."

He's affected me, though I thought he never could. "Oscar, you don't love me."

"I do, Emoni. And it's not going to stop just because Darrin is on the scene."

"See you later, Oscar."

I roll up the window and speed off. I wanted to be mean and nasty to him, but it's hard to do that after someone professes his undying love. I check the rearview, and he's still standing there in the same spot, looking lost.

Am I on a roll or what? Darrin asks me to be his *lady*, and Oscar tells me he loves me? Wow.

I don't even know if all this attention is a good thing. I might start getting a big head and thinking I'm fly or something.

I must be smelling myself when I walk through Mother's parlor, because I don't bother to greet her Women's Leadership Council guests. They call themselves a council, but what they are really is a clique of the best-dressed biggest-diamond-wearing luxury-car-driving women at Freedom of Life.

Mother clears her throat as I float on by them. "Emoni, we have guests."

"Hey, sisters. How y'all doing this evening?"

I watch Mother's face redden. She hates when I talk like common country folk. Especially since she's gone out of her way to make sure her children have no trace of a Georgia accent.

Sister Maggie responds, "Well, we are doing just fine, but obviously not as fine as you."

"That's right," says Oleta. "I hear Oscar has finally decided to make an honest woman out of you."

"Why, that is simply not the case, ladies. As a matter of fact, when it comes to the subject of Oscar, I'd much rather remain dishonest."

Everyone's mouth, including Mother's, falls right open.

"Bye, y'all."

It takes all of the strength I can muster to stifle my giggles. When I get to the top of the stairs, I stop, grab the wall, and let my laughter come in quiet ripples. Sascha is coming out of the bathroom, wiping her mouth. She rolls her eyes when she sees me laughing. "What is your problem?"

"Good evening to you, too, Evilene."

"You smell like doughnuts. Do you have any more?"

I shake my head. "No, Darrin got some Krispy Kremes earlier, but I didn't. And you're too early in your pregnancy to be having food cravings."

"Shhhh! Mother's friends don't know."

"Oh, yes, I forgot. Sorry."

Sascha narrows her eyes in scrutiny. "What's up with you and Darrin? I saw y'all hugged up at Bible study."

"We were not hugged up."

"Might as well have been, the way Bishop was looking at y'all. Oscar, too."

"Ain't nobody worried about Oscar, and Daddy is going to have to get used to us."

"Us?"

"Yes. Darrin just got finished asking me to be his girl-friend."

Sascha gives me a high five. "All right, girl! I'm proud of you. He's fine."

"And rich."

"Even better," squeals Sascha.

An unexpected frown crosses my face. "So what's wrong with him, Sascha? Why does he want me?"

"You're not serious with that question, are you?"

"Yes, I am. He's pretty near perfect so far. There's got to be something wrong with him."

"If you say so." Sascha heads back to her room, then turns for the bathroom again, grabbing her stomach.

Morning sickness is for the birds. I am not having kids.

Chapter Twenty-nine

Darrin

I'm swimming laps, trying to clear my head. Everything's been kind of foggy since I officially asked Emoni to be my girlfriend, because I think we're doomed.

We're doomed because she's destined to find out the real reason I'm in Atlanta and we'll be through after that. No doubt she'll go running off to her prince in polyester armor—Oscar the horrible.

After my tenth full lap, I need a breather, so I pull myself out of the pool. While I'm huffing and puffing, Dorcas walks in, and she's on a mission. Did I say that us living in the same building was a good thing? I recant that statement.

"Hi, Darrin," says Dorcas in a tone that I can't decipher, but it sounds like a cross between saltiness and hateration.

"Hey, Dorcas. What's up?"

"So when did you and Emoni get to be an item?"

"That's what I like about you, Dorcas. You cut right to the chase."

"I can't believe I was so wrong about you," responds Dorcas.

I feel myself getting slightly offended. "What were you wrong about?"

"I thought that we had a connection. Maybe a chance to build a relationship. But after one small disagreement, you're off to the next woman."

I can't believe my ears. "A *small* disagreement? You told me that I was on assignment from the devil."

"I spoke hastily."

"Maybe, but what does the Bible say in Matthew Twelve?" I counter. "'For out of the abundance of the heart, the mouth speaks.'"

Hey, I shocked myself with that Scripture. Bible study is working out for me.

"So in less than a week, you're romancing someone else? I'll repeat: I was wrong about you."

I throw my arms up and concede the conversation to Dorcas. "I've been digging Emoni for over a week, and if you weren't so busy blocking, we would've hooked up sooner."

"Blocking? Who was rubbing whose feet?"

"You told me from the jump that she was dating Oscar, and you knew it wasn't true."

Dorcas is silenced. She wasn't expecting that, but it's true. Emoni had me from the first day I stepped into Freedom of Life. She's the one who caught my attention first. Well, her booty caught my attention, but that wasn't the only reason. She has intrigued and challenged me from our first conversation.

I continue, "But fine. If you want to say you were wrong about me, I can say I was just as wrong about you. We were both wrong."

Dorcas looks me up and down angrily. "What were you wrong about?"

There is so much I can say, but I'm going to hold my tongue. I want to tell her that she can go on somewhere with her deepology—saying I was on assignment was unacceptable.

Instead of saying that, I reply, "Dorcas, I don't want to argue with you. Things didn't work out with us. I hope that one day we can see past this and become friends."

"You don't have to worry about that. Have a nice life," responds Dorcas as she turns and walks away.

I watch helplessly as another woman walks away from me and out of my life. Dorcas was wife material, too. I wonder if I made the right decision in choosing Emoni over Dorcas. Maybe neither woman is right for me—maybe God wants me to be celibate in repayment for all of the stray booty I've gotten over the years.

I say another prayer of repentance before I dive back into the pool. I let the cool chlorinated water soothe my doubts away as I daydream about Emoni's stolen kiss.

Chapter Thirty

Emoni

Darrin is here, picking me up to go to Savannah, and Daddy is not happy. He's got Darrin hemmed up in the corner, interrogating him yet again. Funny, I've never seen him up in Kevin's face like that.

"So what do you have planned for my daughter?" Bishop asks.

"Just doing her a favor, sir."

"Daddy, will you please stop harassing my boyfriend?"

Bishop frowns. "I have every right to. You are my daughter."

"I am your adult daughter, and you need to respect my privacy."

Darrin says, "Emoni, I don't mind answering your father's questions. I'm sure that one day I'll be as protective over my own daughters."

We go outside to Darrin's truck with Daddy following

closely behind. Darrin opens the car door for me while watching Bishop out of the corner of his eye.

Daddy clears his throat and says, "Let me pray for traveling mercies for the two of you." Darrin takes one of Daddy's hands, and I reach for the other one. Bishop prays, "Lord protect these two, your son and daughter, as they travel on the highways and byways. Allow Emoni to find all of the answers that she seeks in meeting with this man. Lord make Darrin and Emoni to reverence you by remaining chaste and holy before you. In Jesus' name."

A little giggle escapes my lips as I say amen, but Darrin does not seem to be amused. He doesn't relax until we're driving away from my house and out of Daddy's view.

When we're a safe distance away, I say, "Darrin, you should've seen your face when Daddy was praying about being chaste and holy."

"You were supposed to have your eyes closed! Why were you looking at me instead of reflecting on the goodness of God?"

That tickles me even more. "My dad is just tripping because he's never seen me with a man before. Plus, he's spooked by Sascha's pregnancy."

"I am insulted. I do not wish to be judged by another man's sins."

"Wow, that was deep."

"I'm a deep brotha."

I see the top of the opened DNA test box in my bag, and I start thinking about what it means if Kumal Jr. is my brother. Is he going to become part of our family, or is Mother still going to pretend that he doesn't exist?

"A dollar for your thoughts," says Darrin.

"A dollar?"

"Well, a penny isn't much money, and you're thinking hard over there."

"I was just thinking about Kumal Jr. I can't believe I might really have a big brother out here. It's mind boggling."

"I've always wished I had a sibling."

Here's my chance. "So tell me about your childhood," I say.

"You're serious?" he asks.

"Yes. We've got a four-hour drive."

Darrin sighs. "There's really not much to tell. I went to a private boys' school and participated in my mother's Jack and Jill club functions."

"Jack and Jill? Y'all must be old money."

"Not really. One of my mother's friends invited her to become a member."

"Still."

Darrin continues, "My father worked a lot, so I don't have many family-type memories. Me and my mother took vacations to Martha's Vineyard in the summertime, and that was fun."

Jack and Jill? Martha's Vineyard? His mother's going to think I'm some country bumpkin. "Do you think your mother would like me?" I ask.

Darrin's right eyebrow goes up. "You planning on meeting her anytime soon?"

"I don't know."

"I'm messing with you," Darrin says with a smile. "She'd love you, even though you're her polar opposite."

"What does that mean?"

"You're independent, free-spirited, and sassy. She's totally dependent on my father, reserved, and very, very polite."

My eyes widen. "I'm not polite?"

"Not really," says Darrin with a straight face.

"What?"

"You're pretty sarcastic."

I cross my arms. "Okay, right. I am sarcastic, I am free-spirited, and I am your boo. What?"

Darrin looks over at me and starts laughing. "You are crazy, girl."

"Enough about me. I want to ask you something, and I want you to be one hundred percent honest."

Darrin takes an eerie pause before responding. "Okay."

"What happened with you and Dorcas? You and her were kicking it strong, and then all of a sudden it's about me and you. What did I miss?"

Darrin grins and drums his fingers on the steering wheel. "I'm not the man she was looking for. It's that simple."

"Oh, you're going to take the high road, I see."

"Nothing bad happened with me and Dorcas. I'm just more attracted to you."

"Mmm-hmm."

"You don't believe me?"

"Sure I do."

Why am I disappointed that nothing "bad" happened? I want something very bad to have happened. Something so bad that he wouldn't be tempted to try things out again with her if things get a little rocky with me.

Darrin puts a CD in the player, and we sing to old-school Mary J Blige and SWV. He knows more of the words than I do, but I've got a better voice. This is fun, and it's helping take my mind off of what's troubling me to the bone.

My pulse starts to race when Darrin pulls up to the restaurant where I'm to meet Kumal Jr. I'm nervous beyond belief and shaking like a leaf.

"Do you want me to go in with you?" he asks.

"Please do."

Always the gentleman, Darrin opens my door. My heart flutters even more when he puts his arm around my shoulders. I'm sure he has no idea how much I appreciate his support.

"Do you think he'll take the DNA test?" I ask Darrin.

"I don't see why not. But don't worry about that at first. Just get to know him."

We walk into the restaurant, and Kumal Jr. is waiting in the reception area. He stands when he sees me and Darrin. It is uncanny how much he looks like Daddy. Right down to the smile he's beaming over to me. "You came," he says. "I wasn't sure you really would."

I stretch out my arms for a hug. "Of course I'm here. I want to know all about you."

"Same here," he responds.

Kumal shakes Darrin's hand, and they exchange greetings. "You her boyfriend?" Kumal asks.

"Yes. Yes, I am."

"Thanks for coming with her."

We follow the hostess to our table, which is a booth. Darrin and I sit on one side, and Kumal Jr. sits across from us.

"So, how is my father?" Kumal asks with a chuckle.

"Daddy is surprisingly fine. Everything is normal at home."

"I'm not surprised. He's known about me since I was little."

I'm about to reply when the waitress comes to take our order. I watch Kumal's mannerisms, and it's like I'm seeing my daddy thirty years ago. Kumal's gestures, vocal intonations, and facial expressions all lend credence to shared DNA.

"So," I say to Kumal when the waitress is gone, "tell me about yourself. Your life, your mother . . . do you have a girlfriend?"

"There's not much to tell. I'm twenty-seven, and I live with my mom. She can't live on her own right now because she's sick."

Darrin asks, "How is it that you knew about Bishop preaching in Savannah that Saturday?"

"I'm a partner at Freedom of Life; I send in my offerings every month, and in exchange, I get to learn a little about my father."

I add, "Daddy's itinerary is on the partner newsletters."

"Why now?" asks Darrin. "What made you want to meet him now?"

Kumal frowns. "Do you question my intentions?"

"I don't know your intentions at all."

The waitress brings our drinks, and Kumal glares at Darrin while taking a long sip of his soda. Things are getting a bit chilly in here, and it has nothing to do with the ocean breeze. I try to lighten the mood. "I'm happy you finally got the courage to come out."

Kumal ignores my statement and responds to Darrin.

"My mother is sick, and we're broke. I was hoping that for once my rich father would acknowledge me and lend some assistance. Does that answer your question?"

"Absolutely." Darrin smiles as if he's proved his point, although I don't know what the point could possibly be.

"We're not rich, Kumal. Is that what you think?" I say.

He laughs. "Come on, little sister, our father has twenty thousand members. I did the math."

I don't know how to prove to him that we're *not* rich, so I keep it moving. "You have a brother named Tyler and an even younger sister, Sascha. She's getting married soon."

Darrin is quiet and looking at the ocean view from the window. I can tell he doesn't trust Kumal Jr. I don't know what to think, either, though I can't do anything but give this a try.

"Right," says Kumal. "My mother told me all about them, and about your mother, too."

"Did Genevieve tell you how she met Daddy? I've been wondering, but I've been too afraid to ask him."

"Wow. You don't know the story? Well, our father and my mother were high school sweethearts. Then she went to college, and he went to the streets. When she was home visiting one holiday, they reconnected, and he shared his new passion with her—crack cocaine. My mother was an instant addict."

I'm shaking my head in disbelief. This was not what I wanted to hear. I wanted to learn that Genevieve had turned my father on to drugs, not the opposite.

Kumal continues, "My mother loved our father, and she still loves him."

"Why didn't she get clean when he did? Why didn't they go to rehab together?" My questions are desperate, begging for answers that I don't want to hear.

"That's the ten-million-dollar question. My mother says she woke up one morning and he was gone. She didn't know he'd gone to rehab or anything. A week after that, she found out she was pregnant with me."

"I don't know what to say. I'm so sorry."

Kumal smiles tenderly. "Hey, it's not your fault. Or mine. We've been dealt the hand."

Darrin asks Kumal, "Will you take a paternity test? We have the equipment right here."

"And I thought we were having a Hallmark moment," remarks Kumal in a sarcastic tone.

I say, "If you take the test, I'm sure I can convince Daddy to help you and your mother."

"He'll help me whether I take the test or not," Kumal says, not even trying to hide his scorn.

Darrin clears his throat. "So, are you taking the test?"

"No."

Now I'm confused. "Why not? You must realize how difficult this is for us! A little more evidence than your mother's word might help the healing process."

"My mother's word is enough for me. To you, she's a crack whore, but to me, she's everything—the only person I have."

I object, "I never said those things about Genevieve."

"But you're thinking them. Just like Diana. She's the one who convinced our father to leave my mother high and dry."

"But they've helped you financially over the years, right?"

"Barely. If you can call it help."

"Kumal, please take the test," I beg.

"No. Put yourself in my shoes. Imagine that your father, whom you've loved your entire life, asked for a DNA test. How would you feel?"

"I'd be devastated, but this is different, and you know it."

"Little sister, I am happy you reached out to me, but I won't take that test." He stands from the table. "Thank you for coming, but I think our lunch date should end now."

"We haven't eaten."

"I've lost my appetite."

Kumal strides away from the table and out of the restaurant. It is my first instinct to follow him, but Darrin grabs my arm. When I turn to him with tears in my eyes, I see that Darrin has a smile on his face. He dangles the plastic bag from the DNA kit in front of my eyes.

Inside is Kumal's plastic straw.

Chapter Thirty-one

Darrin

Just got back from my trip to Savannah with Emoni. The ride home was quiet—too quiet. She didn't want to talk about the lunch date, and I couldn't think of anything to get her mind off of the ordeal.

I had wanted to use that opportunity to tell her my secret. To divulge the fact that I'm here on a mission—or was on a mission. But I didn't have the courage to destroy her mood even further.

I'm checking my e-mail, and I have a note from my own personal fatal attraction. It says:

> Happy Thanksgiving, boo. I wish I could visit you next week and have some of your infamous sausage dressing. I can't wait for you to come home so we can rekindle the flames of our romance.
> Hugs and kisses,
> Shayna

I'm really slipping these days. Shayna is too loose of a loose end to have hanging, but at least I know she's tucked away in Cleveland and still pining after me.

I peek at the catalog sitting way over on the kitchenette counter. When I decided not to write this story, I applied at a culinary arts school in Savannah, but I haven't opened the course catalog or the letter that I received from the admissions department. This is going to be my backup plan when Mathis cuts me off from the funds.

I think I'm waiting to see how things pan out with Emoni. Admittedly, I'm nervous about telling her the truth. More nervous than I've ever been when dealing with a woman.

Emoni has gotten me to a crazy, unfamiliar place. A land where weddings and Darrin Jr.'s reside. A place where spending the rest of my life with one woman doesn't seem strange or impossible.

I think I like it here.

A knock on my door invades my thoughts of Emoni. When I look through the peephole and see Oscar's mean-looking mug, I almost go back to daydreaming. But curiosity, as always, gets the best of me, and I open the door.

"Oscar. Do come in. Have a seat."

"I don't need to have a seat."

I shake my head and roll my eyes. "Sure, then. Stand. I don't care."

"Why are you interfering in the Prentisses' business?" Oscar's tone is harsh and completely unfriendly.

"What, no small talk?"

"I'm not one of your boys."

"To answer your question, Emoni asked for my help."

"Why would she do that?"

"Because you and her father are trying to pretend that everything is fine. It ain't fine, bro."

"You don't know anything about them—especially Emoni. She'll never be yours."

I laugh heartily. "Seems like you're the one who doesn't know anything about her. If you did, you'd be helping her find out about her brother."

"I believe Bishop. He says that the man isn't his son."

"Believe what you want to believe, but I'm supporting what Emoni wants. Period."

"You need to stay out of Emoni's life. I can make things real difficult for you if you don't."

"Fool, you threatening me? In my own crib? You need to bounce."

Oscar sizes me up, and I'm making mental notes about the closest thing I have in proximity to whoop this fool with in case he decides to take the leap. He looks like he might, but then he changes his mind.

"You ain't even worth it," he says.

What is this, high school? I don't respond. I just slam the door in brotha man's face. It is too late in the evening for this foolishness.

I sit down on my couch and exhale. The sound is loud and labored, as if it's the last breath I'll ever expel. I'm under too much stress, because hiding things—that isn't me. I don't keep secrets. I'm straightforward and blunt and honest and all those things that people value in someone's character.

Keeping secrets is not my thing.

Not telling Emoni the truth isn't like me. It's so out of character for me that I'm grabbing my gear and rushing to the pool for a late night swim. Need to work off this energy and clear my head. Maybe I'll think of a way to tell her without telling her.

I almost crash into Dorcas on my way into the gym. We've been doing a great job of avoiding each other. We sit on opposite sides of the church, park on opposite sides of the apartment lot, and work out at opposite times of the day. But tonight is not my routine, so I'm crossing paths with yet another Freedom of Life member who doesn't care for my company.

"Dorcas. Hi."

"Hello. Should one of us move or something? Is it going to be strange every time we bump into each other?"

Dorcas blinks up at me with a soft and angelic smile on her lips. Maybe she's forgiven me for seeing Emoni. Maybe she's just in a good mood.

"It doesn't have to be. How have you been?" I ask.

She smiles. "I've been good."

"Me, too."

"Are you going to Bishop's house on Thanksgiving?"

"I haven't officially been invited yet."

"I'm having a get-together for some of the people in the singles' ministry who don't have families to go to for the holidays. If you don't go over there, you're welcome at my party."

"Thanks. Why are you being so nice all of a sudden?"

"I know that God is going to send me a husband, and I won't have to compete for him. So you must not be the one."

I know it wasn't meant to be, but Dorcas's words sound like an insult. Like she's trying to get the last word.

"I'm glad you've made your peace with the scenario."

Dorcas walks away but then remembers, "Oh, by the way, you have to bring a dish."

Bringing a dish is the least of my problems.

Chapter Thirty-two

Emoni

Darrin has invited me over for dinner. He says that he has to tell me something important. I know it's not the DNA test results. Those won't be here for a few weeks. He sounded so strange when we talked that I'd be lying if I said I'm not nervous.

To keep myself busy until it's time to go to Darrin's, I'm helping Mother prepare the house for her yearly Thanksgiving celebration. She's putting out all of her decorations: turkeys, pilgrims, Native Americans, and every shade of leaf you'd ever want to see.

I'm so fidgety and distracted that I keep dropping things on the floor. What could Darrin want to tell me? What if he wants to break up with me?

I pick up a leaf that has fallen and tack it back in place. Mother smiles at me and asks, "Are you inviting Darrin over for Thanksgiving?"

"I think so."

"He seems like a good catch. His parents really are as rich as he says they are."

"Mother, did you do a background check on him?"

"Of course I did. You should've done it yourself."

"I prefer that he just reveal himself to me."

Mother laughs at me. "No one just reveals himself. Not in a romantic setting. We're all on best behavior."

I remember my mother's words as I walk up to Darrin's apartment. Has he been on his best behavior this whole time? What if he has some ridiculous flaw that is a total deal breaker?

He opens the door before I can knock. "Hey, baby," he says, and kisses me on the cheek.

"Hey."

He rushes back to the kitchen but says, "Get comfortable and sit on the couch. Dinner will be ready soon."

"We're not sitting at the table?"

"Nope. Not tonight."

I glance around the room at the strategically placed candles and the huge blanket in the middle of the floor. On the blanket are elegant place settings and huge, soft lounging pillows.

"Should I sit on the floor?" I ask.

"You can if you like."

I sit down in front of a pillow and rest my head, inhaling the aromas coming from the kitchen. I feel kind of bad that I've never cooked anything for him. But

I'm almost a thousand percent sure he wouldn't like my cooking.

"Dang!" shouts Darrin from the kitchen.

"Is everything okay?" I ask.

"No. I forgot the ginger for the sesame ginger chicken."

I shrug. "So why can't we just have sesame chicken?"

"Because I have my mouth set for sesame ginger, and it's not the same thing. I'll run to the corner and hope they have fresh gingerroot."

I grab my jacket from the couch and start to put it on. "Oh, I can go and do that for you."

Darrin takes my coat out of my hands and kisses me on the forehead. That was definitely a boyfriend move. "What kind of man would I be if I let my woman go out at this time of night? You can relax here until I come back."

"You sure?"

He nods and smiles. "Yep."

"Well, you better hurry up, because I might fix myself a peanut-butter sandwich."

"You better not," threatens Darrin with a laugh.

As soon as Darrin walks out the door and I hear the bolt turn in the lock, I hear my mother's voice in my head. *No one just reveals himself. Not in a romantic setting. We're all on best behavior.*

I'm not too worried about Darrin having anything to hide, because a man who is hiding something does not leave his girlfriend in his apartment alone. Right?

A colorful brochure calls out to me from Darrin's desk in the corner. It's right out in the open, so he shouldn't care if I take a little peek at it.

Why am I looking over my shoulder like there's someone watching me?

I walk casually over to the desk and pick up the brochure. It's for a cooking school in Savannah. I feel a smile stretching across my lips.

Is my man planning on going to school in Savannah? Is he doing this so he can be near me? Is he going to ask me to marry him? We've only been dating a few weeks, but it could happen.

I start doing a little praise-break shout like Sister Rogers at our church. Sister Rogers shouts *every* Sunday. Most of the time she shouts out of her hat. Sometimes she shouts out of her wig.

While I'm in the midst of my shouting, I accidentally bump Darrin's desk, and the computer flashes on. I jump like somebody's caught me, but then I blink and look at the screen.

A Google search page. Nothing exciting.

Then I hear my mother's voice again. *No one just reveals himself.*

I had a friend in college who used to always hit the back button on her boyfriend's Internet browser to see the Web site he'd just looked at. She found out that he had a cyber girlfriend and liked to look at butt-naked video chicks online.

No one just reveals himself.

I feel my hand reaching for the mouse, and before I allow common sense to stop me, I click on the back button.

I draw in a sharp breath when I read the screen, because it's all about my daddy.

DIARY OF A MAD BLACK BLOGGER

Some of y'all want to know which lady I chose, and that's funny to me. I tell y'all about a scandal that could make my career, and all y'all want to know about is which girl I picked!

I can't believe y'all.

Before I tell y'all about the girl, let me give y'all an update about the hypothetical situation.

I actually met the alleged illegitimate son of the bishop. He was believable, and I truly felt bad for the dude.

This has got me even more torn because I was one hundred percent in the bishop's corner until I heard this dude out. I mean, to grow up without your father and then see him on television every week: ouch. That's gotta hurt. Sad thing is, I don't think the bishop is going to acknowledge him or ever be in the dude's life.

That's messed up.

I just know that it won't be me revealing anything to anyone. My mother loves to say, "What's done in the dark will always be brought to light." If God wants to blow the lid off this thing, He will. I've got too much of my own stuff that I hope stays in the shadows.

Anyway, I picked the bishop's daughter, so that complicates matters even more. Gotta think of a way to tell her why I'm really "on location." (Y'all thought I was about to slip and tell y'all the city so you could try to guess the bishop! Wow, y'all are nosy.)

Hit me up in the comments, and y'all . . . pray for me!

COMMENTS

Tyrone 4:55 p.m.

Yeah boyee! You picked the PK. I knew you'd make the right choice. Is she a freak?

Jia 5:12 p.m.

There YOU go, Tyrone. Anyway . . . . I think you should reveal it, because it's too many scandalous preachers out here right now. You can't even go to church without worrying about WHO is praying for you. Tell it! Tell it!

Lee-Lee 5:30 p.m.

Ooh, MBB! How you gone play me like that? You know you supposed to be my boo. But I agree with Jia. That's real talk. Not everyone was called, some of these pastors just WENT.

Sister Mary 6:17 p.m.

If you want to do anything, you nede to be praying for your bishop. He's a man too. You nede to be liftin up the blood stained banner and stompin the devl under your feet.

The room is spinning, and my head feels like it's about to explode. I cannot believe this. So many thoughts going through my head right now.

Why would Darrin do this to me? Why? He's putting my daddy on blast on the Internet, and me, too! Did he know I was gonna give it up from the jump? Does he think I'm a freak?

Why did I give my virginity to this man?

I spin around quickly and grab my coat and shoes. Gotta get out of here before he comes back. I can't look at him. I don't want to see him, because I can't look at him without crying.

And I'm not letting him see me cry over him. But if I don't get out of this apartment, I'm going to fall apart. I'm not strong, and I'm not mature, and I'm not going to be okay after this.

I gave this man my virginity, and we're not okay.

I dash out and rush down the hallway, trying to be unnoticed. The tears have already started to fall.

But the inevitable occurs. I run right into Dorcas in the building's lobby.

"Emoni, are you all right?" she asks.

Do I look all right? I hate when people ask me stupid questions. What she really wants to ask is *What did Darrin do?* or *Did you guys break up?* But instead she asks if I'm all right. Then it occurs to me. She probably knows all about Darrin and his "story." I bet that's why they broke up.

So I was his afterthought. His second choice. His fall back piece of tail. I can't believe I gave this man my virginity.

I respond to Dorcas, "Yes, I'm fine."

I can tell she doesn't believe me. So what? I'm tired of trying to convince people of things about me. Tired of convincing Daddy and Mother that I'm grown, tired of convincing Sascha that I'm not a square.

I rush into my car, slam the door, and start the engine in a fluid motion.

I'm tired of convincing Darrin that he should pick me instead of Dorcas. Pick her. I don't care.

The only person I've never had to convince of anything is Oscar.

Chapter Thirty-three

Darrin

I'm so stupid.

Stupid. Stupid. Stupid.

How could I have been careless enough to leave Emoni in my apartment with her business all over my computer? I'm seriously slipping.

The only person I have to turn to is my boy Leon.

I call him up and tell him how I foolishly left Emoni to get some ginger and then how she went snooping on my computer and found out about my blog. I tell him how she was gone when I got back and how she's not answering her cell phone and how I never got to explain myself.

Leon, for once, is silent.

"Dawg! Did you hear what I said?"

Leon takes a long inhale and a long exhale. "Man, you are in some deep doo-doo."

"Tell me something I don't know."

"I have a question. Did you sleep with this girl?"

I close my eyes and sigh anxiously. "Yeah, man."

"Aw, man! You took the pastor's daughter to bed? What's wrong with you?"

"I didn't mean to. It just happened."

"The real thing you need to worry about is what you're gonna tell Big Mathis at Christmas when he asks about your story."

A groan escapes my lips. "Don't remind me."

"Dude, you have to go and talk to this girl. Go to her house, see her at church. But you can't leave it like this. You gotta let her know what's up."

"Yeah, I know. But tonight I have this Thanksgiving party to go to."

"Can't you go to your girl's house? You know she's gonna be home on Thanksgiving."

I considered this already. Of course Emoni's home. As is the rest of her family, including her brother and father. And probably that fool Oscar. If she told them about the blog, the deck is stacked against me. If she told them we slept together, they might be looking to shoot a brotha.

"Naw. I've got to talk to her on neutral ground. I ain't got no boys down here backing me up."

"I feel you on that. But er . . . uh . . . a brotha like me is trying to watch this here Cowboys game. So you let me know how all this turns out."

"Right. Yeah, all right."

I press End on my cell phone and head to my true sanctuary: the kitchen. I start chopping celery and onions for my sausage dressing, though I can't believe I still plan on going to Dorcas's shindig. But it's something to do, and I've never spent a holiday alone. Been blessed to always have people around me.

Right now, though, I'm alone with my thoughts. Trying to figure out how I let things get so intense with Emoni without telling her the truth. I've never been able to commit, but I've always been honest about it. I've never done anyone dirt, as my West Indian grandma likes to say.

There is a knock on my door. I'm assuming it's Dorcas and hoping it's Emoni. But one peek through the peephole tells me differently. It's Shayna—the woman who is obviously not done with me.

I open the door. "Shayna."

She hugs me and kisses my cheek. "Hey, baby. Happy Thanksgiving. So are you happy to see me?"

I let out a heavy sigh. "Shayna, why are you here?"

She opens her coat to reveal a little black Victoria's Secret ensemble.

I laugh out loud. "I know they didn't let you on the airplane looking like that."

"No. I changed in the airport bathroom. Now tell me about your story! Should I stop sending Bishop Prentiss my tithes and offerings?"

"There's no story, Shayna. Your tithes are safe."

She raises an eyebrow like she doesn't believe me, then goes into the kitchen and eyes my dish on the counter. "What are you cooking?"

"Sausage dressing."

"You're cooking a big Thanksgiving feast? I came just in time."

"I'm invited to a get-together."

"Can I come with?"

I laugh again. "Sure, but it's going to be mostly people from the singles' ministry at church."

She scrunches her nose. "No, thanks. I'll just chill out here. And we can have our celebration later . . . by candlelight."

"I can't have a candlelit dinner with you."

"Why not?"

I want to tell her I'm dating the girl I could be with forever. Thing is, I don't know if Emoni will ever get over what I've done.

I pull myself away from the suggestive conversation and go into the kitchen to finish my dressing. Shayna picks up the brochure for the cooking school from my table and thumbs through it. "What's this?" she asks.

"What's what?"

"This culinary arts school booklet. Is there something you need to tell me?"

I consider telling her the truth. Seeing that my number of confidants has dropped to few and far between, it might help to have a sympathetic ear. But in light of Shayna's background of carrying pertinent and not so pertinent information back to my mother, I swiftly change my mind. "No. That's just some junk mail."

"Oh, okay. You know, I was a little worried about coming down here."

"Why?"

"Only because I've hardly heard from you since you left. I almost thought I'd run into your new girlfriend."

"Hmmm."

"So why haven't you called me?"

"I've been busy," I reply.

"Too busy to call your woman?"

Now she's standing in front of me, putting little kisses all over my face and neck, and I consider not stopping her. I'm torn because my flesh misses this, wants this. I'm feeling so down about Emoni that I would rather wrap myself in Shayna's arms and fornicate my troubles away.

But then I think about Bishop's Bible study lesson about the flesh. About how everything concerning the flesh is the opposite of everything the Spirit displays. My flesh is selfish and would take Shayna right here and right now, even though I don't love her. Don't even want her in my life.

"Shayna. Put your clothes on, baby."

"You don't sound like you mean that."

"But I do."

Shayna takes a spin, modeling her expensive lingerie. "Don't leave me hanging, Darrin."

I close my eyes tightly. The new man I'm struggling to preserve can't look at her standing here in booty-call apparel. I grab my cordless telephone from the counter and start to dial.

"Who are you calling?" she asks.

"Information. I'm finding you a hotel. The downtown Ritz-Carlton, please."

"You're not serious."

"Yes. I'd like to book a suite," I say into the phone.

Shayna rolls her eyes and pulls a pair of pants from her bag. "I don't believe this."

After I make the reservation, I place the phone on the counter and attempt eye contact with Shayna. I ask her, "Don't you see why this is a good thing?"

"It would be a good thing if I were a church girl you were going to make your wife."

Immediately, I think of Emoni. "Come on. I'll walk you to your car."

"So that's it? We aren't even going to spend any time together?"

"I've got this Thanksgiving party, and after that, it'll be late—and dangerous."

"I don't want to spend Thanksgiving alone. Can I come to the party with you?"

I don't want her to come. Dorcas is going to be offended, and the news of my "date" will be back to Emoni quicker than I can blink. But Shayna did come all the way here, and I don't want her to be alone on the holiday.

"Yes . . . you can come, but please don't tell everyone you're my girlfriend, because that is not the truth."

Shayna rolls her eyes again. "Right, I'll just tell them I'm your booty buddy. Or *was* your booty buddy."

"Don't embarrass me, Shayna."

"I know how to act, Darrin."

I go into the kitchen to put the finishing touches on my dressing. Shayna, now fully dressed, is sitting on my couch pouting. I'm sure that going to a sanctified Thanksgiving party was not what she had in mind, but oh well.

There is a knock at my door, and before I can turn from the oven, Shayna is answering it for me. It's Emoni. Who else would it be when I've got my ex posted up in my spot?

I hear Emoni say, "Is Darrin here?"

"Hey, Moni—Emoni," I say as I dash from the kitchen. Shayna asks, "Are you going to introduce us?"

I clear my throat. "Shayna, this is Bishop Prentiss's daughter Emoni. Emoni—"

"I'm Darrin's *friend* Shayna."

She puts a ridiculous amount of emphasis on the word "friend." I should've known she would do that. Emoni looks about ready to lose her composure and go straight to the streets on Shayna. This can only end badly.

Emoni asks Shayna, "Are you from Cleveland?"

There is more stank in Emoni's tone than a Bronx garbage day in the middle of July.

"Yes. I came down here to spend the holiday with my *friend*," says Darrin.

Emoni spits more fire. "Wow, you two must be great friends if you'll come all the way to Atlanta for Thanksgiving."

"You might call us *bosom buddies*."

I have to jump in before this gets out of control. "Emoni, isn't your family getting ready for dinner? We're going to the singles' ministry party."

"I just came by," replies Emoni in a softer tone, "to make sure you weren't spending the holiday alone."

Shayna says, "Oh, he's good."

I grab Emoni by the hand and lead her into the hallway. Shayna gives me the look of death when I close the apartment door in her face.

"Moni, thanks for coming to see about me. I appreciate that."

"I shouldn't have. Not since you're trying to destroy my father and his ministry."

"It's not like that, Emoni."

"I. Saw. Your. Blog." Each of Emoni's words is punctuated with hurt.

"But if you'd read every post—"

"I did read every post, Darrin. You're torn about revealing my father. I get that. But the fact that you even considered it . . . that hurts."

"Moni—"

"Please stop calling me that, Darrin. Save your little endearments for your bosom buddy."

I sigh and run my fingers through my hair. "This is not what it looks like."

"Oh really? Well, it looks like you kicking it with your ex for the holiday. What part do I have wrong?"

"I didn't invite her down here. She came on her own. You've got to believe me."

Emoni takes a step closer and peers into my face. Then she sucks her teeth. "It would be a lot easier to believe you if you didn't have that heifer's lip·gloss all over your face."

I exhale in frustration as Emoni storms down the hallway. I can't explain my way out of this. There's nothing I can say.

"Emoni, don't walk away like this. I think I'm falling in love with you." I'm begging. Ain't never begged a woman for nothing.

She steps into the elevator with tears running down her face. "I want someone who knows he's in love with me."

I watch the elevator close on the one relationship I ever really wanted.

Defeated, I turn back to my apartment, and Shayna's standing there with figurative smoke coming from her nose and ears.

"You love her, Darrin?" she asks, her voice trembling with rage.

"Yeah, I do."

Shayna screams every curse in the book at me as she snatches her suitcase and marches out of my apartment. I don't try to stop her.

"Lose my number, Darrin."

"I'm not the one who keeps calling."

Shayna takes off a stiletto shoe and throws it at me. Her aim is on point, because I don't have enough time to duck out of the way. Manolo Blahnik just busted me in my eye.

Make that two women who are done with me.

Chapter Thirty-four

Emoni

I'm trying to hold back my tears, because I don't want my family to know about me and Darrin. Mother scolded me for not inviting "my man" for Thanksgiving, so I had no other choice but to try and get him to come.

After I rushed home from Darrin's apartment, I calmed down. Then I thought maybe I'd been hasty. I wanted to hear his side of the story. I wanted to hear anything that would erase all of the pain he's caused.

And no, he did not have the audacity to say he *thinks* he's falling in love with me. He must not have been thinking about that when he was playing tonsil hockey with Shayna. Standing in front of me trying to apologize with lip gloss on his neck. He's got me twisted for real.

Sister Ophelia and Kevin are joining us for Thanksgiving dinner, and she is already getting on my nerves. The worst part is that after Kevin and Sascha get married, they are going to be at *all* of our holidays.

We're sitting in the living room, drinking coffee and waiting for the caterer to finish our meal. My mother hires a caterer on every major holiday because the idea of standing on her feet in the kitchen over two hours terrifies her. I'm glad she gets a caterer; the last time she attempted to cook a turkey, it was raw in the middle.

Ophelia says, "Diana, we haven't got a lot of time to plan this wedding. I've been working on a few things."

She hands Mother a notebook that has magazine clippings taped on the pages. Mother flips through the notebook with her nose turned up, as if it smells like rotten garbage. Sascha sits next to Mother and snickers.

"Sister Ophelia, I think me and my mom can handle planning the wedding. All you have to do is show up," says Sascha as Mother hands the notebook back to Ophelia.

"This is my grandson's wedding, too. Y'all ain't 'bout to block me out of everything."

Kevin interjects, "Grandma, I don't really care about this stuff. Let them plan it."

"What do you mean, *let them plan it?*"

Sascha replies for her man. "He means it's not really a big deal who plans our big day. We're happy regardless."

"Well, if it don't matter who plans it, I'll be happy to," states Ophelia. She's angrily smoothing her skirt, and her eyes dart from Mother to Sascha.

Mother says, "Ophelia, for heaven's sake, I'm not going to have my daughter be married in some country ceremony with spaghetti and fried chicken at her reception."

"You think she too good for my ideas? It ain't like she a blushing virgin. Y'all ought to be going down to the courthouse. Who ever heard of a pregnant bride getting married in the church?"

Sascha squirms in her seat, and Mother glares at Ophelia. This is pretty entertaining. It's almost enough to take my mind off Darrin and his date, who will probably be doing who knows what after Dorcas's party. She looked like she could pop, lock, and drop it and everything in between.

Mother is about to respond when the doorbell rings. Sascha springs up to answer it. "I'll get it!"

Sascha comes back an instant later with Oscar in tow. I so don't feel like dealing with him today. "I thought you were at Dorcas's party," I say in an irritated tone that I'm not trying to hide.

He says, "I wanted to be here for you on the holiday."

"How sweet," says Sister Ophelia sarcastically.

"You didn't have to do that." I stand up and walk into the kitchen. Oscar follows me.

"Are you all right?" he asks as he sits down next to me at the table.

"Why does everybody keep asking me that? I'm fine."

"I saw you leaving Darrin's apartment when I was on my way to Dorcas's party. Did he do something to hurt you?"

"I'm fine, Oscar, leave it alone. You should've stayed at Dorcas's party."

So what if that is clearly a lie? Oscar doesn't need to know all of my business. He already has too much information.

"The way I see it, you can either sit around here sulking about Darrin, or you can marry me."

I almost vomit in my mouth. "No, thank you, Oscar."

"What's so wrong with me? You act like I'm nothing."

"There's nothing wrong with you. I just don't look at you that way. You're like a brother to me."

"Would your brother do this?"

Oscar pounces, and I have no time to flee. He kisses me full on the mouth, tongue and all. My first thought is to push him off me, but after the first second, I'm not disgusted anymore. I close my eyes tight, imagine he's Darrin, and kiss Oscar back.

"Now, that wasn't so bad, was it?" Oscar asks after we're done.

There is a real vulnerability to his tone, like he's going to be devastated if I give the wrong answer. Truthfully, he's not that bad. It's just that I want to have a choice. I don't want to think he's all I can get.

"It wasn't bad, Oscar. It honestly wasn't bad."

"So why don't you give us a chance? It could work. All you have to do is fall in love with me, because I'm already in love with you."

I take a huge gulp. Why does he keep saying he loves me? Seriously? I don't know how to respond to this. I wish he were Darrin professing *his* love. Why can't Darrin be the sure thing? I'd much rather share my life with him than settle for Oscar and have not so bad kisses for the rest of my life. I can't imagine having Oscar's children or being married to him forever.

Something in me wants Darrin. The guy who's probably fornicating right now with his hot girlfriend from Cleveland. The something is that Darrin makes my heart beat fast, and he makes me nervous, silly, and giddy all at the same time.

I love Darrin. There. I said it.

So here's the thing. Should I chase the guy I could totally fall in love with or settle for the guy who already loves me? Mother would tell me to choose Oscar. Daddy would, too.

Something in Oscar's manner or words has reached past everything I feel about Darrin and touched my heart. Oscar did love me as the ugly duckling, before Darrin was even a thought.

Still, since I can't respond to Oscar yet, I go to rejoin my family at dinner, with Oscar at my heels. As soon as I'm seated, Sascha frowns up at Oscar and says to me, "I thought Darrin was coming."

"He had a friend in from Cleveland, and he couldn't make it," I answer.

Daddy replies, "Does he know how important the holidays are for this family?"

I make another excuse for Darrin. "His friend dropped in unannounced. He didn't want to impose."

"That's funny. Dorcas told me he was coming to her party," says Oscar. I give him the look of death.

Mother asks, "Is that true, Emoni? Is everything all right?"

"Everything is right as rain." Mother and Daddy both clear their throats at my obvious sarcasm. If they can pretend like everything is fine, so can I.

"Actually, everything is not all right," blurts Oscar.

"Oscar—"

"No, Emoni. Everyone needs to know what a miscreant Darrin is."

Daddy asks, "What are you talking about?"

Oscar ignores my evil eye and continues, "His real

girlfriend is here from Cleveland. That's why he's not here."

I could choke him. Even though Oscar's telling the truth, he didn't need to bring that up here. And judging by the shine of Sister Ophelia's eyes, this is going to be a Freedom of Life headline.

My brother, who has been quietly listening until now, asks me in a menacing tone, "Do you need me to go and see Darrin?"

"No, Assistant Pastor Tyler. I do not." Obviously, I need to remind him that assistant pastors don't go and beat guys down for their big sisters.

"I might be a pastor, but I'm still your brother."

This is getting out of control. I don't think it could be any worse.

And then Oscar says, "Darrin is not the man for you, Emoni." He turns to Daddy and continues, "That's why I'm here tonight, Bishop. To ask your permission to date Emoni."

"Don't you need *her* permission?" asks Sascha with a laugh.

Daddy glances at Ophelia and says, "Why don't we discuss this later. In private."

Oscar takes my hand and smiles into my eyes. I don't let go immediately, but I do avert my eyes. I'm not ready to accept this yet. I think about Darrin and his girlfriend and let out a heavy sigh. Why shouldn't I let Oscar love me? I won't have to chase him or compete with any other women for him. Even if he doesn't make me swoon like Darrin does, I know he will be good to me. And Oscar loves my family—he would never, ever think of doing something to destroy Daddy's ministry.

Chapter Thirty-five

Darrin

I must be a glutton for punishment. It's the Monday after Thanksgiving, and I'm sitting in Bishop Prentiss's office, getting ready to tell him the truth about myself. I seem to have been stricken with some type of honesty virus that can't be cured.

"Son, what can I help you with?" Bishop asks. "Is this about your trouble with Emoni?"

"Well . . . Emoni and I aren't on speaking terms right now, but that's not what I want to talk about."

"What did you want to talk about?"

"Bishop . . . I need to tell you my true reason for being in Atlanta."

Bishop frowns. "Your true reason? You're not here to pursue your writing career?"

"Yes, but you were supposed to be my breakthrough story."

"Me?"

"Yes. I saw you on television one morning, and I was sure you were a money-hungry fraud and sleeping with half the women in your church."

Bishop nods slowly. "I see."

"I never expected to get saved or admire you so much."

"And my daughter?"

I drop my head. "At first I thought that being friends with her would help my story. But the more I got to know Emoni, the more I realized I couldn't hurt her."

"So you lied."

"Yes, Bishop. I lied, but I'm asking you to forgive me."

"Have you written your story yet?"

"I don't plan to write it, sir."

Bishop says, "When you came down for your baptism, the Lord spoke to me. Do you want to know what He said?"

"Be careful?" I ask with an almost chuckle.

"No. The Lord said He'd sent you to Freedom of Life."

"Dorcas thinks I'm doing the work of the devil."

"I know what I heard in my spirit. I'm just wondering what the end of this thing is gonna be."

"Maybe it has something to do with this." I hand Bishop Prentiss the envelope with the DNA test results on Kumal Jr.

"What is this?"

"Emoni and I gathered DNA from you and Kumal Jr. without your knowledge, and we sent away for a DNA test. I was going to give her the results, but I'm giving them to you."

Bishop Prentiss turns the envelope over in his hands several times. "Have you looked at this?"

"No, I haven't. It's not my business."

"I already know what the results say."

"Sir?"

"I've known that Kumal Jr. was mine ever since I first laid eyes on him. When he was three years old."

"Then why . . ."

"Because he doesn't know me as his father. I couldn't claim a crack addict's baby and build a successful ministry. When Genevieve shared their whereabouts, the boy never wanted for anything."

"Except his father," I remark sadly.

"Except his father. You're right."

"I hope I'm not being out of line, Bishop, but I think your son should be more important than building a ministry."

"I agree. But now it is too late for me to be in this young man's life. He's already grown."

This whole conversation is making me think of my own father. Mathis has always been in my life, even if he doesn't agree with most of my choices. Never really thought about what it would've been like growing up without him.

"Grown men need their fathers, too."

Bishop nods. "Well, Darrin, if my forgiveness means anything to you, you have it. Right now I'm not in any position to condemn anyone for telling a lie."

"Thank you."

"I can't speak for my daughter, though."

"I don't want you to. This meeting isn't about Emoni."

I stand up from my seat and hold my hand out to Bishop. Bishop holds his arms out.

"Son, be blessed and thank you," says Bishop as he embraces me.

"For what?"

"For not telling the world about my secret."

"Oh. You're welcome, sir."

I leave the office feeling confused and dejected. How can Bishop be such a mentor and spiritual father to men like me and Oscar and not be concerned about his own flesh and blood?

And here is Oscar marching down the hall. I'm so not in the mood to be accosted by him. "Hello, Oscar."

He says nothing and keeps walking. I know how to take a hint. Didn't want to have that fake conversation anyway. When I'm almost out of earshot, Oscar says in a loud and angry voice, "Why don't you go back to Cleveland?"

"Excuse me?"

He rushes over and stands nose to nose with me. "I said, why don't you go back to Cleveland? Why are you still here messing up everyone's life?"

"Man, whatever." I turn to walk away. I'm not about to entertain this.

"You messed over Dorcas, then Emoni, and now you're trying to ruin Bishop."

I raise an eyebrow. "I'm not trying to ruin Bishop."

"Emoni told me about the DNA test."

I wonder if she told him about the story. "Is that all she said?"

"Isn't that enough? Why don't you leave us all alone? Go home to your little slut in Cleveland."

I feel my blood start to boil and my hand ball into a fist. But I'm not going to do this, not here. I throw my hand up and dismiss Oscar. "Dude, go on 'head with that." I leave Oscar standing there scowling and head to my truck in the parking lot. Dorcas is on her way into the church. What do you know? The gang's all here.

"Hi, Darrin."

"What's going on, Dorcas?"

"You all right? You're all red in the face."

I take a deep breath. "I'm cool."

"Have you heard the latest?"

I laugh. "I don't think I'm in anyone's circle right now. The latest about what?"

"Emoni and Oscar are dating."

I'm blinking and shaking my head. "What?"

"Yes. Ophelia says he asked Bishop's permission on Thanksgiving."

So Emoni gets mad at me and up and says yes to that fool. No wonder he wants me to go back to Cleveland.

"Well, I hope they're happy."

"Me, too," says Dorcas.

I need to end this conversation so I can go somewhere and think or sulk. Mostly sulk. "I'll see you around, Dorcas."

"That sounds like a goodbye."

I smile and wave. Maybe it is goodbye. I don't know. I can't think beyond this moment. I finally find a woman I want to treat the right way, and I mess that up.

Maybe Oscar is right. If I go back to Cleveland, everything will be cool. Emoni will end up marrying Oscar, Dorcas will find a man to make her happy, and no one will ever know about Bishop's secret.

I get in my truck and grasp the steering wheel, trying to decide what to do. When I feel myself crying, I know this situation is beyond my expertise. I start praying. Don't know how to do it like the professional church warriors—I can only say what's in my heart: God, I don't know if you sent me here. I just know that I've been trying to do the right thing, and it's all turning out wrong. Will you show me what to do? Lead me and guide me, because I seem to be making a mess of my life. Thank you, in Jesus' name.

Chapter Thirty-six

Emoni

Mother and Daddy have invited Oscar for lunch, so we can talk about his foolish outburst on Thanksgiving. Sister Ophelia has done her job informing everyone, because I got several congratulations from the church mothers on Sunday.

"Bishop, you don't know how honored I am to have your blessing."

"You only have my blessing if this is something that Emoni wants."

Everyone looks at me, and I shrug. "I haven't decided one way or the other."

Bishop says, "If you ladies will excuse us, I'd like to have a talk with Oscar alone."

Mother and I clear the table and go into the kitchen to clean up. She's looking at me like she wants to have one of those mother-daughter moments. I don't feel like having a moment.

"Emoni . . ."

Oh, no. Here it comes. "Yes?"

"You don't want to date him, do you?" she asks in a whisper.

"I don't know, Mother."

"Did you want to date Darrin?"

I sigh heavily. "Yes, but he lied to me."

"He lied. Did you talk it out with him?"

"Yes, he admitted that he was wrong. But Mother . . . it was horrible, what he did."

Mother nods thoughtfully. "So he made a mistake and admitted it?"

"Yes, but it was too little, too late. Then he was with his ex on Thanksgiving."

Mother sits down at the kitchen dinette. "Emoni, come over here and sit down."

"I really don't want to talk about this. I know what I'm doing."

"Come here and listen to this before you make a mistake you're going to regret."

I slump down in one of the hard wrought-iron chairs. I don't want to hear my mother's advice or anyone else's. She's beautiful *and* married to a man who loves her. What can she say to me?

"Emoni, I'm not going to tell you not to date Oscar."

"You're not?"

"No, but I do think you should make sure things are over with Darrin. Don't go into something with Oscar with unresolved feelings."

I cross my arms over my chest. "I don't have any unresolved feelings."

"Only you know that for sure. But if you do, at the

first sign of trouble with you and Oscar—and there will
be trouble—you'll start thinking you should've made
another choice."

"Oscar has never lied to me."

Mother reaches across the table and asks, "But does
he make your heart sing? Can you see yourself spending
forever with him?"

I don't answer her. I can't answer. Seriously, Oscar
doesn't make me feel anything. Darrin was beginning to
make me feel that way, though we weren't together long
enough for me to know for sure.

"I think I can learn to love Oscar."

"Or you could learn to hate him," Mother replies as
she gets up from the table.

She leaves me alone with my thoughts. I find myself
thinking of how Darrin's lips felt on mine and how much
joy he got out of cooking meals for me. I miss the feeling
of anticipation when I knew I was going to see him; the
almost sick feeling in the pit of my stomach that was a
mix of excitement and adrenaline. I'm glad when Sascha
bursts into the kitchen and snaps me back to reality.

She asks, "Did you look at those dresses I picked
out?"

"Yes. Any of them are fine for me."

"Are you and Oscar going out later? I'm nosy."

"I guess" is my listless reply.

"Girl, what is wrong with you? You sure don't sound
excited about it."

"Maybe I'm just having a bad day."

"Humph. Maybe you're just not excited about the
man."

"Is it that obvious? Mother said something similar."

"I mean, yeah, Emoni. It's obvious."

"Well, I'm dating him. Who needs all that excitement, anyway? It's only lust. Oscar is the right decision."

Sascha's eyes narrow. "You don't feel *any* lust toward Oscar? Not even a little?"

"No!"

"What about Darrin? Bet you felt some lust toward him."

"Seriously, are we even having this conversation?"

"You don't have to listen to me . . ."

I laugh again. This is something I already know.

Chapter Thirty-seven

Emoni

Mother actually got to me with her little "unresolved issues" speech. I think that if I know everything is over and done with Darrin, I'll feel so much better about seeing Oscar.

So I'm sitting in my car outside of Darrin's apartment. I'm planning to go and ring his buzzer as soon as I think of an excuse to be here. I can't just pop up here, seeming all desperate. That is not a good look at all.

I forgot. The DNA results. How could I have forgotten about them? In the midst of all these breakups, the whole idea that I might have another brother has been relegated to the back burner of my life.

Now that I've got my reason, I hurry up to the apartment and ring the doorbell. I shift my weight from leg to leg as I wait for a response. I scan the parking lot from inside. His car is here, so why isn't he answering?

"Who is it?" I finally hear through the crackling loud-speaker.

"It's Emoni."

There is a *very* distinct pause before the door unlocks to let me up. Usually, there is someone else going into the building, and I don't have to ring Darrin's buzzer. But since we're not exactly on speaking terms, it would seem somewhat rude for me to show up at his door. That's something Dorcas or Oscar would do.

I rap lightly on the door after getting off the elevator and walking down the hall. Darrin opens the door wearing a bathrobe and smelling of a manly fragranced body wash. Sascha's words about lust come to mind, but I push them away.

He doesn't invite me in.

"Hi, Darrin. How are you?"

"Good. You need something?"

Wow. I need to go and grab my winter coat for the arctic wind that just blew out of Darrin's door.

"Um, I was wondering if you got those DNA results back. I'd really like to know about Kumal Jr."

"Yes. I got them back and hand-delivered them to Bishop Prentiss."

"Why did you give them to him?"

"Because it was his business and not mine."

"I see."

Darrin asks impatiently, "Anything else?"

"Well, dag, Darrin! Aren't you a little bit happy to see me?" I feel my anger rising. He's supposed to be glad to see me!

"Why would I get excited about seeing another man's woman?"

"About that . . ."

"You don't owe me an explanation."

"Are you going to invite me in?" I ask hopefully.

"No."

"Why? Do you have a woman in there?"

Darrin laughs. "You are welcome to think that, if you want."

"No, seriously. What about your date from Thanksgiving? She still in town?"

"Nope."

"How can I take your word for it? You haven't called since we had that argument. You rush out of church right after the service is over."

Darrin has a small smile on his lips. "You said you were done with me. And now you're dating Oscar. It looks like I was right not to call."

He's playing hardball, and I'm either too proud or too bullheaded to cave in. He wants me to say everything on my heart, but I'm not going to do it. He won't hear that I miss him and that I wish I wasn't even considering Oscar. He won't hear any of that, because I'm leaving.

"All right, then, Darrin. Take care, okay?"

"You, too, Emoni."

The tears are flowing before I even make it to my car. Even if my feelings aren't resolved, his obviously are. The conversation we just had was like talking to a stranger.

I only wish I could erase my own feelings as easily as Darrin has.

Chapter Thirty-eight

Darrin

Man, that was the hardest thing I've ever done in my life."

I'm talking to my boy Leon. This situation is getting too complicated for even my skills. I'm not ashamed to use all kinds of slang: I'm caught up, Emoni's got me twisted, she's got me open, etc. . . .

"So let me get this straight. She came to your crib, and you sent her packing?"

"Yeah, man. I think it was the right thing to do."

Leon asks, "Why? Just because she's dating that other dude?"

"Yeah, because she's dating that other dude."

"But she came to you, right? She wanted you to talk her out of kicking it with old boy."

"Or maybe she needed to make sure we were done. I let her off the hook."

"Do you love her?"

"Man . . ."

"Do you love the girl?"

"Yeah. I love her."

But do I love her more than Oscar does? Would I be better for her? Maybe loving her means letting the best man win.

"Shayna wouldn't put you through all these changes. She really digs you, man."

"Shayna! Please. She just digs my parents' money. When I tell her I'm going to chef school, she'll drop me like a dummy."

"Dude, you down there wilding out! Chef school? I thought you was playing."

If my boy doesn't even take me seriously, I know Big Mathis is going to laugh in my face. But I'm preparing myself for that conversation. Christmas at the Bainbridge mansion is going to be more like the Fourth of July. Fireworks are a given.

"I was not playing. You know I like to cook."

"Man, that's a hobby."

"Tell that to Emeril or Wolfgang Puck."

Leon laughs. "Ain't both of them white dudes? Black men ain't chefs, man!"

"Okay . . . Isaac Hayes on *South Park?*" I ask with a chuckle.

"Him and Tom Cruise is boys. He might be an honorary white dude."

That's why I called Leon. Even if he can't help me make the right decision, he can make me laugh. I need something comedic right about now, because this Emoni situation is downright tragic.

"Man, you've got to come over my parents' house for Christmas," I say.

Leon replies, "So I can watch Mathis explode when you tell him you're going to cooking school? He's gone call you all kinds of sissy."

"That's why I need you there. I think both of us could take him."

"I can *take* you to the emergency room after he stomps your little scrawny self."

"Man, you ain't even right. As many times as I've had your back?"

"All right," Leon acquiesces, "I'll be there, but if things get crazy, I'm that dude who's calling 911. Somebody has to live and tell the story."

Chapter Thirty-nine

Emoni

"How is your dinner?" asks Oscar.

I didn't listen to Mother or Sascha, and I agreed to at least a few dates with Oscar. Honestly, it hasn't been *that* bad. Oscar is a gentleman, sometimes obsessively so, and he has a sense of humor. Okay, so it's been kind of bad, but I'm trying to make lemonade out of these lemons.

He always lets me pick the restaurant. He says it's because he wants me to be excited about our dates. I don't seem excited enough, I guess. I'm trying really hard, though. And my having that un-conversation with Darrin truly helped Oscar's case. He should probably be writing Darrin a thank-you note.

I take a huge bite of the medium-well steak and reply, "It's fine."

"You shouldn't take such large bites," Oscar remarks.

"Thanks, Dad."

"I didn't mean it like that. It's just that I don't want you to choke."

I nod and roll my eyes. "Right, right."

Right when I get ready to be okay with deciding to date Oscar, he goes and does something like this. He pulls out the armor-bearer Oscar. The one who thinks it is his major mission in life to protect the interests of Bishop Prentiss—including me.

"Do you want dessert?" Oscar asks with a sigh.

"No."

He sighs again. Am I getting on his nerves? Whatever. Join the club. He's signaled the waiter to take his dessert order. The cute waiter, who's brown-skinned with thick pretty cornrows that touch his shoulders. I wish I had a tract or something, because I would invite him to church.

"You all want to order dessert?" the waiter asks.

"Yes," says Oscar, "I'd like the crème brûlée."

I roll my eyes again. He *would* pick an uptight dessert. "What do you suggest?" I ask the cute waiter, and yes, I am well aware of my flirtatious tone.

The waiter smiles. It is a welcoming and very sexy smile. "Well, for you I'd recommend something sweet, like the caramel brownie sundae. It'll make you lick your fingers."

"I'll have that."

The waiter grins and leaves with the order. Oscar is furious, but I don't care. He's getting on my nerves.

"Don't you ever disrespect me like that again," Oscar states.

I salute him. "Sir, yes, sir!"

"I mean it, Emoni."

"Get over yourself. I was just being friendly."

He shakes his head so hard that he looks like a big old Siberian husky. "That was more than friendly. I don't want a wife who's going to disrespect me in public."

Okay, so maybe I was a tad bit disrespectful. I'll admit it. "All right. I'm sorry, Oscar. My bad."

"*My bad?* Who are you these days?"

"I am the same as I've always been, Darrin."

"You mean Oscar."

"That's what I said."

Oscar drops his eyes and exhales loudly. I did *not* just say Darrin's name. Not even Oscar deserves that.

"Um . . . I'm going to go freshen up," I say.

I need to get away from this table so I can think for a second. On my way to the bathroom, I pass the fine waiter. His name tag says Will, and he has the audacity to smell good, too.

"You all right, baby girl?" he asks.

"Yes."

"What you doing with that square?"

"Square? Oh, you mean Oscar. He's my . . . uh . . . date."

Will looks me up and down and licks his lips. "For real? Man, what a waste."

I feel myself blushing, so I rush away from him. His smooth and debonair way of speaking reminds me of Darrin. That's probably why I said Darrin's name at the table. Yeah, that's it, because I sure wasn't thinking about Darrin while having dinner with the man I might end up marrying.

I splash my face with water, compose myself, and walk back out to the table with a smile.

"Our dessert isn't here yet?" I ask, totally unwilling to address the faux pas I committed a few minutes ago.

"No, it's not."

"I wish they'd hurry up, because I really feel a sweet tooth coming on."

Oscar replies, "Mmm-hmm. So, how long do you think we should date before we get engaged?"

"Don't you think that's rushing things?"

"I am a man, Emoni. And I've been wanting you for a long time."

"Okay, that doesn't sound right. As a matter of fact, it sounds right nasty."

"No, Emoni, I don't mean sexually," Oscar explains. "Not totally. It's just that lately, I've realized how much I need you in my life. I've been in love with you for years."

I'm speechless. I don't know how to respond when he starts pouring out emotions. The closest thing I feel is pity, and I don't know if that's a good thing.

He continues, "Why shouldn't we get engaged? We know each other well."

"I want us to take our time, that's all."

"Why? Are you waiting for Darrin to come back and sweep you off your feet?"

"What? No. No, I'm not."

I paused. He noticed. Dang.

"You don't sound sure."

"No, I'm not waiting for Darrin to come back. Why would I have said yes to you if I was waiting on him?"

"That's what I'm trying to figure out."

Chapter Forty

Darrin

Man, it's cold in Cleveland. Looks like we're definitely having a white Christmas this year. There's about a foot of the white stuff piled up in my parents' yard. I'd only needed a light jacket when I left Atlanta.

It's Christmas Eve, and my mother's guests are starting to arrive. Every year she has a dessert social with her Jack and Jill buddies. I try to avoid it at all costs, but this year I'm being a good son. I'm going to need Priscilla in my corner when it comes time to talk to Big Mathis.

I stop by Leon's house first to pick him up. He rubs his hands together and says, "You gone hook me up with a top-notch socialite? I'm ready to be a kept man."

"Sure. I hear Shayna's available."

"Nope. Too many miles on that booty. Most of it from you. I need someone a little less driven."

I laugh. Shayna's car is in the driveway. One thing

about her is that she has heart. That girl will go twenty rounds in a fight with a busted lip and a swollen eye.

"What's she doing here, anyway?" asks Leon. "Is she stalking you or something?"

"She's in the Jack and Jill crew. That's how we hooked up."

I'd met Shayna at the Jack and Jill Mother's Day brunch. I'd escorted my mother but left there with Shayna. She'd had very few inhibitions, and the panties had dropped on the first date. After that, I couldn't get rid of her.

Such fond memories.

Leon and I go in through the patio entrance, trying to not make a scene. Well, I'm worried about a scene; Leon doesn't care.

"There's my baby boy!" sings Priscilla as soon as we enter the party.

Leon takes a cup of the spiked eggnog from the caterer and chuckles. "Baby boy?"

"Man, don't start."

Priscilla glides—yes, glides—across the room with Shayna and another young lady in tow. She hugs and kisses my cheek.

"Hello, Mother," I say.

"Why didn't you call and tell me you were near? I was worried sick about you driving here from Atlanta. You should've flown in."

"The drive was nice. I needed the solitude."

Shayna gives me a friendly hug. I'm surprised it's not overly friendly. Maybe she's finally gotten the message.

"Darrin. How are you?" she says.

"I'm great, and yourself?"

She smiles. "Totally renewed."

The other young lady clears her throat loudly. She's waiting for an introduction. Shayna says, "Darrin, you remember Melody, right?"

"Melody Sinclair?"

Melody smiles, revealing teeth that have undergone all kinds of work. A few years ago, the girl's grille looked like the shark's from *Jaws*. Thank God for modern orthodontia.

"You do remember," says Melody.

"I never forget a face."

Melody motions to Leon. "So who's your friend?"

"Oh! I'm so rude. This is my boy Leon. Leon Chambers, meet Melody Sinclair."

Melody takes Leon by the arm and starts to pull him away. She's quite the aggressive one. A snippet of their conversation as they walk off has Melody asking, "So, what do you do?"

To which Leon gives the hilarious reply: "I'm in the automobile industry."

Shayna laughs out loud. "Do you think he's gonna tell her that he fixes cars?"

"Not until after he gets some."

"Some things never change."

"Right."

"Except you, Darrin. You've changed a lot."

"But it's for the better, I think."

"Maybe." Shayna waves at someone across the room. "Come on, Darrin. I'd like you to meet someone." She drags me over to meet her friend—a male friend. Makes me feel uncomfortable, because I'm not in the mood for mingling. I've got too much on my mind.

"Justin, this is Darrin, the one I told you about," says Shayna.

Justin responds, I don't know whether I should punch you out or hug you."

"It's a holiday. Let's go with the hug," I reply with what I know is a confused look.

"Darrin, I met Justin on my flight home from Atlanta. We talked all the way home."

Justin chuckles. "I talked. She cried."

"I was so distraught over you sending me home, but I really connected with Justin. We got home, had a few dates, and the rest is history."

"Wow. I should probably return that tennis bracelet I bought you for Christmas, then, huh?"

Shayna's eyes light up. "That won't be necessary."

"I was just playing, girl. Congratulations, you two."

I walk away, leaving Shayna to pick up her face off the floor and explain to her new boyfriend why she still wanted my gift. I hope she wasn't trying to make me jealous. Because she oh-so-miserably failed.

I sneak away from the party to my father's study. I know he'll be in here, hiding from Priscilla's friends. And he is here, doing his usual, drinking bourbon and smoking a cigar. I might as well get this showdown over with.

"Son. You made it in."

"I just got in a little while ago."

"So, tell me something good."

I give a nervous chuckle. "I joined this really nice church in Atlanta . . ."

"I'm being serious, boy. Let's see this career-launching story! I've been waiting all day to feast my eyes on it."

"Dad, I couldn't write that story. It would've hurt too many people. People I care about."

"I thought that was the idea. Find a scandal . . . blow the top off of it . . . ruin some lives . . . build a career. Wasn't that the plan?"

"I guess, but I didn't expect to get in so deep."

Mathis grins. "No story, huh?" He tosses an office furniture catalog from his desk.

I catch the heavy book and sigh. "What do you want me to do with this?"

"You can start picking out the furniture for your office. I've got a nice one waiting for you. Great view of the lake."

I sit down at the chair next to his bookcase. "Dad, I'm not coming to work for you."

"Then what? Do you need a letter of reference for a job? Because I'm not giving you another cent."

"I'm going back to school."

Mathis seems to brighten a bit. "For what? Your MBA? That would really help you in the business. I'm all for it."

I reply in a barely audible voice, "No, I'm going to chef school."

"Boy, you're going to have to speak up, because I think I heard you say chef school."

"You heard right."

"Get out of my office. I can't look at your face right now."

Since he's looking more than menacing, I do just that. Priscilla is waiting right outside his door, and her expression is a combination of anxiety and anticipation.

"Did you tell him about the story?" she asks nervously.

"Yeah, and he wasn't happy. I also told him about chef school."

Priscilla gasps. "You should've saved that for tomorrow. Now he'll be totally inconsolable for the entire holiday."

"He'll get over it."

"Did you do what I told you to do?"

"Yes, Mother. I purchased everything that I need for school and took cash advances on all of my credit cards."

"That will have to hold you over until he calms down."

I kiss Priscilla on the forehead. "Thank you."

Christmas dinner is a strained occasion. There are frowns all around. Mathis's is from my revelation; Priscilla's is due to Mathis being such a wounded bear about the whole thing. And mine has nothing to do with them. I'm still thinking of Emoni's last visit. I've been thinking that maybe I should've handled the whole thing differently. It could be the loneliness talking, or the holiday spirit, but I definitely wish I were introducing her to my parents this weekend.

The only person not frowning is Leon, who is enjoying all of the catered food. "Mrs. Bainbridge, you really know how to give a Christmas dinner," he says through a mouthful of turkey.

"Thank you, Leon."

Mathis's jaws are slamming into his turkey like it's a piece of leather jerky. I know better than to open my mouth now. Better to let him implode rather than explode.

"Mathis, did you congratulate your son?" Priscilla asks.

He glares angrily and ignores the question. I'm trying to send my mother a telepathic signal: Mother, please don't poke the bear.

"Did you hear me, Mathis?" Obviously, my mother is not telepathic.

"I don't have a son," grumbles my father.

"Well, I think it's great that Darrin is going to do what he loves. So many people spend their lives unfulfilled."

Mathis retorts, "Many of those fulfilled people are living in poverty."

"Darrin doesn't have to worry about that."

Why does she continue with the poking?

I interject, "I'm going to work my way through school."

"You don't even know what that word means," Mathis says.

Now I'm getting angry. "Your definition of work is sitting in some boring office, looking at the four walls and firing people at will. That ain't me."

"You hear him, Priscilla? That *ain't* me! All that money you spent on his private school education, and he can't even put together a proper sentence."

I stand up and throw my utensils to the table. "How's this for proper? Mathis Bainbridge, I need neither your money nor your approval."

"You're not man enough to call me by my name," barks Mathis.

I'm getting ready to respond in kind when my father starts to pull at his chest. He drops his fork and tears the napkin from his shirt. He gasps and struggles to catch his breath.

"Dad? Are you okay?"

He cannot respond. Priscilla's eyes widen. "Oh, Lord! Darrin, call the paramedics."

Mathis shakes his head furiously, but we ignore him. Leon tries to check my father's pulse, but he pushes him away. He even fights the paramedics when they get here, and it takes all three of them to overpower him and get him on the stretcher and into the ambulance. We follow close behind in my truck.

"Mother, don't worry. He's going to be fine."

She's wringing her hands and praying. I'm sending up my own silent petitions to God, but I'm not letting Priscilla see that I'm worried.

When we get to the hospital, my father is being rushed into a trauma room, and we're being ordered to stay calm and stay outside the room. I've watched enough *ER* to know that when a code is being called, it's serious. A whole team of doctors and nurses come flying around corners and rushing into the room with my father.

"Oh my Lord . . . help him, Lord! Lord, send your angels right now," cries my mother as I hold on to her hand tightly.

After the most tense moments in my life, a doctor emerges from the trauma room. And he's smiling. Smiling is a good thing.

Mother asks, "How is he?"

"Mrs. Bainbridge, your husband is going to be fine. He had a heart attack, but not a massive one. From the tissue scarring, I'm assuming he's had several miniature attacks in the past year or so. He probably thought it was indigestion."

"So our argument didn't do this?" I ask.

The doctor shakes his head. "High cholesterol did this."

"When can we see him?" Mother is already standing, ready to move any- and everyone out of her way.

"We've got him sedated right now so he can rest. You'll be able to talk to him in a little bit."

I let out a sigh of relief and leave my mother and Leon to take a walk around the hospital grounds. Need to blow off some steam and get my head right before I see my father.

If it weren't Christmas Day, I'd call Bishop Prentiss. I need some prayer or counseling or both. Maybe I just need some reassurance that I'm doing the right thing in defying my father's wishes. I don't know.

When I'm done with my walk, my mother is gone from the waiting area, but Leon is still there.

"She's in with your father. Room 2157."

I have to blink back tears when I see my father with wires coming from his nose and an IV dripping into his arm. He has always looked so intimidating, but now he seems small and vulnerable.

"How you feeling, Dad?"

"Been better," he says with a light smile.

I go over to the side of the bed and embrace my father. I can't remember the last time we hugged. Yes, I do—it was at my high school graduation.

"I'm sorry, Dad." I try to make my voice steady, but it comes out sounding like I'm five years old.

"Me, too, son. Live your life."

"Thanks for your blessing."

He clears his throat. "You have my blessing . . . not my money."

Can't help but laugh. It takes more than a heart attack to loosen Mathis Bainbridge's purse strings.

Chapter Forty-one

Emoni

"Merry Christmas, Emoni."

This is Sascha, waking me up at the crack of dawn like she used to do when we were little girls. I smell biscuits baking. Not homemade, but Mother can put her foot in some Pillsbury.

"Merry Christmas."

"Ooh . . . you need to go back to sleep and try that again. You look and sound like the Grinch."

That about sums up the way I feel. Downright Grinchy. I'm not looking forward to spending the day with Oscar breathing down my neck, harassing me about getting engaged, not to mention that Ophelia and Kevin will be here, too.

Fun times. "Wake me up when breakfast is ready."

Sascha shakes her head. "No can do. You have company. Oscar is here already and asking for his lady love."

I throw a pillow at Sascha. "There should be rules about this!"

Sascha giggles and closes my door. Pregnancy has made her entirely too pleasant. It's a good thing her wedding is in two weeks, because her little bump is going to be a big bump real soon.

I drag myself out of the bed and look for something festive to wear. I select my Christmas sweater and a long jean skirt. I stomp down the hall to the bathroom with all of my shower essentials.

"What is wrong with you?" asks Tyler, who is coming out of the bathroom.

"Nothing. Merry Christmas."

He gives me a juicy kiss on the cheek. "Merry Christmas to you, too."

"Wait a minute. Why do you look dressed to leave? Where are you escaping to?"

"I'm not escaping! Love Outreach is delivering Christmas presents at five area women's shelters."

"Can I come?"

"Now, wouldn't that be rude to leave your man here? I'll be gone all day."

I shrug. "I don't know. Maybe."

"I'll see you later on. Save me some of that turkey!"

"Sure thing."

After a ridiculous amount of stalling, I come downstairs, trying to look as chipper as possible. Oscar stands to his feet and kisses me on the mouth. My immediate reaction is to wipe it off. I restrain myself from doing this, because everyone is staring at me.

"I'm glad I brushed my teeth," I grumble.

"Merry Christmas, Emoni," says Mother as she puts biscuits on a plate.

"Merry Christmas, all. Where's Daddy?"

"I'm not sure," Mother replies. "He left in the middle of the night, said it was urgent. I'm guessing one of the church members was in trouble, because he was being very secretive."

"Can't he at least be off on Christmas Day?" asks Sascha.

Mother answers, "That's my bishop. I just wish he'd hurry back so we can open our presents."

Oscar says, "Emoni, can I talk to you alone for a few minutes?"

"Sure . . . I guess."

Oscar and I go into the front parlor and sit on Mother's pretty couch. Since this is Oscar's idea, I let him start the conversation.

"Emoni, I just wanted to give you your present in private."

"Oh, is that all? Okay."

Oscar frowns. "What did you think it was?"

"I don't know. So where's my present?" I'm so relieved that this whole thing isn't about setting a date for our wedding.

Oscar hands me a gift bag, and I take it with a smile. But as soon as I open the bag, my smile fades. This man has given me a wedding planning portfolio.

"What is this?" I ask with much attitude.

"I thought you'd like something that would get you organized in planning our wedding."

I let out a long sigh. "Oscar . . . this is too much. I haven't even agreed to being engaged yet."

"So what are you saying?"

"I'm saying that I need you to wait for me to get all of this sorted out in my mind."

He frowns again, deeply. "What is there to sort out? You either want to be with me or you don't."

"Oscar—"

Before I get a chance to finish my thought, Daddy opens the front door and saves me. I've never been happier to see him! As he steps in the door, I see why he left so early in the morning.

He's gone to pick up my brother Kumal Jr.

I squeal, jump up from the couch, and hug Kumal Jr. He hugs me back and says, "It's good to see you again, little sis."

Mother and Sascha come into the parlor to see what all the commotion is about. I guess Daddy feels this is the time to make proper introductions.

"Everyone, I want y'all to meet Kumal Jr. . . . my oldest son. Kumal, this is your stepmother, Diana, your youngest sister, Sascha, and Emoni's boyfriend, Oscar."

Kumal Jr. hugs Sascha and Mother and shakes Oscar's hand. "It's wonderful to meet you all. I've never had a family Christmas, so I'm looking forward to this."

Mother looks ill and sits down on the couch next to Oscar. Oscar asks, "Are you all right, First Lady?"

"No. I'm feeling faint."

Daddy says, "Diana, I apologize for shocking you with this, but it was something I needed to do on my own."

"Fine," Mother replies. "Kumal Jr., how is your mother?"

"She was doing horribly, but Dad talked her into entering an in-patient detox center. We dropped her off before we came here."

"Wonderful," says Mother as she rises from the couch. "I'm going to check on dinner."

Sascha and I look at each other and laugh; there is nothing to check on. The caterers are preparing the food and bringing it later this afternoon. All Mother has to do is serve cookies.

Kumal asks, "Emoni, is this the young man who was with you in Savannah? I'd like to apologize for my rudeness that day."

"N-no. That was someone else."

Oscar states, "That was her ex-boyfriend. I doubt if you'll get a chance to see him today—or ever, for that matter."

I roll my eyes and say to Kumal, "You might see him at Sascha's wedding. You are coming to Sascha's wedding, right?"

"Am I invited?"

Sascha gushes, "Of course you are! I can't wait for you to meet my fiancé."

"Someone is missing. Where's my brother, Tyler?" asks Kumal.

I answer, "He'll be back later. He's off doing some charity work with his church."

"He doesn't go to Freedom of Life?"

"That is a long story, and not one for a holiday," Sascha replies.

The doorbell rings again. This time it's Kevin and Sister Ophelia. Sascha kisses Kevin full on the lips while everyone watches.

Ophelia sucks her teeth. "Y'all can at least not fornicate on this day that we celebrate the birth of our Lord Jesus!" She marches through the parlor and sits down on the couch. Kumal Jr. takes a seat next to her. Ophelia narrows her eyes and looks Kumal Jr. up and down. "Who are you?" she asks.

Kumal Jr. extends his hand. "My name is Kumal Jr. I'm Bishop Prentiss's oldest son."

Ophelia looks from face to face in the room for an explanation. When none is offered, she says, "Emoni, baby, go and get me a glass of water. I'm feeling a little dehydrated."

I'm glad to escape the room so I can let loose the floodgates of laughter. Ophelia looks like she just saw Lazarus rise from the dead and push the stone from in front of his tomb. Somebody's going to have to clear things up for her before she puts her own spin on it.

Daddy is in the kitchen, fixing a tray of cookies and cocoa for everyone. He is humming to himself, and there is a peaceful expression on his face. He looks truly happy.

"Daddy, what made you reach out to Kumal Jr.?"

"I had a conversation with your friend Darrin. I felt convicted about not being a father to my son."

"Wow. I'm glad the two of you talked."

"Me, too. Where is Darrin, anyway? I haven't seen him lately."

"I'm not sure, but I think he went home to Cleveland. I haven't really talked to him since Oscar and I got together."

"That's a shame. He's a nice young man."

I nod in agreement. "He is."

Daddy draws in a long breath. "Emoni, you know I

don't like to get in your business. You're an adult and quite capable of making decisions . . ."

"But?"

"But are you sure you want to date Oscar?" Daddy pulls out a chair and motions for me to sit down.

"Why are you asking me that, Daddy?"

"Because I know you, and you're not happy. You should be ecstatic about your relationship."

"I want to be happy! I do! But I just keep thinking I might be making a big mistake."

"Honey, there is no harm in waiting until you're sure. If Oscar loves you like he says he does, he'll wait."

Tears fill my eyes. "Thank you for saying that, Daddy, because he's been pressuring me a little. I'm just not ready."

Daddy's face darkens into a frown. "Do you need me to handle him?"

"No, Daddy. I can handle it."

"All right."

I stand up and get Sister Ophelia's bottle of water, and Daddy heads for the parlor with the cookies and cocoa. Mother walks into the kitchen with puffy eyes and a distressed expression.

"Diana, what's wrong?" Daddy asks.

"You had to bring him here? You had to bring that drug addict's son in my house?"

"Diana . . ."

I try to sneak out of the kitchen, but Mother says, "No, Emoni, you stay. You need to hear this, too."

"Okay . . ." I whisper.

"You all might think I'm being hateful by not wanting to deal with that young man. But I just don't believe that he is your son," Mother says.

I want to say, "The DNA doesn't lie," but I don't. Mother already looks like she's coming undone.

"Diana, I can't just not be a father to him because it makes you uncomfortable."

"Why not? You've done it for over twenty years." Mother snatches a cookie from Daddy's tray and goes back upstairs.

Daddy calls after her, "You spending the holiday upstairs?"

"Don't worry about me. Go raise your grown son."

Daddy sighs and shakes his head. I try to encourage him a little. "Daddy, she's being a drama queen. She'll come downstairs later."

But she doesn't. Even after the caterers arrive and Tyler comes back from his charity work. She stays in her room while everyone eats the turkey and side dishes that she ordered. She doesn't come down to open gifts, even though this is her favorite part of Christmas.

While Daddy and Sascha set up the yearly game of Pictionary, I grab Oscar's hand so we can slip out of the family room. I need to have this conversation with him now, while I have the nerve and before I think too hard about being dateless and manless for yet another New Year's Eve.

"What is it, baby?" Oscar asks.

I cringe at the endearment. It's a reflexive cringe. I couldn't have stopped it if I had tried. "Don't call me that, Oscar."

"I can't call my girlfriend baby?"

"No. This is going in, like, warp speed. We went from Sister Emoni to baby in, like, five seconds."

"What's your point?"

"My point is this: You aren't the one for me. I've known that for a while. I've been selfish."

Oscar's face contorts into a mixture of pain and anger. "You've known?"

"Listen, you caught me when I was having some mixed-up emotions—"

"Caught? You act like I trapped you!" Okay, now he's angry. Fists balled up and eyes looking wild.

I take a few steps back. "In a manner of speaking, you did. But I'm not angry. I just think we should end this before someone gets hurt." I hand him the wedding planner that he gave me as a gift.

"So that's it? You're done with us?"

Why is he asking me this? Why is the ball always in my court, as if I know anything? I don't know anything.

"Yes, Oscar. I'm sorry, but I am done with this." I can't bring myself to say "us."

Oscar takes his coat from the rack and goes right out the front door. I see the wetness in his eyes, so I don't try to stop him.

I thought that I would be cool with this. But watching Oscar walk out of my house is like saying goodbye to my future. Maybe he could've been my future. In a few years we probably would've had two kids and a house.

I go back into the family room to finish the holiday. Kevin and Sascha are gazing into each other's eyes. Even with all of the mistakes they've made, they're giddily in love. They act like there's no one in the room but them. That's what I want.

Not someone who can only make me say maybe.

Chapter Forty-two

Darrin

"Praise the Lord, Brother Darrin."

"He's worthy, Sister Ophelia."

I'm back in Atlanta, and it's New Year's Eve. Not at a party; don't have a date. Sitting up in church like somebody saved for real. Talking to Sister Ophelia and not the pretty girl who just smiled and winked at me.

Ophelia cocks her head to the side and comments, "Didn't think I'd see you here tonight. Baby saints usually backslide on this particular holiday."

She's unbelievable. I smile and reply, "Must be the Holy Spirit."

"It's *something*." She walks away from me and to her seat because service is about to start. It's a full house, like Sunday-morning worship.

I scan the sanctuary, trying to get a glimpse of Emoni. She's not with Oscar. He's sitting in the pulpit with a sour look on his face. Tyler's there, too, and wearing a preaching robe. This brings a smile to my face. Maybe he and Bishop have worked some things out.

There's Emoni. She's with the lovebirds Sascha and Kevin. It's so funny that they don't care if the whole congregation is talking about them. They sit front and center, hand in hand, like, "What y'all looking at?"

Bishop Prentiss comes out of his office and stands before the congregation, carrying only his Bible. He wears a serene smile.

He starts to sing: "'Jesus . . . Jesus . . . Jesus . . . there is something about that name . . .'"

The congregation, including me, joins in. The song is beautiful, moving, and touching, all at the same time.

Bishop leads the congregation in singing the song again. Tears are flowing down his cheeks, and he makes no effort to stifle them or wipe them away. Bishop raises his hands toward heaven and rocks back and forth. He's worshipping as if only God is in the room and not thousands of his members.

After he composes himself, he speaks into the microphone. "Praise God this evening, everyone."

The church replies with a thunderous round of applause. Bishop waits for the fervor to die down and then continues, "I have a confession to make, everybody."

The congregation looks confused, but I'm on the edge of my seat. He goes on, "I am guilty of not using what God has put in my own house."

He motions for Tyler to stand. Bishop says, "Some of you may know that my son Tyler is now one of the assistant pastors at Love Outreach."

The applause starts again. Tyler grins a little. Don't think he expected any of this.

"He's over there with a heart on fire for evangelizing and winning souls. He's doing what God has called him to do. But I've got a confession for you all . . ."

Bishop smiles. "I never told y'all that this young man can *preach*! So, I present to you all . . . my son . . . who makes me proud to be called his father. Pastor Tyler Prentiss!"

The entire church bursts into spontaneous praise again. Bishop hugs Tyler and steps to the side so Tyler can stand in front of the podium. Emoni is on her feet, clapping and stomping with everyone else.

Tyler says, "Good evening, y'all. I stand before you this evening feeling blessed to be here. I am humbled by my father's words, because he has truly been an example for me. Not only as a pastor but as a loving father who accepts everyone into his heart. Thank you, Bishop." He then asks, "Can y'all sing with me? 'Walk with me, Lord . . . walk with me.'"

The congregation joins in with singing and clapping. Everyone seems to feel the Spirit moving through the sanctuary.

Tyler claps his hands and shouts. "This is New Year's Eve service, but I'm not going to preach about resolutions. Nor am I going to preach about all the sinners who are going to hell for partying tonight." Laughter fills the church.

"Tonight I'm going to talk about forgiveness. Because . . . let me say . . . I count it all joy to serve such a loving and forgiving God." Tyler whispers, "'Cause I've backslid a couple of times . . ."

When he doesn't get a response from the congregation, he continues, "Oh, I must not be talking to anybody up in here. Y'all some sanctified folks out there! Well, all right, then, I'll preach this message for me."

A woman stands from her seat and shouts, "You betta preach! You ain't by yoself!"

I stand up and clap along with the woman. If anyone can cosign about backsliding, I can.

"I've seen many tests of my faith, saints," Tyler goes on. "And I haven't passed them all. This walk hasn't been a straight line. I've taken some detours and had a few crashes. But oh . . . thank Jesus . . . that He's been with me on this walk. Amen, somebody?"

"Amen!" is the congregation's unanimous response.

"Saints of God, please turn your Bibles to Matthew Eighteen and start at Verse Twenty-one. That is where the Holy Spirit led me when I sat down and prepared this message."

After the rustling of pages dies down, Tyler reads: "'Then came Peter to him, and said, Lord, how oft shall my brother sin against me, and I forgive him? till seven times? Jesus saith unto him, I say not unto thee, Until seven times: but, Until seventy times seven.'"

After a moment of reflection, Tyler preaches. "Our Father in heaven demands that we forgive one another. For the large transgressions and the small transgressions, saints. From stealing your husband to sharing a small secret. All of it. And really, when we think about it, isn't it all small?"

Members of the congregation nod their amens and wave their hands high. Normally, the congregation would be a lot more animated and noisy, but it seems as if everyone is savoring Tyler's every word.

"It's all small compared to how He's forgiven each and every one of us. The stain, filth, and stench of sin is on us from birth. I sometimes wonder how disgusting we must be to the Lord when we are in the midst of our sins. It reminds me of how my mother took care of me and my sisters when we were little.

"I remember one time when all three of us were ill with the flu. We had all sorts of disgusting fluids coming from both ends. I had never seen my mother clean up so much nastiness. But she did it without a word. Why? Because her babies were sick, and she loves us. She rocked us to sleep even though our breath reeked of vomit. We were not disgusting to her.

"God is like that, y'all know that, right? We're His children, and He loves us no matter how disgusting we are. Even when we fail to live up to His holy standards. Even when we take His forgiveness for granted."

Bishop Prentiss seems overwhelmed by his son's words. He falls to his knees right there in the pulpit and cries out to God.

The congregation takes Bishop's lead, and people all over the sanctuary lay prostrate before God, crying out and giving their lives to Him. It's the most moving display of worship that I've ever been part of.

During the beautiful chaos, Kumal Jr. walks into the church and down the center aisle. He walks up to First Lady Diana and holds both arms out wide. She pauses for a moment but then gingerly embraces her stepson with tears in her eyes.

Emoni crosses the sanctuary and joins their embrace while Bishop continues praising God. This is the type of story that only God can write.

"Happy New Year, Brother Darrin!" Dorcas gives me a jolly church hug. I'm shocked.

"Happy New Year, Dorcas."

She asks, "You going over to the breakfast buffet?"

"You know it!"

"You need to be over there helping with the food?"

She's right, but I say, "Ophelia wouldn't want me over there telling her she can't cook!"

"True." Dorcas sees some of her friends and waves. "I'll see you over there, okay?"

When I make it through the crowd and over to the fellowship hall, I save myself a seat and head straight to the buffet line. I know how it works at these church buffets. You snooze, you lose. And a brotha could use a little sustenance right now.

I feel a light tap on my shoulder. I turn and face the tapper—Emoni. The girl throws me totally off balance by giving me a hug. And it's not the I've-got-a-man-but-you-still-my-brother-in-Christ hug, either. She's smiling and holding me in her sexy gaze. "How was your Christmas, Darrin?"

"Action-packed but good." Okay. I need to pull myself together and think of something interesting to say before Oscar jumps out from behind a door somewhere.

"I'm glad. Mine was good, too. Daddy brought Kumal Jr. to our Christmas dinner."

"Are you serious? That's great! So I guess the test was positive."

"I guess so. Daddy said that he did it because of you."

"What? I didn't do anything special."

"It was something you said. I just want to thank you."

I give Emoni another hug because I want to touch her again. "You're welcome."

She and I both hold on for a second too long. She pulls away first. She's blushing. This could be a good thing.

"You coming to Sascha's wedding?" she asks casually.

"Didn't know I was invited."

"Silly! The whole church is invited."

"Oh. Then sure, I'll be there."

"You got a date?"

I burst out laughing. "Um . . . no. Why? Do you have any suggestions?"

"You could—I mean, we could go together."

"What about your man?"

"Don't have one."

This is awkward. She's standing here waiting, like she couldn't care less if I say yes or no. She's casual and non-chalant, but I'm about to explode. I don't want to seem too excited. Brotha got to save a little face.

"Yeah, sure," I reply. "I guess that would be okay."

"Okay, then, I'll see you there. One o'clock Saturday."

"Cool."

Emoni sashays off like she knows I'm watching. Like she owns my attention. And she would be . . . absolutely correct.

Chapter Forty-three

Emoni

It's the day of the wedding, and I'm excited for my sister. She's going to be a beautiful bride, pregnant and all. Actually, I think she has that pregnancy glow going on.

It seems as if there are a thousand people at Freedom of Life, and they're only the ones setting up for the wedding. The wedding isn't scheduled to start until one o'clock, and it's only eight thirty in the morning. The entire bridal party is in the women's lounge, making final adjustments to their dresses while a hairstylist primps everyone's 'do to perfection.

I'll admit that I have butterflies. Darrin is my date for the evening, and I can't wait to slow-dance with him at the reception. I'm so looking forward to him holding me in his muscular arms. I don't care that everyone is going to wonder what happened with Oscar. Let them wonder. I just know that I'm not going to let anything come between me and Darrin this time. Not Oscar, not Darrin's old girlfriends in Cleveland—nothing.

Mother sits down next to me on the tiny embroidered love seat. Without a thought, she straightens the velvet throw that covers one side.

"Mom, why are you always doing that?"

"Doing what?"

"Fixing, cleaning, straightening. It's annoying."

Mother folds her arms and looks me up and down. "What is your problem?"

"Nothing."

"Oh, it's something, because you're sitting up here talking to me like you forgot that I'm your mother."

My tone becomes apologetic. "I'm sorry, Mom. I guess I'm nervous about seeing Darrin again today."

"So now it's back to Darrin? When did this happen?"

"I don't know if anything has happened. Darrin and I are going to try and reconnect today."

"I'm not surprised about that."

"You're not? I thought everyone expected me to take the safe route and marry Oscar."

"I knew you weren't going to marry him. You're a daddy's girl, but your personality is like mine."

Um . . . I'll listen, but I beg to differ. Mother has a touch of obsessive-compulsive disorder.

"You be careful, Emoni. Make sure the Lord is leading you on this one."

"I will, Mother. Thank you."

It's crazy that I haven't been praying on any of this. It's probably why I agreed to date Oscar and had no empathy when Darrin was trying to make things right. I obviously don't know what I'm doing, not just about men but for my life in general.

Mother walks away to talk to Sascha, and I bow my head in a silent prayer. *Lord, please forgive me for not seeking you in my life. I want to do what you feel is best for me. If Darrin is the man for me, I know you will confirm it in my spirit. If he's not, then I'm going to trust you enough to send someone who will love me, mind, body, and spirit. Thank you, Lord, for understanding me with all my flaws and loving me in spite of them. I pray for your perfect peace.*

At last, the time has come to start the wedding ceremony. The bridesmaids are scrambling around, trying to find their places in line, and I'm leaning against a wall watching the commotion.

I hear a knock on the ladies' lounge door, so I open it. Yippee, it's Oscar. "Yes?"

"Is everyone ready? It's nearly time to start."

"Yeppers. Just about." I start to close the door in his face, but he holds it open.

"Emoni, are you going to talk to me?"

"We don't have anything to talk about."

Oscar has been trying to talk to me all morning, but I've been able to successfully dodge him and his unrelenting conversations about nothing. I especially don't want to be bothered with him now that I have prayed and feel a release in my spirit from him.

"Emoni, I spoke rashly on Christmas. I promise, I'll

give you all the time you need; just don't say that this is the end for us," Oscar pleads.

It's falling on deaf ears. I step out of the lounge to talk to Oscar face-to-face. He obviously doesn't care about putting the entire bridal party in our business.

"Oscar, this is not the right time for this conversation. Why don't we leave it alone?"

He doesn't look happy with my reply, but it's the best I can do. I don't want to see him hurting, but I'm not going to let sympathy cause me to make the wrong decision. Plus, on top of everything else, I've got a date.

I go back into the lounge and deliberately push the image of Oscar's worried face out of my mind. I need to think of something pleasant to get me through this long day. I close my eyes and think about Darrin in the gray suit that he's wearing. I caught a glimpse of him as he walked into the church, and he's looking right scrumptious.

The shrill sound of Ophelia Moore's voice rudely jars me from my fantasy.

"What do you mean *she's* going down the aisle first?" Ophelia rants as she points in Mother's direction.

We went over this in rehearsal, so it shouldn't have been a surprise, but Ophelia is acting as if this is something new. I feel my face tighten with anger, probably because I've been taken away from my lovely vision to listen to Ophelia's nonsense.

"Sister Moore, that's the way the program has been set up. We're going to walk the mother of the bride down first," Mother says.

Ophelia's arms flail angrily. "Everybody knows that the groom's mother always walks down first! Why should we change it here?"

"Ophelia, calm down," Mother says in an exasperated tone.

"You calm down! You think that just because you all paid for everything, you're running the show."

Mother laughs. "Pretty much."

"You ain't running nothing!" hisses Ophelia.

"You know what?" says Mother, still laughing. "Go ahead and walk down first. I don't even care."

"Now you're letting me walk down first? Because you said so?" Ophelia continues to rage.

After my initial irritation, I find myself watching this argument with sick amusement. Seeing Ophelia's nostrils flare out like a demented bull's is the funniest thing that has happened all day.

"Ophelia, you do whatever will make you feel important," says Mother with a dismissive wave.

If questioned on a witness stand about this incident, I could only tell the jury that after Mother's statement, Ophelia has spontaneously combusted. Her eyes have bulged out of the sockets, and her fleshy red lipstick covers lips that are trembling madly.

Sascha, bless her heart, makes the horrible mistake of trying to intervene. "Why don't you two walk down together? The aisle is big enough."

Ophelia snaps her head in Sascha's direction. Sascha jerks as if the action has caused her pain.

Ophelia says in front of twenty church members, "Oh, you shut up, you little slut. We wouldn't even be having this shotgun wedding if you hadn't got knocked up by my grandson."

Jaws drop all over the room, including mine. Mother swiftly steps to Ophelia, looking as if she's ready to do battle. Ophelia plants her feet and places both hands on her hips: a worthy opponent.

Mother hisses, "Ophelia, you're going to go along with the program as rehearsed, or I will have you forcibly removed from the premises."

"You wouldn't dare," replies Ophelia, but her voice has clearly weakened.

"I would dare. I'll have security parade you out of here in front of all your guests. And then we'll go on with the wedding."

I watch silently as Ophelia meekly lines up with her escort. Even though Mother has won this little battle, Ophelia has a triumphant smirk on her face. I shake my head and glare at that hateful woman. She's probably been waiting for the perfect opportunity to blurt out Sascha and Kevin's secret.

I dash over to comfort my sister, who has burst into tears because of Ophelia's harsh words. A small team has assembled to try to save her makeup, but little streaks of supposedly waterproof mascara are running down Sascha's cheeks.

"Stop crying," I whisper to Sascha. "Everyone was going to find out about the baby anyway. It's no big deal."

"How could she do that on my wedding day?"

"Why does the black widow spider eat her mate? We're talking about Sister Ophelia. It's just what she does. Pull yourself together. This is your day."

Sascha takes a deep breath. "Okay, I'm fine now. But Mom looks mad."

"Mad" is much too benign a term to describe the expression on Mother's face. Her perfectly arched eyebrows are dipped severely toward the bridge of her nose, and her lips are drawn into a tight line. Her meticulously applied matte makeup is overpowered by an angry red undertone that has taken her over from the neck up. It gives the illusion that her blood is literally boiling.

I nod in agreement with Sascha. "Ophelia is going to regret ever saying that."

But Mother's wrath will have to wait. We have a wedding to put on, and Mother would never let the congregation know that Ophelia has ruffled her feathers. She takes the arm of her escort and glides out of the women's lounge, taking her place as the first lady of the church and the mother of the bride.

I hold Sascha's hand until it's my turn to walk down the aisle. Then I step gingerly into the sanctuary, trying not to make eye contact with any of the thousands of pairs of eyes staring in her direction.

Inadvertently, my eyes rest on Oscar. He's scowling. I feel a smile teasing the sides of my lips, because the only thing that would have him *that* heated is Darrin looking at me.

Though I scan the crowd as I walk down the aisle, I can't find Darrin among the masses of big hats and fancy suits. But the more Oscar scowls, the more desperately I search.

I make it to the front of the church and stand beside the other bridesmaids and directly across from Tyler, the best man. I look out at Oscar again—both of his hands grip the armrests with an intensity that has turned his knuckles white. I follow the direction of Oscar's darting eyes and finally spot my date.

Darrin is seated next to my brother Kumal Jr., and

he's smiling at me. When we lock gazes, Darrin gives me a wink and mouths, "You look wonderful."

When Sascha emerges from the rear of the church, all eyes shift in her direction.

All eyes except mine and Darrin's.

We gaze at each other; I'm trying to communicate a thousand apologies. I think Darrin's eyes are apologetic, too, although I need more than a heated stare to know there may still be a chance for us. But I feel nothing but peace in my spirit about choosing Darrin.

The ceremony seems to go on forever, with Daddy happily preaching about marriage and family. He looks out at Kumal Jr. with hope in his eyes when he tells Kevin and Sascha how important forgiveness is to a successful and long marriage. I think Daddy wants to make things up to Kumal Jr. He wants to erase the fact that he's been missing in action for Kumal's entire life.

I feel a twinge of relief go through my body when Kumal Jr. returns Daddy's smile. He seems reluctant at first, but he can't hide his pleasure. This is the best thing that could have happened from that trip to Savannah.

When the ceremony is over, I stand in front of the church alongside my sister, waiting to greet the guests and accept congratulations. As Darrin approaches, my entire body trembles with anticipation. All thoughts of anger and hurt have disappeared. I just want to wrap my arms around Darrin's neck and say that all is forgiven.

Chapter Forty-four

Darrin

Emoni looks so beautiful. She's standing in her sister's receiving line, and she has the most welcoming look on her face.

I have to say that I was apprehensive about accepting a date with Emoni. So afraid that I'm going to ruin things again. But my feelings for Emoni are starting to run deep. I only want to be near her.

After my father had his heart attack, I'd considered going to a culinary arts school in Cleveland or somewhere closer. But something was pulling me back toward the South. I know now what that something is.

I'm in love with this girl.

She's not just another one-night stand or another someone to *do*. I know I want to have a relationship. I want to see where this thing leads. And if we end up having a wedding ceremony of our own, I'll be glad about that, too.

I see Oscar staring me down, but I'm not going to mess with the brotha. I did steal his woman. He's probably got a right to be mad at somebody. I don't mind if it's me.

I step to Emoni and pull her close. "Hey, girl."

"Darrin, you are making me blush."

"Is that all? Wow. I meant to make you weak in the knees."

Emoni laughs. "You think you got it like that?"

I whisper in her ear, "I know I do. But you've got it like that, too."

Reluctantly, I let her go and promise that we'll dance the night away at the reception. On my way to the back of the sanctuary, I see Kumal Jr., and he gives me a hug.

"I see you're back in the game," he says with a laugh.

"What? Oh, you mean with Emoni? Maybe I am."

"Man, you're in there. She had me confused at Christmas, though, talking about how she was with that other guy."

"I wasn't worried at all."

Kumal Jr. lifts an eyebrow. "Really?"

"Okay, so I was worried, but I'm good now."

"That's what I thought." Kumal's face turns serious as he continues, "Man, I want to apologize for how I acted that day in Savannah."

"Totally unnecessary. It was a stressful situation. I'm just glad y'all worked everything out."

"I know. People keep looking at me all weird, like they can't believe that I'm Bishop's son, but he's claiming me like I've been a part of the family my whole life."

"Bishop is a good man. He's taught me a lot about Jesus."

One of the flower girls walks up to me and gives me a note. I excuse myself from Kumal and go to read it in private. It says, "Meet me in Bishop's office in five minutes."

The note is in Emoni's curly handwriting, and I can't help but grin. I take a look at my watch and will those minutes to fly by. I fold the note back up and put it in my pocket.

When I notice that Emoni has abandoned the receiving line, I make my way to Bishop's office. She's there already and perched on the edge of her father's desk with both arms folded. "Close the door," she says.

I obey and then wait for her to start. She bites her lip and says, "Darrin, tell me something."

"Anything."

"Are you trying to be with me, or am I going to have to share you with the entire singles' ministry?"

I answer truthfully. "I am only interested in you, Emoni."

"How do I know that's the truth?"

"All I can do is give you my word. Is that enough?"

Emoni laughs. "No. That is not enough. Your word has been suspect from time to time."

"So what do you want me to do?"

"Why don't you seal it with a kiss?"

I stare at her for a moment, waiting for her to say that she's playing. But Emoni is dead serious. She's put it out there, and she's waiting for me to rise to the occasion.

"In your father's office? Isn't that blasphemous?" I ask.

"He's the bishop, not Jesus!"

I pull Emoni from her father's desk and give her a

chaste hug. She closes her eyes in anticipation, and I place a tiny peck on her lips.

"What was that?" she asks.

"A kiss! You doggin' my kiss?"

She rolls her eyes. "I can't stand you."

"Yes, you can."

Emoni walks around her father's desk, looking like she's ready to start fussing, when she and I both notice at the same time the brown envelope that holds the DNA results for Kumal Jr. It looks undisturbed, like it hasn't even been opened.

"Is that what I think it is?" she asks.

"Yes. I gave that to your father before Christmas—"

Emoni interjects, "And he still hasn't opened it."

"Then how does he know about Kumal Jr.?"

I can answer this question for myself. Bishop had no need to open those results. His heart told him that Kumal Jr. was his son. Reminds me of Tyler's New Year's message.

Emoni snatches the envelope. Obviously, her heart needs some hard-core proof. "Should I open this?"

Something feels wrong about this. I just keep thinking about Tyler talking about how God loves us like a parent loves his children. I've even got that song that he sang in my head: *"Walk with me, Lord . . . walk with me . . ."*

I shake my head. "No, Emoni, I don't think you should—"

Emoni ignores me and opens the metal tab on the envelope. Seems like the results should be sealed, but they're not, and that's perfect for Emoni's curiosity. No one will ever know that she looked. No one but me.

"Walk with me, Lord . . . walk with me . . ."

She doesn't have to tell me what the results say; her expression tells it all. Her mouth falls open, and her eyes widen as she drops the stack of papers to the floor.

She whispers, "He's not Daddy's son. He's not my brother."

"*Walk with me . . .*"

Emoni is frozen in place, so I pick up the results and place them back in the envelope. I take both of Emoni's shaking hands in mine. "It's all right, Emoni." I encircle her with my arms and rock her while she sobs into my chest.

Guilt kept Bishop from opening that envelope. Guilt at leaving Genevieve to the crack cocaine. Guilt at maybe having a son he didn't know and guilt about not trying to find out.

"Should I tell Daddy?" Emoni asks after her tears have dried.

"No. Bishop Prentiss is a spiritual father to a lot of people. Why not Kumal Jr.?"

"*Walk with me . . .*"

Emoni and I walk out of Bishop's office hand in hand. It feels wonderful having her beside me, like this has all been destined from the beginning of time. Her smile tells me that she's here for me, like I'm right here for her.

Chapter Forty-five

DIARY OF A not-so-MAD BLACK BLOGGER

What's good, cyber homies and homettes? I know it's been a good minute since I updated y'all, so here's the scoop.

The pastor I told y'all about earlier doesn't really have an illegitimate son, but he's adopted the young man into his church family and real family. That's a true man of God, right? I'm still not telling y'all who it is, because I've decided that some things are best left secrets.

But what I will tell y'all is that I've fallen hard for the bishop's daughter. I'm talking 'bout tripped-on-a-banana-peel-and-busted-my-head-open type of falling. She's digging me, too, . . . so, sorry, ladies, I'm taken.

My posts are going to be few and far between for the next few weeks, because I'm in culinary arts school. I'm gonna be a chef. Chef Boyarbro, if you will. I'll keep y'all posted on the important stuff.

Mad Black Blogger signing off . . . hit me up in the comments!

Discussion Questions for
The Bishop's Daughter

1. When Darrin decides to pursue his story, Shayna quotes Psalm 105:15, which says, "Touch not mine anointed, and do my prophets no harm." Are Christians prohibited from revealing scandal when it comes to church leaders?

2. Darrin cringes when Shayna mentions the word "relationship." Do you know any relationship-phobes? Do they exist inside and outside of the church?

3. Emoni describes herself as "not pretty." Do you think she's being honest with herself or just superficial? Has her attitude kept her from having relationships?

4. Read Romans 14:16: "Let not then your good be evil spoken of." How does this apply to finances in the church?

5. Are Emoni, Tyler, and Sascha the typical pastor's kids? Should a pastor's children be held to higher moral standards than other youth?

6. Freedom of Life's singles' ministry has an unfair ratio of women to men. Is this an accurate depiction of singles' ministries in general?

7. What are your impressions of Oscar and Dorcas? Would they make a good couple?

8. How did you feel when Genevieve presented her son to Bishop Prentiss?

9. Kumal Jr. is offended when Darrin and Emoni suggest a paternity test. Are his reasons rational? Do you believe he and Genevieve had good or bad intentions in coming to the church in Savannah?

10. Darrin calls himself a WIP Christian, as in "work in progress." Is there such a thing? Were Darrin's sexual missteps with Dorcas and Emoni realistic, or was Darrin simply not submitting to Christ?

11. Was Darrin right to conceal his story from Emoni? Do you think she would've understood had he told her instead of her discovering the truth?

12. When Emoni learns the truth about Darrin, she agrees to date Oscar. Do most women take the safe route in relationships, instead of following their heart?

13. Should Emoni and Darrin tell Bishop Prentiss the truth about Kumal Jr.'s paternity?

Turn the page for a preview of

In the Midst of It All

a new novel by

TIFFANY L. WARREN

Prologue

Zee, are you going to get that?"

Zenovia blinked a few times, glanced at the clock, and shook her head. "Three a.m. It's not good news."

She closed her eyes and buried her head under the covers; tried to escape the ringing telephone. Her husband reached over her and took matters into his own hands. Zenovia was grateful that he was home. This kind of news didn't need to be left on an answering machine.

Audrey lay in a pool of her own diluted blood, but the room is permeated with the scent of lavender. Pink bubbles float on top of the pool. Scented by lavender; stained by blood.

Zenovia's husband talked for a few moments, then pressed the End button on the cordless telephone. He touched Zenovia on the shoulder. She jumped. She was expecting him to wake her; to be the town crier of her misery, but she was startled nonetheless.

"That was your stepfather. Your mother has passed away."

"How did she die?"

"He says in her sleep."

Zenovia rolled her eyes. "He's a liar."

"Did you see it?"

She nodded. "But not in enough time to stop her."

Zenovia turned away from her husband and buried her head in the pillow. A salty river of tears trickled down her face, but Zenovia was not ready to share them with her mate. She wanted two minutes of private grief.

She heard him pressing buttons on the telephone.

"Who are you calling?" she asked.

"Bishop. You can't preach in the morning."

"I'm preaching."

"It's okay, Zee. He'll find someone else. You need to handle your mother's affairs."

"That can wait. I've got a word from the Lord that cannot."

Chapter One

Zenovia heard knocks on the door.

They were not the soft knocks of the children in the apartment next door. There were two of them—a boy and a girl. Always dirty, with unwashed faces and mismatched socks, if any. Their mama was on crack, and they visited Zenovia and Audrey every morning looking for breakfast. But it was ten a.m. and they were probably plopped in front of their television, watching the Saturday morning cartoons.

Zenovia waited for the knock again. This time it came with a voice. "Hello? Is anyone home? We'd like to share the Gospel with you today."

Zenovia laughed. She had been thinking that the person behind the door was a drug boy running from the police or a crackhead hustling some stolen property. But it was a lady, and she wanted to share the Gospel. No harm there.

Still, she didn't answer the door.

Audrey rushed from the bedroom of the one-bedroom apartment. She was wearing a ratty-yet-colorful housecoat. Wild red hair framed her face like a flame, perfectly complementing her freckles and green eyes.

"Why don't you get the door?" she asked.

She didn't wait for a response, but went to the door herself. She swung it open wide and smiled at the two ladies who stood before her.

"Good morning!" sang Audrey.

"Well, good morning to you, too!" said the lady who'd knocked.

Audrey asked, "Did I hear y'all say, y'all was talking about the Gospel this morning?"

"Yes, you did. The Gospel of our Lord and Savior Jesus Christ."

"Well, come on in and keep talking! Zenovia, something told me we were going to have good news today."

Zenovia felt a smile tickle the sides of her lips. That *something* was a vision. Audrey had been having them since she was a little girl, and Zenovia had started having them when she'd turned twelve. They were haphazard messages, sometimes future, sometimes past. Usually there wasn't enough information contained in the visions to do anything useful. Most times, Zenovia was annoyed by the visions; treated them like unannounced visitors. Just like the two Bible ladies.

Both of the ladies stepped gingerly into the spotless apartment. Their eyes darted back and forth, inspecting. Their nostrils flared, inhaling the scent of the ocean breeze candles that Zenovia had lit. Zenovia watched their facial expressions change from caution to pleasant surprise.

Zenovia narrowed her eyes. "You can sit down. Although I'm sure you saw roaches in the hallway, none of them have taken up residence here."

The ladies smiled nervously as they took a seat on the worn but clean sofa. Audrey sat across from them in her leather recliner.

"My name is Charlotte Batiste," said the lady who'd knocked.

Audrey's smile beamed. "Charlotte. Like the little pig in that book."

"Actually, the pig's name was Wilbur," Zenovia corrected. "You're talking about the spider."

For a fleeting instant, Audrey looked irritated, but it quickly faded. "Well, that doesn't matter. My name is Audrey and the smarty pants is Zenovia."

Both ladies looked from Audrey to Zenovia with tight-yet-friendly smiles on their faces. The second lady, not Charlotte, actually wasn't a *lady* at all. She was a girl, no older than Zenovia, but she was dressed in a much older woman's apparel: a long corduroy skirt and a turtleneck sweater. At their feet were little bags stuffed to the hilt with tracts and pamphlets.

"Well, it's nice to meet you both. This is my daughter Alyssa," declared Charlotte with yet another smile.

She never seemed to run out of smiles. Zenovia wondered if her face was sore.

Charlotte continued. "I am here this morning to share a wonderful thought from the Bible. Do you have a Bible?"

"Of course!" replied Audrey.

Audrey reached into a side compartment on her recliner and pulled out a huge, white, leather Bible; the kind grandmothers pass down to their grandchildren with the family tree on the inside cover and the picture of Jesus in the center. There was no family tree in the front of Audrey's Bible; only her name, in big block print.

"I'm going to read you some verses in the Book of Revelation Chapter 21. It's the last book of the Bible."

"Oh, I know where Revelations is," said Audrey.

Zenovia cringed. She wanted to say, *It's Revelation, not Revelations*, but since she had already been labeled as a smarty pants, the critique went unspoken.

Charlotte read. "And I heard a great voice out of heaven saying, Behold, the tabernacle of God is with men, and he will dwell with them, and they shall be his people, and God himself shall be with them, and be their God. And God shall wipe away all tears from their eyes; and there shall be no more death, neither sorrow, nor crying, neither shall there be any more pain: for the former things are passed away."

Zenovia liked that scripture. No tears and no sorrow sounded like just what she needed. Apparently, Audrey liked it too, because there was a tear in the corner of her right eye.

"Well, I can't wait to go to heaven and see Jesus. He's going to take away all sadness and death. I believe that," stated Audrey with conviction.

"What if I told you that this scripture was talking about a paradise here on earth?" asked Charlotte.

Zenovia almost slipped from her usual academic self and said *What you talkin' about, Charlotte?* like Arnold querying Willis on *Diff'rent Strokes*, but she held her tongue. She wanted to hear Audrey's response.

Audrey asked, "This scripture ain't about heaven?"

Charlotte went on to explain how God was going to make the earth over into a big park and that believers were going to live there in a utopian nirvana. She said that children would have lions and bears for playmates and go unharmed. Zenovia was a little skeptical, but Charlotte flipped through her little orange Bible with such skill that she had to be telling the truth.

After she was done, Charlotte let out a loud sigh. "Now, Audrey, don't you think God wants you and your sister to live in paradise and not squalor?"

Audrey looked confused, but Zenovia laughed. It was not the first time that she and her mother had been mistaken for sisters. Audrey was a young-looking thirty-one and Zenovia was a mature-looking sixteen.

"She is my mother, not my sister," said Zenovia.

"Oh," replied Charlotte, and then . . . with recognition, "*Oh!*"

Audrey dropped her head. "Had her when I was fifteen."

"Well, that's all right," said Charlotte cheerfully. "That doesn't matter once you give your life to God and get baptized."

"I've been baptized," replied Audrey defensively.

"Oh, but not like this. When you get baptized with us one of the Brethren of the Sacrifice, your life will surely be changed."

Zenovia cleared her throat. "I've never heard of the Brethren of the Sacrifice. What denomination are you?"

"We're not a denomination at all. We are *true* Christians, teaching *true* Christianity." She said this with such conviction that Zenovia wanted to pump her fist, yell *Power to the people!*, and hand her an afro pic.

Charlotte turned her attention back to Audrey. "Would you like to come to one of our services?"

"I'd like that," responded Audrey eagerly.

Zenovia rarely saw her mother get excited about anything, so, again, she held her tongue. She wanted to object and tell Charlotte that she and Audrey had a church home. First Gethsemane Baptist church, up the street, was where they had fellowshipped for the past two years.

But maybe it was time for a change. Audrey had gotten into a particularly embarrassing scuffle with one of the usher board members. The usher, Sister Brown, had told Audrey that she couldn't sit on the Mother's row. Audrey had responded by accusing Sister Brown of being jealous because Audrey was pretty and Sister Brown was "black and greasy."

After the altercation, Zenovia had done what she always did. She apologized to First Lady Benson and Sister Brown. She'd explained that Audrey had just been prescribed new medication for her schizophrenia and that it had not yet taken effect.

All that happened a month ago, and they hadn't been to church since. Zenovia liked to let things die down before they returned to worship. Admittedly, though, she missed the anointed singing of the choir and the spirited preaching.

Audrey looked over at her daughter. "What do you say, Zee? You want to join a new church?"

Zenovia shrugged and answered her mother's question with a question. "Why not?"